Relative Secrets

HELEN STANCEY

FAIRLIGHT BOOKS

First published by Fairlight Books 2021

Fairlight Books
Summertown Pavilion, 18–24 Middle Way, Oxford, OX2 7LG

A CIP catalogue record for this book is available from the British
Library

1 2 3 4 5 6 7 8 9 10

ISBN 978-1-912054-86-2

www.fairlightbooks.com

Printed and bound in Great Britain by Clays Ltd.

Designed by Fairlight Books

1999

CHAPTER I
Lucy and Mary

'And she's such a beautiful baby,' said Lucy's grandmother proudly. 'Look. Oh – look at her.'

In padded armchairs lining the front room of the care home, frail comatose figures sagged, curled and listed, several covered in multicoloured blankets crocheted by the Home's Friends. Behind the chairs, wallpaper clematis bloomed, fancifully luxuriant in the overheated atmosphere. A ledge above the absent fireplace held Busy Lizzies and African violets, along with brass ornaments, one belated Easter card and a red plastic feeding cup, temporarily forgotten.

Lucy stared at the empty space on the carpet.

'Yes,' said Lucy. 'She's beautiful.'

'A delight. A constant delight. How could you have any regret? You couldn't. She's a blessing.'

'I haven't any regret,' said Lucy. Her voice cracked and she swallowed.

'Not you, my dear. Me. A blessing. I have no regret.'

'Like the song.'

'Is it?'

'Help me. Help me. Someone, please help me.' At the other

side of the room, one of the frail figures leaned forwards, clutching the seat of her chair. Up to now, all had been quiet and for the moment the staff members were occupied elsewhere.

'Help me, someone. Please.'

The old lady's legs stretched and jerked. One slipper had come off and lay, sole upwards, at a distance from its bunch-toed foot. Lucy left her grandmother's side and crossed the room to pick up the slipper.

'Shall I put it on for you?'

The old lady glared.

'Shall I?'

No reply. Lucy bent down and tried to ease the stiff contorted foot into the powder-blue velour. The foot jerked and kicked out.

'Don't you dare!' shouted the old lady. 'Leave me alone!' Her hand jabbed towards Lucy. 'Get off me! Get off!'

Rattled and embarrassed, Lucy went back to the chair by her grandmother and took her hand again. No one else stirred.

'Oh help me. Help me someone. Please help me.'

Lucy concentrated on her grandmother.

'Are you comfortable? Can I bring anything for you?'

'Yes, we are comfortable. It worked, you see. We managed it. I have no regret.'

'Help me. Help me someone.'

A middle-aged nurse, wearing the Home's green uniform, came through the doorless doorway. 'What is it, Hilda?'

'I tried to put her slipper on for her,' said Lucy, 'but she wouldn't let me.'

'No. She's frisky today. All right, Hilda, all right. Is that your gran? She's settling in nicely, isn't she? Hello, Mary. How are you, my sweet?'

'Very well, thank you.'

'She's a lovely lady, your gran. Very easy. All right, Hilda. We'll dress that leg in a minute. It's quiet today, apart from Hilda. She does have these little episodes now and again. Fortunately, not too often.'

The nurse left the room, smiling companionably at Lucy and Mary, and giving Hilda a pat on the shoulder as she passed. Hilda snarled. From the television set in the corner came the Sunday morning service. The screen filled with shining countenances, singing joyously.

'That's a cheerful hymn,' said Mary.

Lucy turned in surprise. Her grandmother's hazel eyes were alert, were present.

'It is,' she agreed enthusiastically. 'Do you like it?'

'I don't know that one, so it's fortunate I don't have to sing, isn't it? I'd disgrace us.' She chortled roguishly. Lucy joined in a little.

'Ssh.' Mary lifted a finger to her lips. 'We mustn't disrupt the service. We'd better behave. At least we've kept awake. Unlike them.' She indicated the slumbering bodies opposite. 'Fast asleep in church! I expect it's because these pews are so cushioned.'

The hymn ended and prayers began. Mary closed her eyes and repeated the Our Father along with the television congregation. 'Amen.' There was a pause for private prayer.

'I'd disgrace us all,' she said sadly. 'Disgrace us all.'

'No, you wouldn't,' said Lucy urgently. 'It wouldn't matter one bit. Besides, we didn't have to sing, did we? It was a hymn for the choir by themselves.'

Mary's eyes remained shut.

'It's fine, Grandma. We did what we were supposed to do. We were like everyone else.'

'Ah yes.' Mary's eyes opened. 'Like everyone else. We were like everyone else.'

'Help me. Please help me.'

'I'll help you, my love.' The nurse entered with a dressing. 'I'm going to see how that sore on your leg's getting on.' She knelt and began to roll down Hilda's knee-high stocking.

'Get off me. Get off me. Get off.'

'I won't hurt you.'

'Get off.'

'It's got to be done, Hilda, my love.'

'Get off. Get off.'

Hilda lunged and grabbed the nurse's hair, tugging it to and fro with each beat of her chant. Appalled, Lucy shot over, then hesitated, unsure of how to deal with an old lady's attack. Head forced down, the nurse was attempting to disentangle Hilda's fingers from her hair. Lucy tried to aid her. As each finger was dislodged, Hilda re-hooked the previous one with considerable strength. Together they succeeded, Lucy guiltily holding the fingers as each was prised off. Not firmly enough: as the nurse was finally freed, Hilda wrested her hands free from Lucy's grasp and lashed out before the nurse could duck.

'Get off.'

'She's scratched you,' said Lucy. 'I should have held her tighter. I didn't think she'd be so strong.'

'No, it's surprising.' Flushed, the nurse dabbed at her temple. 'You can't imagine where they could get it from. See her now.'

Hilda was slumped as if suddenly switched off.

'All passion spent,' said the nurse. 'I'll leave her till later though. Thanks for your assistance. She used to be a headmistress, you know.'

Lucy smiled wanly and again traversed the room of insensible bodies to her grandmother.

'Good morning,' Mary greeted her. 'I was admiring your singing. Have you been in the choir for long?'

'For quite a while,' humoured Lucy, sitting down.

'Do you know, I must have heard you sing before. There's something familiar... Where could I have heard you sing before?'

Lucy tried reality. 'I used to be in the choir at school, Grandma. You used to come to the concerts at Christmas and in the summer term.'

'Of course I did.' Mary's face brightened in sudden understanding. 'You're Lucy, aren't you? My darling little Lucy.'

Thrown by this unpredictable reappearance of recognition, Lucy began a weak joke about not being little any more, but the ray of comprehension was already fading.

'Do you still sing at school, dear?'

'I've left, Grandma. I'm going to university in the autumn.'

'It may work out for the best. Leaving. It can, you know. It can work out. You can worry about what to do, worry and worry, and then it can work out.'

'There's no need for you to worry, Grandma,' Lucy broke in. 'We'll take care of you. Mum and Daniel and I. And Adam when he's here. And the nurses. We'll take care of you.'

'Take care. Yes, we must take care. We must be careful. Keep quiet. Keep quiet.'

'We will. We'll be quiet.'

'Mum's the word. Yes, that's it.' She began to chuckle. 'Mum's the word.'

Her gurgles of amusement slowed and died. The vivacity drained from her. 'Oh yes,' she repeated softly. 'Mum's the word.' She pressed her lips together, gazing inscrutably out.

Lucy stroked her grandmother's cheek, to no reaction. The television vicar was talking about renewal and hope, linking the renewal of springtime with hope for the forthcoming new millennium. At the other side of the window, a car parked in the driveway of the house opposite. A man got out. A woman. Two children. Car doors slammed. The man rang an inaudible, invisible doorbell and a woman came, followed by a man who was holding a baby over his shoulder. Kissing, man-hugs and petting of children. The family of four went in. A tub of daffodils bobbed and waved by the porch.

Mary moaned. Her brow furrowed and an expression of determination came over her. She picked up the hem of her skirt and pleated it, folding the material back on itself with exactitude, ensuring that the pleats were of equal size. She held up the wodge, inspected it, clicked her tongue and put the pleats down again, smoothing the material over her knees. Her forehead, relaxed as she contemplated the replaced skirt, puckered again and she started to rub the arm of the chair with short fast moves as if scrubbing a stain. After a while, she stopped and began a longer, slower action, moving her fingers from the wrist as if painting.

The congregation was filing out of church as the credits rolled. Lucy watched the vicar shaking hands with the members of his flock, their genial open faces predominantly female. She wondered how many of them would wind up crumpled in chairs round the periphery of a hot room in a converted suburban villa. Wondered if she herself would.

Two care assistants came in with a folding wheelchair. Each crooked one of her arms under Hilda's and in a continuous movement swung her out into the wheelchair with cheery encouragement.

'Come on, Hilda. Lunchtime. You like your lunch, don't you?'

'Do I?'

'Juicy slice of lamb with peas and mash.'

'Do I?'

They wheeled her away, returning after a short interval for another load.

'Hello, Joan. How are you today?'

Twitching silence.

'Come on, Joanie. Time for lunch.'

Lucy touched her grandmother's arm.

'I have to go,' she said. 'They're taking everybody in for lunch.'

Up and down. Up and down. Mary continued the rhythmic painting, hunched forwards in concentration.

'I'll come again.' She kissed her grandmother's cheek.

Up and down. Up and down.

'Bye. Goodbye. I'll see you soon.'

She stood up to go. Instantly, her grandmother left off and clasped Lucy's hand, fixing her purposefully.

'We managed it,' she enunciated. 'We did manage it.'

'We did, Grandma. We did.'

Mary gazed intently into Lucy's eyes, then loosened her grip. She sank into the chair, put her head on one side, smiled.

Lucy went out into the hall with its picture of sunset in the Highlands and its artificial flowers on the table. The front door wouldn't open.

'You'll have to unbolt it,' called a voice from behind her. A care assistant was returning with the empty wheelchair. 'We have to keep it locked,' she explained. 'Some of them are wanderers and they might get out if we didn't. If you tell one of us when you're about to go, we'll lock it again after you.'

The bolt was high up on the door. The carer took a stick from a nook behind the radiator and knocked the bolt from its staple.

'Bye. Thanks for coming.'

Spring sunshine. Cool fresh air.

The bolt clicked into place.

CHAPTER II
The Family

'How was she?' Lucy's mother, Beth, was ironing in the kitchen of their flat. The oven was on, the radio was on, it was 12.45 and Beth was tired. She switched the radio off to attend to Lucy's answer.

'She seemed happy enough when I left.'

'How was she before that?' asked Lucy's younger brother anxiously. He was leaning against the fridge, about to take a gulp of orange juice from the carton.

'Use a glass, Daniel,' said Beth.

'Sorree.' He headed to the cupboard. 'I wouldn't wash-back into it, you know.'

'I should hope not. It's disgusting.'

Daniel poured a large glass of orange, and Beth returned to her questioning.

'Was she better than last time?'

'Oh yes, much better.'

Beth bit her lip as she relived that last time, the day after her mother's removal into residential care. Mary sat with her eyes closed, screwed-up closed, and kept them so for the entire visit. Beth held her hand, regaling her with this and that hearty snippet of information, prattling with increasing desperation. Mary shut it out, whether deliberately or not she couldn't tell, and was still unsure when, as she, Daniel and Lucy rose to go, Mary said, 'Don't leave me. Please don't leave me,' and opened her eyes to release tears, which dripped onto the purple cardigan she had never liked.

'Was she tearful?' Beth asked.

'No. She even had a giggle when she thought everyone was asleep in church.'

'Asleep in church? Who?'

'They had the morning service on the television. She must have mixed that in with those poor old things asleep around her.'

'It's a bit depressing there,' said Daniel.

'As long as they're kind to her,' said Beth, folding a blouse. 'As long as she's comfortable. As long as she's as peaceful as she can be.'

'She said she had no regrets.'

'Did she? Did you ask her?'

'She said it by herself. She kept saying things like, we'd managed it, and that it would work out for the best, and that she had no regrets.'

Beth rubbed her forehead with the back of her hand.

'We had to do it, didn't we, Lucy? We couldn't look after her here any more, could we?'

'No, we couldn't, Mum,' said Daniel gently, stroking her arm. Then, more cheerfully, 'And we'll have our own bedrooms to ourselves again.'

'You have yours to yourself all the time,' Lucy pointed out.

'Not when Adam comes home.'

'That's only occasionally.'

Beth emptied the iron and let down the ironing board.

'Here, Daniel. Put these away.' She indicated the pile of his clothes on the table. Lucy took the others, and Beth began to cook the vegetables.

She couldn't have coped any longer. She couldn't. Although Lucy had been a gem and Daniel lent a hand, it wasn't fair to lay too much on them. Possibly there had been some slow deterioration before their grandfather died; after his death it got much worse. Muddling names. Becoming vague in conversations. Losing track of time. It was grief, naturally. She'd lost her beloved husband Tom, to whom she'd been so devoted. She didn't know what to do without him. Her life had lost its landmark. It would take a period of mourning to adapt. She would recover, they thought.

She didn't. She turned on the oven and forgot to turn it off. She ate nothing besides biscuits and the meals on wheels Beth arranged. She fell and hurt her leg. Fell and hit her head. Wandered up the road in her nighty and was brought home by the dustbin men. Beth moved her mother into the family flat and Mrs Abbott was paid to come in each day while everyone else was at school or work. Mrs Abbott was friendly and efficient, despite calling her Mary instead of Mrs Pearson, which Mary found unacceptable at the times she was able to notice it. She was no longer mobile enough to wander and most of the time didn't know where she was. Mrs Abbott said that lifting Mary's weight was beginning to strain her own back: she'd have to leave. The doctor and psychiatric social worker stepped in. It was time for her mother to enter a care home.

Although Beth had done her best, she felt guilty. And she felt guilty, too, about the way she also felt relieved. As Daniel had realised, much as she loved Lucy, it would be a liberation just to have a bedroom to herself again, even more so for Lucy, at her age. And if Mary didn't know where she was, did it matter where she was, as long as she was properly cared for?

Lucy came into the kitchen.

'Did she recognise you? Did Grandma know it was you?'

'Once, briefly. The rest of the time, not really.'

Lucy set the table, Beth called Daniel to make the gravy, his speciality, and they sat down to eat.

'Next,' said Beth, distributing portions of chicken, 'we'll have to decide what to do about the house.'

'Grandma's house? Do what about it?' asked Daniel.

'We can't continue to leave it there with no one living in it. We're lucky it hasn't been broken into already. I didn't like to do anything about it when she was staying with us. We'll have to now.'

'That does sound heartless,' said Lucy. 'It's like taking her home away from her behind her back.'

'I know. That's what I felt. But we haven't any choice. We have to top up the care home fees, and that's where the money will have to come from.'

'What are we going to do?' asked Daniel. 'Sell it?'

He put one bean on his plate and reached for the potatoes.

'Or rent it out to start with. You should eat more vegetables, Dan.'

'I'm eating potatoes.'

'They don't count.'

'They're vegetables.'

'I mean vegetables like carrots and beans and tomatoes.'

'Tomatoes aren't vegetables. They're fruit.'

'You have to eat more fruit too.'

'I drink orange juice.'

'Don't I know it.'

Daniel put a few more beans on his plate. 'Will we get loads of extra money if someone rents Grandma's house?'

'Not for us. It goes to the Home. That's how it works.'

'I can't imagine other people living among Grandma's things,' said Lucy, starting to eat.

'I know. All the same, I'd prefer to rent it out at first, rather than sell it immediately.'

'If we've got to do something, renting does seem less mean to her than selling it,' Lucy admitted.

'How do you rent it out?' asked Daniel.

'I'll give it to an agency. Most estate agents do lettings. Some people rent a house while they're waiting to buy their own.'

'What people?'

'Young professionals might be interested. Downsizing older people whose families have left home. It's an attractive house. Too small for us, though.'

'Good thing Grandma only had you,' said Daniel.

'Well, both of us stayed there when we were little, Dan,' said Lucy. 'And Adam too.'

'How did she fit us in?'

Beth had been too overwrought at those times to pay attention to practical niceties. There were only two bedrooms, but her father had been a restless sleeper so there were separate beds in the larger room, and her own was wide enough for two at a pinch. Perhaps that was how they'd done it.

'I slept with Grandma in your old bedroom, Mum,' said Lucy. 'I liked it. She used to sing me songs. She said they were the songs her mother had sung to her.'

Beth knew what they were.

'There was a tailor had a mouse,' she sang.

'Whoopsy diddly dandy dee,' Lucy joined in.

'And Burlington Bertie.' Daniel pushed his plate aside to strike a pose. 'He walked down the Strand with his gloves on and then he took them orff. Grandpa drew Burlington Bertie for me. Like a cartoon. I thought the Strand meant he was on a beach with the owl and the pussycat, until Grandpa explained when he drew it.'

'Ah – sweet,' teased Lucy.

'Shush. I was sweet. I wonder what happened to the cartoon?'

'It could be somewhere in the house,' said Beth. 'We might find it when we go through her things.'

'That's intruding,' objected Lucy.

'What else can we do? We can't leave the whole lot there, whether we sell or rent.'

'Do we own this flat?' asked Daniel thoughtfully.

'Some day,' said Beth. 'Some day my prince will come. Until he rides up it belongs to the building society. Only yoghurt pots for dessert, I'm afraid.'

'It's ours,' said Lucy, as Daniel looked discomfited.

'Your prince,' he said to Beth. 'Oh yes. You haven't told Lucy the news.'

'Told her what?'

'Telephone call.'

'Ah.' Beth began to clear the dishes. 'Your father rang while you were with Grandma. He's going up to see Adam. He wanted to know if you and Daniel would go with him.'

Lucy hesitated. 'It depends when. I don't want to take time off work for it.'

'You don't have to decide straightaway,' said Beth. 'Think about it.'

'I didn't need to think,' said Daniel, heading for the fridge. 'Oh no. I'd like to visit Adam, but not with him. I'm not going anywhere with that old git.'

And so say all of us, thought Beth as she put the dishes in the sink. But she managed to keep it inside her own head. Just.

CHAPTER III
Daniel

Daniel took the largest, newly washed, pan from the kitchen cupboard and set it on the hob over a low heat. Into the pan he deposited six candles: four of them the ordinary household white, broken into chunks but clinging to the string wick; two of them squat exotic swirls of red and green. These were perfumed, the survivors of the box he'd bought from the dodgy shop to improve the atmosphere in his bedroom. Beth had been unenthusiastic about this, partly because the heavy scent filled the entire flat and gave her a headache, mainly because she had no desire for her laboriously won and sustained home to go up in flames. Daniel's candles were forbidden. Also the joss sticks that he tried as an alternative. Although joss sticks were less liable to set fire to everything, they were alight and therefore came under the same edict.

Daniel watched his candles soften in the pan, fishing out the wicks as the wax melted. He added half a packet of butter and a lavishly prolonged squirt of washing-up liquid. Patiently he stirred with a wooden spoon until he obtained liquid homogeneity, which he poured into a mug lined with cooking foil. He placed the mug in the freezer, the pan in the sink, his feet in his blades, strapped on his pads and, with a shouted 'Bye' to his mother in the sitting room, hobbled down the stairs to street level and skated off to the roller rendezvous – a short flight of steps leading to a council estate half a mile away.

'Neal. Ade.' He greeted his friends with a statement of their names.

'Dan.'

'Dan.'

Neal was grinding the steps. He stood at a distance, pulled in his concentration, and skated forwards in long swoops. As he approached the steps, he leapt, catching the gap between his skate wheels on the edge and sliding along with arms out. At the end, he jumped off, landed and circled to a halt. The other two muttered approval.

'Wants more wax,' said Neal. He took a lump from his pocket and rubbed it along the edge of the steps. 'I'm almost out.'

'I've got some,' said Daniel. 'And I made extra before I came so I'll have plenty for next week.'

'Did it work?' asked Ade.

'It seemed OK.'

'Mine was skank. It went into layers. The bottom was runny and the top was crumbly.'

'You've got to get your proportions right,' said Neal.

'I can never remember what they are.'

'That explains it, dunnit.'

Neal ground the freshly waxed step, then Daniel, then Ade. Neal took a swig of his Red Bull and passed the can around.

'These steps are too short,' he said. 'You've no time to do anything. Let's bash the rail.'

The rail was the handrail. Daniel and Ade knew they weren't up to it.

'I'll give it a wax,' said Neal.

A window was flung open in the overlooking flat.

'Oy! What are you doing here?' An irate female voice hurtled down, saving Daniel and Ade from humiliation.

Neal went on waxing.

'Clear off. Scarper, the lot of you. You've been told before. Get out of it.'

'We can be here if we want,' returned Neal.

'No, you bloody can't. Making those steps a death trap. I'm warning you. Get out before I call the police.'

'Oh fuck off,' said Neal.

'What! What was that? You giving me lip? Just you wait! I'm calling the police.'

'Come on,' said Daniel. 'Let's go.'

'She'll not do it. She's all mouth. She can't stop us.'

'No. Come on.'

'I don't want no aggro,' agreed Ade. 'Come on, Dan. Let's go.'

'Coming Neal?'

'Miserable old cow. She's jealous because she's too old and fat and ugly to do anything except goggle TV and moan on. Where are we going?'

That was the problem. Daniel and Ade led the way out of the danger zone, Neal slouching along with exaggerated nonchalance. But at Sainsbury's, people with trolleys got in the way of the raised flowerbed. In the park, slabs had been taken out of the low walls to form grind-thwarting crenellations. Skates weren't allowed in the adventure playground.

'Boring,' pronounced Neal. 'I'm going home.'

Daniel and Ade lay on the grass, skates and pads by their sides. The Sunday spring afternoon had brought friends and families out of doors. Games resembling football, rounders and cricket were being played on the open tracts of the park. A man whirred a remote-control plane in the skies above a group of onlookers. Joggers jogged the paths, cyclists cycled, everyone circumnavigating the recreational skaters. In the enclosed area, adventure playworkers kept tabs on the timber frame runs, while in the adjoining part, younger children clambered over colourful wooden trains or called to their elders to push them on the swings.

'Neal's going to get a Nokia,' said Ade.

'What?'

'A Nokia. The red one.'

'He says.'

'Yeah. He says.'

'Who's paying?'

'Dunno.'

'So – he says.'

'Yeah.'

Daniel was watching a small boy and his father negotiate the rickety bridge to the curly slide. The boy, who had climbed up the ladder happily enough, stood by the posts at the beginning of the bridge timidly eyeing its unstable length. Two older boys ran across in the opposite direction, whooping as the curve bucked and rolled, its slats rattling. The timid boy retreated further, shaking his head at his father, who stood by the side, encouraging him. A queue had formed, and a girl, the next in line, squeezed past and moved gingerly along, stepping sideways and waiting, after one foot joined the other, until the bridge steadied again. She got to the end this way and crowed in triumph. Her friend followed, facing forwards but eyes down, holding tightly onto the chain rail. The boy and his father waited till she reached her friend on the platform, the two girls jumping up and down joyfully before vanishing down the curly slide one after the other. The father spoke to the boy, who took two steps along the bridge, faltering again as it began to dip. The father held the boy's hand, and he started out yet again. Daniel watched the sequence of hesitation and encouragement, refusal and coaxing, anticipation and the final roar of achievement when he made it. The child shot down the slide to be caught as he landed and swooped through the air in congratulation. Once replaced on the ground, the boy ran to the beginning of the slide for another go, pulling with him the jovial dad.

Daniel watched with bitter envy. Along the path came another small boy on his bike, stabilisers off, wobbling. At his side was another presumed father, equally engaged, ready to catch if necessary.

Where had Daniel's father been when Daniel's courage deserted him in a playground? Nowhere, that's where. Shouting and whinging and gone. It was Grandpa who had taught him to ride a bike, who had played a bit of football in the park. Not that Grandpa was athletic. He was artistic, what with his painting and having an art shop and everything. And he'd been knocking on – well, he was a grandpa – but he'd done his best. He'd bothered. Not like the Git. Scraping in when he felt like it, if he felt like it. Trying to get you to go to a film with him, asking about school, what's it got to do with him. Trying to get in with you. The creep. Off to try it on Adam this time. Hope Adam tells him to get lost.

'What do you reckon?' asked Ade.

'What?'

'What do you reckon? Can he do a Topside Acid?'

'Who?'

'Neal, you fish. Who else have we been talking about? He's forever going on about it, but I've never seen him do one, have you?'

'Never.'

'You know he's saying he's going to get sponsored?'

'Who by?'

'Senate, he says.'

'Not likely.'

'He says he's done it with Karen Beale.'

'He says.'

The boy had fallen off his bike, was being cuddled by his father. Families were beginning to leave the park. A queue formed by the ice cream van.

'What shall we do?'

'Dunno. We could see if Matthew's in.'

'He's at his dad's this weekend.'

'Dunno then.'

'I'd better go home. I've got some stuff to do for tomorrow.'

Outside the park, they shared a can of Irn-Bru from the ice cream van, then set off on their individual journeys home. In a residential road on his route, a long high kerb drew Daniel's attention. Unimpeded by parked cars, uninterrupted by driveways, it ran smoothly between a shiny green Range Rover and a BMW. The road was empty.

Daniel applied his wax. He went out into the road at an angle, skated diagonally towards the kerb, jumped with both feet together. He slid fast and faultlessly along the edge, landing with precision. Bliss. He skated out into the road and executed another perfect Grind. He did a Soul next, less accurately but adequately. The second attempt was better. Topside Acid? Actually, he couldn't simply Topside itself yet, but it was worth having a go, and what if he did manage it and could outdo Neal?

He skated diagonally in from the road again, jumped and locked on almost perfectly, but his skate stuck and he flew over, sprawling. No. He couldn't. Not to worry, he'd get the hang eventually and he wasn't hurt, not even his dignity since there had been nobody to see. He sat a minute or two getting his wind back, scrambling up as he heard a car approach. The car stopped a few yards distant, then drove slowly down the road. Returning to the pavement, Daniel took no notice until:

'That was stupid, wasn't it?'

The car had pulled up alongside him, window down, the male driver leaning over the passenger seat with cocked chin and narrowed eyes.

'I don't think so, thank you.'

'Don't you? You could have caused an accident, out in the middle of the road like that.'

'I wasn't in the middle of the road. And you were nowhere near me. I'd already heard you.'

'You were endangering others as well as yourself.'

'I don't think so.'

'That's the problem. You don't think. If you were my son, I'd make sure you did think – about your responsibility to other people.'

'Your son? I bet you're impotent.'

The retort was lost as the car drove away again. Son? Son? Another pushy wannabe dad shooting his interfering mouth off. He picked up a stone from the gutter and chucked it against a garden wall. It ricocheted back at an angle, hitting the Range Rover.

Oh.

Do it good. Idiot car to have in town. It's designed to be jolting over rough terrain with pebbles bouncing off it. Make it feel less out of place.

He put on some speed and skated home.

CHAPTER IV
Beth

At her desk in the large open-plan college office, Beth gave vent to the baleful thoughts she had quelled at home in the presence of her family. Her computer screen was filled with the names of students who were, theoretically, candidates for the biology modular examination, several of whom hadn't paid their entry fees. Beth's eyes studied the list but saw instead her erstwhile husband.

Why won't he bog off altogether and be done with it? she fumed inwardly. He decamps, we get life sorted again and what do you know, he comes smarming in as if we'd been in suspended animation since his previous glorious drop-by. If he still kept up with the money, we'd be better off if he otherwise removed himself from our lives. Completely.

'Hello! Anyone at home? Hello there!' called her colleague, Desree, from the desk opposite where she was registering samples of coursework that the lecturers had been bringing into the college office.

Beth glanced across. 'Did you say something?'

'I was asking you what's wrong. You're a bit grim this morning, babe.'

'Tony's back on the scene. He rang up yesterday.'

'God. At least when Carl walked out of our house he did me the favour of never walking back in again. What's Tony after?'

'He's going up to see Adam. He wanted to take the others with him.'

'Will they go?'

'Doubt it. Daniel called him an old git.'

'That's my lad.'

Desree swivelled her chair to answer the telephone, and Beth interrogated her database. She found the name she was supposed to be reviewing. No, he hadn't paid, so technically wasn't a candidate. If he didn't pull his finger out, he'd have to pay the additional cost of a late entry. Not sensible, and the less spare cash he had, the less sensible it was.

It was tough for these students on low incomes, but she had been one too, not all that long ago, and got through. An adult returner, refreshing her office skills. At this same college where she was currently employed, although she hadn't got the job here immediately after completing the course. There had first been the boring job in the builders' merchants, and after that the one shared between the bookshop and the junior school, which was entertaining until the bookshop went bust. Finally, she got this one, working in the examinations section of the college registry. It could be fraught at times, but Beth could cope. She was no longer the self-effacing creature of her past. The intervening years had made her hardy. It had been either that or go under, and she had chosen to survive.

The head of English came into the office and leaned against Beth's desk, looking frazzled.

'It's no good,' she said. 'I'll have to withdraw her, Beth.'

'Which one's that, Anne?'

'Charmaigne. The one we talked about before. She's been absent for ages. I've written twice. I've rung three times. Her tutor's been on to it and left voicemails. Nothing.'

'Yes, we've got to withdraw them when they go off radar. We can't afford them and you don't want them counting against you in your statistics.'

'Absolutely. We can't have anything dragging down the pass rate. It's frustrating, though. She could have done it. She's intelligent and has a real feel for literature. Lacking in stamina, unfortunately.'

'Stamina, huh,' grunted Desree, stapling forms together.

'Is that OK, Beth?'

'Yes, I'll withdraw her. You'll send her the notification of withdrawal, won't you?'

'I'll do it at once. Thanks, Beth. See you.'

Beth went through the withdrawal procedure, tapping keys and moving mouse. Meanwhile Max Fisher teetered towards Desree with a pile of sociology projects. She gestured at the floor by her desk. Max dropped the scripts over-quickly and knelt to tidy up the stack.

'Cutting it fine, Desree,' he said. 'Sorry. I was waiting for Likkit's. He's had a lot of problems this year, but he's kept going. It would be awful if he blew it at the eleventh hour.'

'Don't worry. You're not the only one. Not quite.'

'Also – Beth, there's an invigilation I can't make so I've done a swap with Palak. I'll memo you about it nearer the date.'

'By that time, Max, I shan't care if it's a team of dancing elephants covering the exams as long as they abide by the regulations. Have you seen how many clashes there are this year?

We've never had so many students who'll have to sit the exams out of the scheduled time.'

'With all that supervision between their exams to be organised,' sympathised Max.

'And a lot of overnight supervision this year too. I'll be begging for volunteers. I should have asked Anne while she was here. She usually comes up trumps.'

'It's a nightmare job, yours,' said Max, leaving. 'Teaching can be bad enough, but what you do would give me a nervous breakdown. We're fortunate you two are so well balanced.'

Beth accepted the compliment ruefully. Nervous breakdown. It sounded fidgety and anxious. It hadn't been like that though. She hadn't had enough energy to fidget, not enough sensibility left for anxiety. She had lived in a flat, grey world drained of meaning. The past had been locked in a brightly lit box, and although she could open the lid and observe it, like a scene in miniature, it had no connection with her. At that time the future hadn't existed; the present rolled on and on, and featureless wide spaces were filled with an endless now. The streets were vast and noiseless. In the unchanging steely light, pedestrians floated past her and cars lilted slowly along in silence. No shadows, no contours. The pavements bucked like a shaken shawl. She might skid and fall down the rabbit hole but to nowhere, for ever. She'd had to tread cautiously to avert this, tiny steps, test the ground. No. Stand motionless in case the long expanse moved again. Out, out the space. Too much space. Too far away. Too cold. Better to sit inside. Not to provoke.

Post-natal depression, they'd said. Hormones. Channelling into agoraphobia. 'And you have a beautiful baby, the image of yourself.' Daniel. Blue-eyed, dark-haired Daniel. 'And two other lovely children. And your mother to take charge of them while you concentrate on getting better. And your husband to rally round.'

It wasn't only the hormones. There was something she almost knew but couldn't allow herself to acknowledge: that he was at it again. The promises made after Lucy's birth, when that affair was discovered, had twisted and retracted. Oh yes, he had kept his promise to break off the extramarital relationship. It was what he'd promised, hadn't he, and he'd done it. However, the promise didn't cover starting up future relationships. They weren't part of the bargain, so no dishonesty there. The conscious discovery of another infidelity lay in Beth's future, as she held the newborn Daniel in emptiness and heard the voices of her older children distantly on the borders of another land.

'Hi, Beth. Hi, Desree.'

'Hello, Mehmet. What can we do for you?'

'I've got one dyslexic, one for large print, and one who'll be using a computer. All above board and medically certified.'

'Give me their exam info and the certificates and I'll see to it.'

Gradually she made a partial recovery, the older children staying long stretches with her parents, her mother calling on Beth and Daniel daily, Tony around some of the time, when he couldn't get out of it.

She lived warily for months, unwittingly waiting for the inevitable future distortion of her world when what she had not been facing up to would become certain. It was almost a relief not to be waiting any more but to be confronted with the incontestable evidence of the latest of her husband's flings.

She found a birthday card in Tony's jacket pocket. It was a suggestive card from someone called Cheryl who had written inside it a titillating note for her Big Boy.

'You didn't turn out to be much fun, did you?' he commented when challenged.

Fun? What was 'fun'? She had shrunk in misery at first, then wrath rose. Fun? She had three children to bring up. He was no use. He came and went as he pleased. He left her to do everything. Fun? What could he expect?

Obviously more than she was capable of giving, he responded. Unimaginative. Unadventurous. Boring.

She collapsed under the assault on her personality. Raged. Collapsed again. The children lived with her parents while the fighting continued. She separated from him, ultimately divorced. She got the flat; he had access. When he felt like it. If he felt like it. On those occasions, he arrived confidently, increasingly prosperous, flashing gifts at the children, her children, all that shielded her from the fearful beyond. Beth he treated with disdain.

Daniel started school.

'You've done it,' said another mother in the playground. 'You're a strong woman. You've held it together. What are you going to do next?'

Beth was gobsmacked. 'A strong woman.' Was the scrimpy, clinging-on creature she felt herself to be really a strong woman? Perhaps she was. She began to adopt the new view of herself. She had coped and could go on coping. She could do something. She could be independent, returning to the office world she had been able to handle before her marriage. If she could do it in her youthful inexperience, she could definitely do it tempered by her older harsh experience. She reverted to her maiden name, enrolled on the adult returners course and became a student for a year, her mother having the children after school when necessary, although not routinely because the course was designed for women like her on the basis of a short day. But sometimes it was enjoyable to sit in the college canteen after classes and talk with the other women, learning about everybody's mishaps and struggles, grimacing and consoling and joking. That was fun.

'No fun for him,' Desree was saying. 'We'll have to refer him to student services. We can't take responsibility for something like that.'

'No. Not our pigeon,' agreed Beth.

'It's not as if we haven't got enough to do. Before long they'll be telling us to shove a broom up our bums and sweep the floor as we go.'

'Such lovely bums too,' murmured a passing IT boffin, on the way to his own section. 'No – delete that. I didn't say it. I definitely did not say that.'

CHAPTER V
Lucy

Lucy folded the sweaters that customers had pulled out of the pile for inspection and dumped in disarray. She rearranged the shoes on the racks. She sprayed the display cabinet with glass cleaner. At these times an image arose of the apron that the mother of one of her sixth-form friends used to wear in the kitchen. It pictured a woman in a mortarboard washing up, surrounded by the legend 'What a degree did for me'. Lucy hadn't hit the university scene yet, but her high exam grades weren't noticeably relevant to her present source of income as a clothes shop assistant. Nevertheless, this was what she did for the time being, and she wanted to do it properly. She was glad that her father had never rung back to find out if she and Daniel would go with him to visit their elder brother. It could be that he had lost interest in going. It could be he hadn't got round to explaining that it wasn't convenient for Adam. Whatever the reason, Tony's latest disruption had fizzled out.

Lucy's colleague, Maya, was on placement from a merchandising course, which gave her a certain panache in the way she adjusted the clothes on the hangers. Their supervisor, Niomi, was in the stockroom. Selling was slack.

'How did you wangle getting off early today?' asked Maya, stroking the lapels of a jacket.

'I'm owed it. I did extra last month.'

'Lucky for some.' Maya made space on the rail for a crushed skirt. 'Got anything planned?'

'Doing my bedroom.'

'Oh-kay. Is there nothing better on offer?'

'It's not as bad as it sounds. It's the one my grandmother was using. It used to be mine. When she came to live with us, she had it, and I shared with my mum. Now she's gone into the Home, it's mine again. This will be the first chance I've had to move all my gear back.'

'My grandmother lives with us,' said Maya. 'Makes fantastic chapattis but we have to share rooms too. It must be brilliant to have your own. What are you going to do with it?'

'I haven't decided. There's still a bit of stuff left in there. I'll sort that first to see how it goes.'

'You want to check out the magazines – *Elle Decoration*, something like that. See what they're doing so you can have the same.'

'What with? I won't be employing an interior design practice.'

'Oh, you know what I mean. You'd pick up some ideas and do it yourself. It's like clothes, isn't it? The originals come out, which no one can afford, but once you've seen them in the magazines you can create a similar outfit for yourself with cheaper things.'

'Or not, as the case may be.'

'If you're someone who can't be arsed. You don't get anywhere that way.'

'No.'

'I'll be wearing designer clothes one day. That's my dream. You've got to be sure about what you want, and I'm aiming high.'

'Yes. I know you are.' Maya's single-minded determination could be a conversation stopper at times.

'If you don't go for it, you'll never get it.'

Lucy wondered if this were true. When she read interviews with famous people, it often sounded as if they'd got where they were by a fortunate coincidence of events. Perhaps that was pretence in order to appear attractively nonchalant as opposed to raveningly ruthless. Or perhaps events do arrange themselves advantageously for people who already possess a purpose. Or perhaps it's one explanation for one person and something different for someone else.

'What's yours?' Maya kept to her theme.

'My what?'

'Your dream. Your aim. What are you going out to get?'

Lucy wished she knew.

'Next,' she said, 'I go to university.'

'Then what?'

What indeed. She hadn't been able to project herself further than getting the university place, and that hadn't been the result of a mission, like Maya, more like riding a rolling wave which, provided you hung in there, deposited you on the shore of higher education. It was a wave of assumption produced by others – teachers, her mother and even Adam, who had rolled in before her. According to her school reports she was perceptive and conscientious, which were apparently required attributes, but Lucy also recognised that some years ago, not long after getting the junior school job, Beth had suddenly become more involved in her own children's academic achievement. She started to check that their homework had been done, even though Lucy didn't need to be monitored. That summer a copy of Adam's GCSE examination timetable was attached to the kitchen wall and, with furrowed brow and a lapful of exercise books, she tested him on what he should have revised. Daniel was told not to play near Adam, because he was doing important work. Although Adam resisted at first, their mother was strangely relentless. He got good results, which filled him with amazed pride, and the demands of this new self-image carried him on through A levels to business studies at university and out the other side to a job in his northern university town.

Meanwhile, Lucy did her homework, revised for tests and passed her exams creditably, according to assumption. Presumably, she would be safe to press on in that manner for a further three years on the psychology course, but where it was leading to was another matter. She hoped she would find out as she went along.

'Looks as if you need to get it organised,' commented Maya.

'What?' said Niomi, stepping briskly into the shop from the stockroom.

'Life,' said Maya.

'Oh that,' said Niomi, who was having difficulty in finding a reliable man. 'It doesn't make any difference whether you organise it or not. It goes its own way. I thought you were talking about the shelves. No, don't worry – they're good enough. Do you want to go, Lucy? You can if you want. We're faffing around here.'

As Lucy left, Maya was telling Niomi about some new quick-drying nail varnish that had transformed her life vis-à-vis her manicure routine, and Niomi was expressing scepticism as to whether that was transformation enough. The arrival of a lone customer interrupted the conversation; two more were lingering with intent outside on the high street, and Lucy scurried off before she could be recalled in case of a mini rush. She wanted to get on with her room.

She caught the bus outside Putney station, noticing a trifle guiltily that the number of shoppers was increasing, and sat downstairs for the short journey home. They lived in a low-level block of between-the-wars flats, separated from the road by a hedge and belt of flowerless grass. The building was rendered white, its metal window frames painted green. Adam said it looked as if it had been made from a 1930s child's construction kit.

Lucy walked up the path and punched in the code to open the front door. The morning's mail lay on the entrance hall floor. Lucy picked out the letters for her family from the litter of fliers for pizzas, discounted carpet cleaning and minicabs, and put the ones belonging to the other five flats on the communal table. There were window envelopes for her mother, with one letter for herself, posted in Lyon, from her friend, Rebecca, who was spending her gap year as an au pair and who sent regular updates about how her French life was turning out.

At first, Rebecca had written about being homesick. Monsieur and Madame, the young couple who employed her, were good-humoured but they worked long hours, were tired and basically wanted her to get on with it. The older child, Cyrille, was uncooperative and mimicked her non-native French disparagingly. Also, she hadn't realised that babies were so exhausting. She had thought she wouldn't be able to stick it for long. However, she did stick it, and Cyrille now boasted to his school friends that he could speak English;

the baby, JoJo, was cute; there were advantages in Monsieur and Madame being busy; and she had a boyfriend, Serge, who appeared, judging from the photos, enticingly mean and menacing, but fortunately liked children, which produced the extra advantage that she could combine childcare and other activities without too many complications. She couldn't bear to imagine what she would do in England without him.

Au pairing for a year was what Lucy had intended to do originally. She had been allocated to a family in Rouen. They had exchanged photographs, everything was shaping up, and then her grandmother massively deteriorated. Beth moved her into the flat, where it was easier to keep an eye on her, and Lucy, seeing how demanding this was, withdrew from the au pair scheme in order to be around to help at home, although Beth told her it was unnecessary.

So this was her gap year. Her friends at university, or somewhere or other around the world, and Lucy not knowing if she could make anything of the rest of this year, let alone, as Maya exhorted, having any coherent plan for the rest of her life.

Lucy climbed the stairs to the first floor and let herself into their flat. She went into the kitchen, put her mother's bills in a pile on the table, made a mug of coffee and a cheese sandwich and sat down to read the latest instalment of the children's antics and Serge's passion.

That could have been her too, she thought as she read. By this stage, she might have been fluent in French and romantically attached. Somewhere, living a life in Rouen, was the mean man who might have been hers. Someone who didn't even know it. Neither did Lucy herself, come to that. She was on a ludicrous speculation. She wasn't particularly good-looking, with her fawn hair and pale eyes. She hadn't managed a boyfriend here in London and there was no reason why Rouen should have been any different. Pull yourself together girl. Get back on your own planet, where a bout of cleaning is a major satisfaction.

Obedient to her own commands, Lucy folded the letter and put her plate and mug in the sink on top of the breakfast crockery. She went into the bedroom she had been sharing with her mother and changed out of her fashion-shop worker clothes into old jeans and T shirt. Taking the radio with her, she went to her own room, previously lent to her grandmother and now hers again.

It was uncharacteristic, the smell that hung behind the door. It wasn't how her grandmother had smelled when she was younger and active, when she had taken them home for tea after school or when they had stayed with her in her tranquil, shiny house. She had smelled of pink soap and floral hand cream – honeysuckle or damask rose. Her house smelled of polish and fabric conditioner, wafting from cushions when you sat down, and from the curtains when they were drawn, and from the bedding if you were sleeping there. Mary's room in the flat had a different smell: stale, sickly, static. They had kept her and the room clean, encouraged her to move around, ventilated, sprayed air freshener, yet the decaying scent lingered. Lucy opened the windows as wide as they would go, an act of disloyalty, as if it were an attempt to eradicate her grandmother's aura. With one foot on the bed and the other on the window ledge, she took down the curtains and put them in the washing machine on a delicates cycle.

The wardrobe held one dress and some old-fashioned padded coat hangers. Lucy folded the dress and put it outside her room to take to the Home. Opening the chest to line the drawers with scented paper that Rebecca had given her for Christmas, Lucy found Mary again, for a pair of stockings was rolled up and pushed into a corner next to a little pile of greetings cards they had given her on her birthday, separately to produce the impression of more, and a flower-spray brooch with a broken pin. It was the brooch her grandmother used to wear on the lapel of her jacket when Lucy was a child. Noticing that the Queen wore jewellery on her coat collars, Lucy had felt that she was walking with royalty when she was out with her grandmother. Now its broken condition seemed to echo her grandmother's state, and Lucy cradled it in her palm before putting it on the bed to keep among her own things later. She went through the birthday cards. The one from Adam was a dapper cat in a sharp city suit. Daniel's was a cartoon cat. Beth's cat snoozed on a cottage doorstep, and Lucy's gazed out to sea from an indoor window ledge. Although Mary loved cats, she could never keep one as a pet because they made Tom wheeze and go red. The family's birthday cards were a yearly substitute.

A scraping of keys, banging and thud indicated that Daniel had arrived home from school. His bag was lying in the middle of the hall, his shoes wide-angled a yard apart, his sweatshirt dumped on the kitchen table, and Daniel himself in the process of tugging the lid off the biscuit tin.

'Hello,' he said, surprised. 'Why are you here?'

Lucy explained.

'Right,' said Daniel. 'Bye.' He made off to his bedroom with a handful of biscuits and a carton of orange juice.

Lucy replaced the cards and brooch in the newly lined drawers and picked up the stockings to add to the dress outside. They looked rather old and felt strange, a little knobbly, and she began to unroll them to see if they were in good enough condition to be worth taking for her grandmother. As she unrolled, the end of a tarnished silver chain slid out. What on earth was that doing there? Further along, the chain had caught on a snag, then, as she continued to unroll, Lucy could see that an entire locket and chain had been wrapped up with the stockings. It was as if it had been hidden away from burglars or from prying eyes. Lucy disentangled the chain and held the locket up. It too was tarnished silver, oval, and etched with a curly pattern round the edge. What an unusual and pretty thing to find in a pair of old stockings! She dug her thumbnails into the join to open it. Inside was one browning photograph of a woman, who seemed familiar, despite the clothes and the hairstyle and the general old-fashioned demeanour; familiar because she had the same features as Lucy's mother. Lucy peered at the photograph. How weird to see her own mother in this unknown person. Who was she? Lucy put the locket in the drawer with the brooch and cards to discuss with her mother later.

Sticking to her plan, Lucy transferred the curtains to the dryer, remade the bed and moved her clothes into the drawers and wardrobe from their squashed housing in her mother's room. She made another mug of coffee, and drank it asking herself whether she wanted to repaint the room. No. The sounds of a computer game bounced from behind Daniel's door. Lucy shut her bedroom window and sniffed the air. She couldn't tell, having been in there all afternoon, but it must be better.

'Come on, Dan. You'd better start your homework,' she called at his door, then returned to the kitchen, where she began to make pasta sauce and salad.

When Beth came in the washing up was done, the hall was tidy, the pasta was ready to be cooked, and Lucy was explaining to Daniel what she could remember of the electro-magnetic spectrum.

'You are an angel,' said Beth, sinking into a chair. 'I'd forgotten you were coming home early. Did you enjoy your afternoon?'

'I moved my stuff into my room,' said Lucy. 'There's plenty of space for you to spread out again.'

There was a pause while neither of them said how good it would be to have their rooms to themselves. An image of Mary hung in the silence.

'And, Mum,' Lucy was reminded, 'I found something when I was doing out the chest of drawers.'

'When's dinner?' asked Daniel from the depths of his physics book.

'Any moment.' Lucy headed to the sink to fill a large pan with water. 'Can you guess what it was?' she continued.

Water sloshed into the pan, and the entryphone buzzer sounded in the hall.

'Expecting a friend?' asked Beth of Daniel.

'Nope.'

She levered herself up. 'I'm nearest. I'll go.'

The security receiver clicked. Beth spoke, and spoke again. The buzz sounded to open the door.

Beth returned to the kitchen.

'Well, what do you know?' she said blithely. 'It's your father. He's on his way up.'

CHAPTER VI
Tony

'Hydy ho, campers!' said Tony, rolling into the room. 'Looks like I've come at the right time. What's for supper?'

He stood in the doorway, rubbing his hands together and beaming round. He wore a leather bomber jacket, and had cropped his hair to minimise the recession.

Lucy gestured half-heartedly towards the pan on the hob.

'Nothing,' said Daniel. 'We don't eat here. We've evolved beyond that stage.'

'Have you? That's a retrograde step. Eating is one of life's pleasures. And drinking. Speaking of which...' He went out into the hall again – a brief intermission during which Daniel pulled a face and Beth shrugged at Lucy – and returned with a bottle of wine.

'Here we are,' he said, brandishing it. 'First goodie. Highly recommended in the Sundays. Daniel – get a corkscrew. Train your manly skills on that.' Thrusting the bottle at Daniel, he began opening and shutting a succession of cupboard doors in search of glasses. 'You've moved them,' he complained. 'What have you done with them? Can't find a thing.'

Beth opened a cupboard and indicated the array of glasses.

'Cloth?' said Tony. 'Clean cloth?'

Lucy handed over a tea towel, and Tony sniffily withdrew a series of not-quite-matching wine glasses, polishing each one and holding it up to the light before putting it on the table. Meanwhile, Daniel was in a tussle with the cork. He hadn't slit the capsule and was battling to push an old-fashioned corkscrew downwards. He changed tactic and pulled, the bottle between his knees. The wooden handle came off, leaving the screw in the cork.

'Haven't you anything better than that?' asked Tony, casting aspersion from the glasses cupboard.

Beth stood by with a screwpull. 'Shall I do it?' she whispered. Daniel shook his head, scarlet.

'You'll need pliers,' said Tony.

Lucy had realised this and was ready with a pair from the DIY drawer. Daniel took them from her, gripped the bottle with his knees and attached the pliers. The screw came slowly out, fragments of cork clinging to the spirals, the main cork with its new borehole obstinately stuck in the neck of the bottle.

Beth held out the screwpull, but Tony had finished with the glasses.

'Give it here,' he said in world-weary tones. 'I don't know. We'll be straining the cork through our teeth now.' He opened the bottle, poured out four glasses and handed them round. Daniel shunned his and made for the door.

'Just a minute, just a minute.' Tony raised his hand. 'There are more goodies. Wait your rush.' He put down his glass and went into the hall again. Daniel determinedly avoided noticing that his mother was signalling for him to stay. Tony returned with full arms. There was a large bunch of irises, tied up with a raffia bow. For Daniel there were copies of the latest editions of the skater magazines and a set of new wheels. For Beth and Lucy there were bottles of scent.

'Been to Costa Packet,' he said as he gave the perfume. 'No. Barcelona, if truth be told. That was holiday. But I'll be going to Los Angeles soon, Daniel. Daniel!' Daniel was squirming out of the door. 'Plenty of skating there. Keep in with me and I might be willing to take orders.' He patted the side of his nose. Daniel left.

'Why are we standing?' cried Tony to Lucy and Beth. 'Never stand when you can sit, my old granny used to say. Have you any nibbles to go with this, Beth? I feel like a nibble or two. Oh, forget it.'

He sat down at the kitchen table. After a moment, Lucy did too. Beth leaned against the draining board.

'Mmm,' said Tony with a wide, closed-mouth smile. 'What a treat it is to see you. Here's to you both.'

He raised his glass in salute, picked out a speck of cork, and drank. 'Difficult age.' He jerked his head to where Daniel no longer was. 'Early teens – difficult. Best to take no notice, Beth, that's what I say. Ignore it. Don't let him undermine you. You've got our lovely Lucy here at your side. And Adam's doing himself proud. I expect Daniel will grow up a bit to take Adam's place in the family now he's going.'

'Now who's going where?'

'Adam,' said Tony. 'Now he's going to Singapore.'

'What do you mean – now he's going to Singapore?' Beth approached the table and stood before him, stunned.

'Hasn't he told you?' Tony rearranged himself, throwing the ankle of one leg over the knee of the other. 'Hey ho, these young ones. So full of their plans that they forget to keep in touch.'

'Apparently he kept in touch with you. Did you go up to visit him? How do you know about this?'

'I was involved, you see. I heard of this job, via a business contact, and I thought that it would be beneficial for Adam at this stage of his career. He's got a good degree, a bit of experience here, he just has to build up his CV, take a long view, plan a few steps in advance. I put it to him some time ago, and he went ahead. He doesn't let the grass grow. Daniel will make it too eventually. Don't let him worry you.' He took another drink. 'Not bad this, is it?'

'Daniel doesn't worry me.'

'Bravo.'

'But what about Adam?' Beth sat down. 'Had you heard anything about this, Lucy? Did you know?'

'No, I didn't.'

'What about "What about Adam?"? That's it. I've given him a leg up to a job in Singapore. He's good enough to be offered it and he's sense enough to accept it. He's going, but I'm not sure when. He's an adult, Beth. He's got his career to develop. You can't cling on to him.'

'I've no intention of clinging on to him. I'm saying it would have been better for me to know.'

'You do know. I've told you.'

'Yes, you have.'

'So what's the problem?' He refilled his own glass, and stretched the bottle out to Lucy, who covered her glass with her hand. Beth's was on the draining board, untouched. Tony rolled his eyes at it and began to work on Lucy.

'What are you doing with yourself nowadays, lovely Lucy?' he said, hanging his arm over his chair. 'What young man is going to go weak at the knees when you swan in smelling gorgeous?'

Lucy answered flatly, aware of her mother's pain.

How could, Beth was thinking, how could Adam have kept this to himself? Except it wasn't kept to himself, that wouldn't have hurt as much. It was kept between himself and Tony, excluding Beth while they fixed it. She had been so gratified by Adam's success. Now he was in cahoots with Tony and didn't consider her worth discussing his plans with or even keeping informed. Tony had taken him over and she had been kept out.

She watched Tony attempting to flirt with his own daughter. It came to him as second nature. Years ago, he had courted Beth extravagantly. At the time, she couldn't understand what he saw in her, passive and unoriginal as she was, and never understood it throughout her married life. It wasn't until recently, in middle age, coming across some photographs of her young self, that she realised how pretty she had been. An ambitious, spirited go-getter, who wanted his life adorned, supported and not defied, might find her ideal at first. It's regrettable, she thought, that she hadn't appreciated what potential power her looks gave her. With greater confidence and ruthlessness, she could have been the one calling the tune, and the subsequent misery, or at any rate that specific variety of misery, would not have occurred. If she hadn't been impressed by Tony's purposefulness and exuberance. If she hadn't found him exhilarating in contrast to the respectable inertia of her home life. If she'd had more of those qualities within herself and hadn't needed them from him, she might have married someone else.

But in that case, there wouldn't be Lucy, Daniel and Adam. It was impossible to imagine the non-existence of these three solid beings, so important in her life. It was equally impossible to imagine the children who might have been their replacements. She re-called into existence her dear Lucy and Daniel and clever, thoughtless Adam. That felt better. They were beyond value, regardless of the rest of it.

'When someone sits looning at a table, you'd assume the wine had been well tipped down their throat, not left on the draining board,' said Tony. 'What's amusing you, Beth?'

'Oh nothing,' said Beth, lightly. 'A thought.'

'What thought?'

'Nothing. It doesn't matter. How's business, Tony?'

'Ah, good, good. One or two things in the pipeline.' He worked his shoulder blades into the chair, pulled at his jacket and stood up.

'I must be getting on. I only called to drop off the presents.'

'They're very nice.' Beth stood up. 'Thank you, Tony.'

'Don't mensh, you're welc.'

Lucy stood up too and followed them into the hall.

'Goodbye, Lucy.' Tony kissed her flamboyantly on both cheeks, and stepped back, holding on to her elbows. 'You're as lovely as ever.'

He let go of her. 'Goodbye, Daniel,' he called to the blank array of doors. No reply. Tony sniffed, unsmilingly acknowledged Beth and left. Daniel came out of his room.

'Has he gone?'

'He has.'

'Thank God for that. It's a pity the millennium bug didn't strike early and drop his plane out of the sky. What's he keep crawling in for? Can't we tell him to sod off and never come here again?'

'No, we can't.'

'Why not?'

'He's got the right to see you, Danny. You know he has.'

'Whose right?'

'The legal right.'

'And what if I don't want to see him?'

Beth put her arm round Daniel and walked him into the kitchen. 'Oh, Dan. It's not often. We can put up with that.'

'Why should we put up with it? Not often! We don't see him for ages, thank God, then he rings up and asks us out and never rings back, not that we wanted to go with him, but it would have been the same if we had wanted to. Then he turns up when he feels like it, not because we've asked to see him, and expects us to be all over him.'

Lucy removed the used glasses and handed Daniel the cutlery to set out.

'He kept doing that when we were younger,' he continued, holding a fistful of forks and spoons, 'he'd say he was coming to take us out – and not turn up. Don't you remember, Luce? We'd be ready, waiting, and where was he? Eh? Missing. AWOL. Isn't that true, Mum?'

Beth relieved him of the cutlery and laid the table while Lucy cooked the pasta.

'We were going to the funfair once. He'd got it set up for us like a big deal. And he didn't turn up. Don't you remember, Luce?'

Beth passed him the salad dressing to mix.

'Grandpa took us later on,' said Lucy.

'I know.' Daniel jerked the oil and vinegar violently around. 'Grandpa was the one who mattered, not him.'

'And you're the ones who matter to me,' said Beth. 'He's gone, Danny. We've done it for the time being. Let's have supper and talk about something else.'

'Like what?'

'We'll find something.'

CHAPTER VII
Mary

I must keep things clean. Tom says, You don't have to do so much. So much dusting and washing and tidying. But I want to. It feels better that way. I don't feel at ease if there's a mess. He's saying that about the cleaning for my sake, to save me from doing too much, not as a complaint. Because he's such a loving man. So even-tempered. Never a cross word in all these years. Always to be relied upon. And he's tidy himself. He's neat about his person, and he doesn't leave things lying around, and he'll do those jobs which keep the house in good order – decorating, trimming the hedges, keeping everything maintained.

Appearances are important. When everything is clean and in condition, people respect it. It's solid. Everything as it should be. Nothing amiss.

There's a mark on the carpet there. I'd better—

'Yes? Hello, dear. Tea? Yes please. Biscuits? Thank you. How am I? Very well, thank you. And you? Oh good.'

I used to make most of Beth's clothes. Bonnets and jackets when she was a baby. Such an enchanting baby. When she was older, at school, there was a fashion for them to wear boleros and pleated skirts. I made her those. The boleros were angora, soft and fluffy, though the fibres got over you when you were doing the knitting. I made the skirts too. They didn't take long, those little things. You just had to be meticulous in measuring the pleats accurately. I did cardigans, too, in different stitches with fancy buttons in the shape of flowers and Scottie dogs. She liked the Scottie dogs best. I made her a bag with Scottie dogs on. I did ribbed cardigans with plain yokes and embroidered them with lazy-daisy stitch. Black patent shoes with ankle straps, cotton frocks that tied with a bow. Red sandals.

People used to compliment me. Oh Mrs Pearson, they'd say. You do dress Beth beautifully. She's as pretty as a picture. She was too. The apple of Tom's eye. They looked captivating together. Not like me, with my hair the colour of nothing and more heavily built. I take after my father in that respect. Unfortunately.

What's that, Father? Rice pudding tonight? Yes, Father, if that's what you'd like. Rice pudding tonight.

It isn't what I had planned. I was going to make apple pie, but it's Father who holds the reins. He's the head of the household and he won't countenance being crossed. If he wants rice pudding, rice pudding it will be, despite the apple pie being already in the oven. Which it isn't. I exaggerate. It's too early to be cooking dinner, and even he knows it takes time.

Rice, sugar, weighed out and scooped into strong blue paper bags. Butter, though it was margarine during the war and austerity.

I'm convinced it was the prospect of war that finished Mother. She was grieved, so grieved. She'd lost two brothers and an uncle in the trenches the first time round. She couldn't bear for it to be starting up again. That suffering.

The shop assistants, my father's employees, are affable to me. Polite but kind too. I don't think it's because of my father. He wouldn't notice. The polite part – he would expect that absolutely – but the kind part is a non-obligatory extra. I'm grateful for it.

I don't know. I don't know...

I wanted Beth to have pretty clothes because I didn't. Father wouldn't let me have anything fashionable. I put on some lipstick once – one solitary time, as far as he was aware.

Face of Jezebel! he bellowed, and made me rub it off on the spot. I'm not having my daughter done up like a strumpet.

An old-fashioned term, though that didn't strike me at the time. I was too upset. Mother was upset as well. She didn't wear make-up, but she was beautiful without it.

A strumpet.

'The red badge of courage.' That's what they used to call lipstick during the war. It would have taken more than courage to wear it in our house, at any time.

I'll wash the cups and tidy round. The sun is lovely. Isn't the sun lovely? Oh, it shows a streak on the window. I'll do that in a minute.

He shouldn't have called me a strumpet. You shouldn't say things like that to a young girl. Or an old girl either.

Chuckling? What am I chuckling about? I don't know. I don't know.

Mother. Mother, it's me. It's Mary. How are you? Carry says you fell in the garden, she doesn't know why. Did you stumble? Does anything hurt?

Dizzy. You suddenly came over dizzy. And your head aches. I'll draw the curtains. Is that better? Have you had an aspirin?

I'll bring you a drink. No, no, Father's not home yet. I've just got in from school.

I won't be going back.

I never went back.

I was nursing Mother. Father thought she was malingering, but she wasn't.

'Full fathom five thy father lies.' We used to sing that at school. 'Ding, dong, bell.'

Ding, dong, bell. Pussy's in the well.

Dick Whittington. Let's do *Dick Whittington.* He went to London to seek his fortune. Good idea. Who's going to be Dick Whittington? It will be a feat to do that pantomime but it will be all right on the night. We'll sing songs. We always sing songs along the way. Who will be Dick? It's me! Principal boy – me! Off to London to seek my fortune.

I'll need some boots. The principal boy wears boots. 'Hello dear – I need some boots.' Boots with heels on. 'No, I'm not going out walking. They're for Dick Whittington.' He'd have tights too. High-heeled boots and tights! I hope I'm not flaunting myself. But if that's what the principal boy wears I'd be more noticeable if I didn't wear them. You have to play the part. You have to keep up the appearance. High-heeled boots and tights. They won't be unseemly in the panto. They're what the audience expects. 'I'll have boots and a cat.' Lord Mayor of London? No, I'm not that!

Chuckling again? What am I chuckling at? Delusions of grandeur, that's what. Perhaps I'd better play the cat. The cat was clever.

Cats are clever.

They know how to manage it. They get on with their lives without intruders. They're polite – cats are gracious – but you don't presume with a cat, you wouldn't enquire too deeply, you're circumspect.

I'll be the cat.

I'd like to wear the boots, though.

'What's that, dear?' *Puss in Boots*! That would solve the problem. We could do *Puss in Boots*.

But I must go to London.

I've got to go to London.

Not *Puss in Boots*.

Dick Whittington.

Thank you, anyway.

London.

CHAPTER VIII
The Family

They were going to Tom and Mary's house to clear it up for letting. Although this was the pragmatic solution, it was a painful decision for Beth. It entailed facing square-on the fact that Mary would never be living there again: that part of her life was over. Worse, since Mary was incapable of giving consent, it felt like a betrayal, a furtive usurpation. Beth told herself realistically that Mary's loss of awareness was all to the good in these circumstances, as disposal of the house couldn't matter to her. Yet it felt cruel and she pinched her nose to stop the damp coming through.

'It's good of you two to give me a hand with this,' she said, as they walked to the car. 'Do you want to drive, Lucy?'

'Oh no. Save us, preserve us,' said Daniel.

'In that case, yes I will drive,' said Lucy. She took the driver's seat. Daniel and Beth got in, Daniel with mock trembling as he climbed into the back. Lucy started the engine and moved off.

'Death took the road as Lucy took the wheel,' said Daniel. 'Londoners take cover.'

'I'll take a hatchet in a minute,' said Lucy.

'She's a very competent driver,' said Beth. 'And don't forget that there's an ejector button for disruptive passengers.'

'Ooo errr,' said Daniel.

There was silence for a few minutes before he said, 'How long will we be?'

'We haven't got there yet,' said Lucy.

'About a couple of hours this morning,' said Beth. 'We won't be able to do more than make a start, I should imagine. When you're both fed up, we'll leave it.'

'OK,' said Daniel.

There was silence again until Lucy, thinking of her bedroom, said, 'It's going to feel funny doing this.'

'I know.'

They arrived in the street of modest Victorian terraced houses. Lucy parked as near as she could, some yards from number 12.

'I'd better tell the Marriotts we're here,' said Beth, taking a holdall from the floor by Daniel's feet. She went to knock at number 10 where the retired couple lived who were on the alert for unwarranted happenings next door. By the time Lucy had locked the car and made her way up the road with Daniel and a roll of black plastic bags, Beth had left the Marriotts and was walking towards Mary's.

Tom and Mary's house was built of London stock. The solid wood front door and windows were painted white. Nestled between the curve of the bay and the dividing fence was a dustbin, which the Marriotts obligingly put a bag of rubbish into each week to make it appear that the house was still inhabited. Beth unlocked the mortice and the Yale and pushed the door open over the heap of junk mail. The smell from their childhoods rolled over them as they entered. This was her grandmother's smell, thought Lucy, not the one she'd tried to eradicate.

The hall had the original black and white tiles stretching past the staircase to the kitchen, whose door was three-quarters open, drawing the eye across the room to the window, through which the green of the garden could be seen. A long time ago, her grandmother had suggested that the hall would be cosier if it were carpeted. Grandpa, liking the Dutch Interior perspective of the tiles, had been against the idea. His own paintings hung along the walls, intricate river scenes and views of the common.

'What's the plan?' asked Daniel, moving down the hall.

'It would be quicker if each of us dealt with a separate room,' Beth said. 'Could you do the kitchen, Dan? It should be straightforward.'

'What do I do?'

'Look in the drawers and cupboards. Any tins or packets that are past their date, throw into a black bag and put in the dustbin. If there are any that are within date and we might use, put them on the side. Leave things like washing-up liquid and cleaning products. We'll need them on a future trip here.'

'OK,' said Daniel. 'Where are the black bags?'

Lucy tore off a couple for him and he went to the kitchen, plugging in his earphones as he went.

'Me?' questioned Lucy.

'Shall we do the rest of this floor? You do the front of the room and I'll do the back.'

It was what estate agents term a double reception. There was a dining table and chairs in the back room, a china cabinet and a built-in cupboard at the side of the chimney breast. This was where Christmas dinners were eaten, important, more extensive meals than those taken at the kitchen table. After scanning and rejecting the china cabinet, Beth started on the cupboard. Lucy stood in the middle of the front sitting room. Sofa, chairs, television, shelves and another cupboard built into the alcove.

'What do we do about books and ornaments?' she asked.

'Leave them for the moment. We'll decide about them another time. Throw out anything that's obviously rubbish and set aside anything that's personal – like photos or letters or any of your grandfather's sketches. We'll take those with us. Like this – oh, Lucy.'

She was gazing at a pencil drawing of a woman, sitting on a wooden chair. A large-eyed baby on her lap stared out with solemn curiosity.

'That's Grandma,' said Lucy.

'Yes, so that must be me.'

'Oh, Mum, you are adorable. And Grandma looks, she looks sort of thankful.'

Beth examined the picture of the young mother, her mother, appreciably younger than Beth herself was now. She felt a surge of protectiveness towards that comfortable and – yes – thankful-looking figure. That cuddly baby too, who became herself. Innocent of their futures. She wanted to dive into time past and smooth away the forthcoming rucks. She knew what was lying in wait for that baby. She was at the other side of it. She hoped.

'There's nothing else to do in this cupboard, Lucy. It's tablecloths and things like that, which we can leave. This sketch was with some stationery. I'll put it here on the table to go with us.'

She put down the canvas holdall and went to see how Daniel was getting on in the kitchen.

'You're doing a good job there, Dan.'

Daniel, his back to her and his earphones in, couldn't hear. She touched him lightly on his shoulder to get his attention. Startled, he whipped round.

'Aargh!' He freed one earhole of wiring. 'What's this sneaking about, Mum?'

'I was saying that you're doing a good job,' said Beth. 'Could you do the bathroom afterwards? Same principle, but it should be quicker.'

'I've ditched most of the things here,' said Dan. 'The tins of soup and things like that were OK.' He pointed to a cluster on the table. 'There wasn't a lot in the cupboard.'

'There won't be much in the bathroom. There won't be many clothes left either. We brought most of Grandma's when she came to live with us, and Grandpa's were given away after he died. We're just doing the odds and sods today. We'll come another time to get it ready for letting.'

'OK,' said Dan. He dropped a packet of bran buds into the black bag and took it upstairs with him to the bathroom, glancing through the open sitting room door as he passed.

Lucy had found a photograph album in the cupboard and was sitting on the floor, absorbed in its pages.

'Are we clearing or not? Some of us have already done a whole room, you know.'

'Yeah yeah. I got distracted. I'll save it for later.'

She put down the album and delved on.

This was a cupboard of things to take with them. A wooden box was filled with tubes of paint. She took out a burnt sienna and squeezed it to see whether it felt squidgy enough. Daniel might be able to make use of them, though she hadn't seen him painting for ages. She replaced the tube and put the box on the floor by her side. Another box was full of cotton reels, a cough lozenge tin of pins, a packet of needles, a tape measure and a pair of embroidery scissors. Behind it was a pair of cutting-out scissors, some pinking shears, a wallet of knitting needles and a plastic bag of old patterns. Lucy pulled one out, a mawkish child in an embroidered cardigan, holding a kitten. An unfinished box of milk chocolates lay deep in the cupboard, some of the soft centres oozing into the paper cups, and flat on the shelf under the pattern bag and chocolates was a sheet of paper, which proved to be no other than Burlington Bertie. There he was, an elegant if threadbare figure, with monocle and head held high, his gloves orff and carried gracefully.

'Dan!' called Lucy.

He was upstairs, plugged in, and couldn't hear. She put the drawing on the table for him and returned to the next box, a box of – of what wasn't immediately apparent, because it was locked. It was the size of a hand, dark green leather, scored and worn at the corners. A strap with a metal tip attached the lid to a gold-coloured clasp at the front. Lucy jiggled it. There was a slight movement within and the lid slid up and down as if the catch were weak.

Would there be more jewellery inside, Lucy wondered, like the intriguing locket she'd found in Grandma's drawer and hadn't had a chance to ask her mother about yet? She chose the largest pin from those in the cough lozenge tin, stuck it in the keyhole and wiggled both it and the loose lid. With a degree of tweaking around, it opened to show some newspaper, folded like padding and nicotine-yellow. Lucy removed the newspaper and found more padding, this time made of folded tissue paper. She lifted that out to reveal not jewellery, but a piece of card with a watercolour portrait of a small boy, sitting cross-legged against a background of green leaves. Lucy picked up the card and turned it over. On the reverse was written: 'My darling son Tom, aged nine years'.

Grandpa! Grandpa as a boy, painted by a parent. And Tom himself went on to sketch his own child when he became a man. This family life, generations of it, preserved in drawings and in love. The portrait had been well protected, thought Lucy, and laid it safely back in place on top of the further tissue paper pad that lined the bottom of the box. As she did so, her fingers caught the edge of the pad, raising it slightly. Something was underneath, and she took her grandpa's portrait and the padding out again to see what it was. Again, no jewellery. The tissues had been covering a second piece of card, similar to the one she was holding, except that on this one was a portrait of a small girl, also sitting cross-legged in front of green leaves. The reverse of that card: 'My darling daughter Mary,' it said, 'aged six years'.

Lucy stared transfixed, her logic clunkingly fitting together the chain of items that led to the conclusion it had already leapt to grasp. Tom, Mary. Son, daughter. Brother, sister. Grandfather, grandmother. Her grandparents, the father and mother of her own mother, were brother and sister of each other.

They couldn't be. There must be other Toms and Marys. They weren't unusual names.

In disbelief, Lucy pulled the photograph album towards her and held each child's portrait against the photographs of the adult Tom and Mary. Although the two children in the portraits were unlike each other, they were inescapably like their older selves.

Did her mother know? Was it Beth's secret too, or a secret that had been kept from Beth? Surely her mother couldn't have been told; it would be too terrible an admission to burden your daughter with. Yet Beth might have found out accidentally, as Lucy had, and kept the secret close. How could Lucy possibly ask her – what if her mother hadn't known?

But it might be that Lucy was monstrously mistaken, and the family background was the normal set-up she had always assumed. How she hoped her interpretation was wrong.

'My darling son Tom.' 'My darling daughter Mary.' The same writing and the same leafy setting. The same parent.

'How's it going?' Beth came in, lugging a full black bag and escorted by Daniel with another. 'What's that?'

'It's Burlington Bertie, Dan,' said Lucy, sliding the portraits of the children under the photograph album, heart pounding. 'I found him in the cupboard.'

Daniel took the drawing from the table and inspected it with a grin.

'Isn't he magnificent!' said Beth. 'Monocle and all!'

'There are some photos and paints and things too,' said Lucy. 'I'll pack them to take with us.' She carried them to the other part of the room and stowed the album, portraits and leather box at the bottom of the canvas bag, putting the other things on top.

'These are for the Salvation Army,' said Beth, indicating the bags that she and Daniel were carrying. 'We'll drop them off on our way.'

'Are we going?' asked Daniel hopefully.

'Yes, we've done enough. I was wondering about calling in on Grandma though, since it's not a big detour. We could pick up a sandwich en route. But you two don't have to if you don't want to.'

'I'll come,' said Lucy immediately.

'That's nice of you. Dan, we'll drop you off at the bus stop if you'd prefer.'

'I'd like to see how Grandma is,' said Daniel. 'Afterwards, can I go round to Neal's?'

'Be home by dinnertime, won't you?'

'I will. And will you take Burlington Bertie for me? Can you put him in my room?'

'I can.'

'And keep him flat, won't you. Don't fold him.'

'No, I won't. I'll take care of him. Come on,' said Beth. 'Let's go and visit Grandma.'

CHAPTER IX
Mary and the Family

'She's been in a panto, haven't you, my love?' said the nurse.

Mary's head was propped on her hand. The nurse bent over her and spoke more loudly.

'*Puss in Boots*, was it, or *Dick Whittington*? Why don't you tell your handsome grandson here about it?'

Daniel scratched his head in embarrassment and looked away. With increased embarrassment, he looked back again quickly. The old lady opposite, sprawled with feet together and knees apart, skirt ridden high, was groping thoughtfully between her thighs.

'I'll get you another chair,' said the nurse. 'It's squashed for you here, isn't it? Shall we move her into the other room? There's more space there.'

'I won't need a chair, thanks,' said Daniel. 'I'm not staying very long.'

'I can move her if you like, all the same,' the nurse said to Beth.

'No, no. We won't disturb her,' said Beth.

She and Lucy sat in front of Mary, Daniel hovering between them. Lucy gazed at her grandmother, feeling confused. A fundamental stratum of life had been shattered and hurled into disarray, and yet at the same time nothing had changed.

Her grandmother continued to be as she was nowadays: frail, mostly befuddled but occasionally with a disorienting shaft of clarity. The nurse patted Mary's shoulder.

'Mary, Mary. There's your family here. A lovely little group. Aren't you lucky?'

'*Dick Whittington*,' said Mary.

'There we are, you see. At the panto.'

'Hello, Mum,' said Beth. 'How are you?'

'The best that can be expected, thank you.'

'I'll leave you to it,' said the nurse. 'We'll be bringing tea round in a minute. You're welcome to have some.'

She went, straightening the clothing of the old lady opposite as she passed.

'I've got to go to London,' said Mary.

'Grandma,' said Lucy, doing her best to sound normal. 'You are in London. That's where we live.'

Mary's eyes widened. She sat up.

'I'm in London? We're here?'

'Yes, we are.'

Mary relaxed. 'Thank goodness. A new life.' Her voice sobered. 'Yes, a new life.'

Before Beth or Lucy could respond, she caught sight of Daniel, and was transfigured.

'Tom!' she cried. 'Shouldn't you be at the shop?'

'I'm Daniel, Grandma.'

'Mum,' said Beth. 'That's Daniel. That's your grandson.'

Mary's face folded in puzzlement.

'Hello,' said Daniel. 'How are you, Grandma?'

'The same as when this lady asked a few minutes ago.'

Emma, a resident, entered the room. She was tall and thin

and carried one of the crocheted blankets with her as she shuffled along, the edge of it hanging to the ground.

'I am awaiting my cab,' she announced. 'Would you be so good as to enquire as to its whereabouts?'

Taking a couple more precarious steps, she hailed Daniel.

'Young man! Young man! Would you assist me? Please find me my cab.'

'She isn't really waiting for one,' whispered Lucy. 'Pretend, Dan.'

'Pretend what?'

'Say you'll find it for her. Go out, come in again and say it's on its way.'

'But it isn't.'

'Go on, Dan.'

'Would you, please?' Emma was saying.

Daniel went pink.

'Yes, I'll go,' he muttered, casting a mortified expression at Lucy.

'A gentleman,' said Emma. 'It's rare to find one in modern times. I'm worried that my cab hasn't arrived yet, or I wouldn't impose on him.'

'Are you going far?' asked Beth, drawn into the charade.

'Home, my dear, home. And how I want to go. It's been a delightful sojourn but, as they say, there's no place like home. I've been away too long.'

Daniel came back in, rosily sheepish.

'It's on its way,' he said. 'I think.'

'You could sit down until it arrives,' Beth encouraged.

'Yes.' She surveyed the chairs, each with its insensible occupant. 'Full to the brim here. I'll go into the parlour.'

She revolved in a semicircle, the blanket dangerously around her feet. Lucy picked up the corner and tucked it into the main bundle.

'My thanks to you,' said Emma, oscillating one regal hand at them as she retreated.

'I'll push off,' said Daniel.

'Yes, you go,' said Beth. 'Say goodbye to your grandma before you do.'

'Oh Mum, she doesn't know who I am any more.'

'She knows there's someone here, love. Be a friendly, polite person, even if she doesn't know which person.'

Daniel leaned over Mary.

'Goodbye, Grandma,' he said. 'I'm going now.'

Mary put her hand up to his cheek with deep affection.

'Goodbye, Tom,' she said.

'I'll let you out,' said Lucy, familiar now with the exit routine.

'Be home in time for dinner, Dan.'

'I will.'

Lucy went with Daniel into the hall. Jumping up, he yanked at the top bolt.

'Jesus, Luce.'

'I know.'

She found the stick behind the radiator and knocked the bolt into its socket after him. When she returned to the front room, Beth was holding Mary's hand and attempting to convey a remembrance from the Marriotts.

'Has he gone?' asked Mary, as Lucy sat down. 'Has Tom gone back again?'

'Yes, Grandma, he has.'

'That's good. I'm always happy when Tom's around, but it's

not worth the risk for him. He'll be in hot water if he's not at the business when he should be.'

Lucy listened with particular care, hoping for clues to disprove the charming, appalling evidence. Beth reassured her mother.

'It's his business, Mum,' she said. 'He can do what he likes.'

'His business! It will be one day. Not that he wants it.'

'Doesn't he?' Beth was surprised. 'I thought he loved that shop and the things in it, the art materials.'

'Humph!' Mary's eyes shut, and she let out a snore.

'He did love it,' said Beth to Lucy in a low voice. 'I'm sure he did. He used to bring paints and crayons for you when you were children. Do you remember? And I used to help out sometimes when I was a teenager, when Uncle Stefan was alive and still owned the shop. I served on the till. Not that it was normally crowded enough for them to be in need of another person, but I liked it, and Dad was really at home there. He kept on working after he could have retired.'

Lucy thought she could make a tentative sounding.

'Maybe she has something else in mind.'

She studied her mother for signs of secret knowledge.

'That's quite likely. It certainly doesn't fit with what I know.'

'What we believe we know could be inaccurate,' pursued Lucy. All her life, it had been Grandpa Tom and Grandma Mary, but now there were the watercolours labelled My darling son Tom, and My darling daughter Mary. 'It could be an illusion.'

'You're getting in deep.'

'Yes, I might be.'

Emma shuffled in again. Lucy dragged her mind onto what she would say about the taxi this time – keep up with the pretence that it was on its way, she decided. It wasn't necessary: Emma had forgotten. Clutching the crocheted bundle before her, she shuffled then stopped, shuffled then stopped, each time gazing blankly around the room. She shuffled up to Lucy.

'I'm so lonely,' she stated. 'So, so, lonely.'

Lucy moved to speak, though what to say against such bleakness? Before she could summon up any words, Emma had revolved again more nimbly than Lucy would have thought possible and begun the shuffle away. At the door, she met a care assistant with the tea trolley.

'Come on, Emma,' said the carer. 'Let's sit down with a nice cup of tea. We'll go to another room, shall we?' Emma was guided off.

'It's sad,' the carer said, returning after an interlude during which Beth and Lucy had looked at each other in dismay. 'Emma lived with her sister all her life. Neither of them married, and they stayed together in the house after their parents died. On the posh side, I reckon, but not a lot of money. The sister's passed away and Emma's got no one, so she's here. Breaks your heart. Here's your teas. I've put Mary's in a spout to make it easier for her.'

'Here's your tea, Mum.' Beth put Mary's hands round the handles and lifted it up to her mouth. Mary sucked in a desultory fashion.

'I can't bear the story about Emma,' said Lucy.

'No. It's terrible. After so many years together. It would be enough to send anyone peculiar. That's when your grandma got noticeably worse. After Grandpa died.'

'He meant a lot to her, didn't he?'

'They had the best marriage I've ever come across. Not that I'm an expert on marriage, as you doubtless know, my little one. It's a difficult institution, but they knew how to make it work.'

Mary's eyes opened. Directing them at Lucy, she shut one in a massive wink, the tea-spout paused in her mouth. The other eye closed again, and she sucked forcefully.

What did that wink mean? thought Lucy, startled. Simple amusement at being praised, or something more? Did her grandmother, in one of her brief leaps into consciousness, realise the praise was being directed at an illicit relationship? But even if she'd mustered enough awareness for that, she couldn't know what Lucy had discovered, so why wink at her as if in collusion? Or was it just another of her odd bits of behaviour, like the skirt-pleating?

'I must go to the loo,' said Beth, getting up. 'Then we'll be on our way, if you're ready, Luce.'

As soon as Beth went, Lucy leaned forwards as near to Mary as she could. She touched her elbow.

'Grandma,' she said. 'Grandma, please – who is Tom? Who is he?'

Slowly Mary put down the spout and opened her eyes again.

'Why,' she said, 'he's your grandpa. You know that, Lucy.'

'You recognise me! Did you recognise Mum?'

'Mum, mum. We must keep mum.' Her eyes closed.

'Grandma, please, was there another Tom?'

Little Tommy Tucker
Sings for his supper.
What shall we give him?
White bread and butter.'

'Did you have a brother called Tom, Grandma?'

How shall he cut it

Without any knife?

How shall he marry

Without any wife?'

'Grandma, you know it's Lucy. Tell me, please.'

'*Half a pound of tuppenny rice,*

Half a pound of treacle.'

'Pop goes the weasel,' said Beth, returning. 'That's jolly singing, Mum.'

'Help me. Help me. Someone, please help me.'

At the end of the room, Hilda had woken up, her mood shifting fast from pleading to headmistressy reproval.

'I'm waiting.' she called imperiously. 'I'm waiting.'

The carer gave her some tea.

'That's right,' said Hilda. 'And none too soon either. I strongly advise you to smarten up your attitude, my girl.'

'I'll try, Hilda,' said the carer benevolently. She poured out a beaker for the adjacent resident.

'We'd better be going, Mum,' said Beth, bending down to kiss her mother's head. 'Ready, Lucy?'

'Bye, Grandma,' said Lucy.

'I must go to London.'

'You can, Grandma. We'll visit you there.'

'Do I make myself clear?'

'I'm going to London. To London.'

'Goodbye.'

'Help me.'

'To London.'

'Goodbye.'

CHAPTER X
Mary

Mother and Tom I loved. That was all. I liked Carry too. She did the daily domestic tasks and she was very good-natured, but that's not the same.

Mother liked to paint. She did watercolours and sketches, when Father wasn't around. She never said that she was hiding her painting from him, but I knew. Children pick up things like that, whether or not the adults realise it. Children easily pick up what's going on. You have to be on your guard. Father thought it was a waste of time. He was strict, my father. Things had to be done the way he said or there was hell to pay. When she died, I went through her belongings and took out the paintings, the paints, everything. I hid them so that he wouldn't find them. She was a gentle woman, my mother. She was worthy of better.

Weren't we all?

After Mother died, there was just Tom. And Carry. But that's not the same.

Carry brought me a kitten when I was small, from her yard. Her family lived in a yard at the other side of town. I don't know where. There was a well in that yard, she said, with no cover over it. Isn't that dangerous? my mother said. Oh no, said Carry. Everyone knows about it. What about the children? said my mother. They know about it too, said Carry. But she did tell me, years later, that a man from the yard was coming home drunk late one night and fell into the well and drowned. At any rate, they assumed he was drunk, because he invariably was on Saturday nights. So Mother was correct – it should have had a cover. But Carry said, No. They were glad to get shut of him. He was a brute. The well had done them a service. You could see the difference in his family, she said, after he'd gone. They filled out and got quite chirpy. A miserable, scrawny lot they were before, and who could blame them? That was what Carry said. I didn't know them. I didn't know where the yard was. We never went there.

One of the cats in the yard had kittens and she brought me one. She carried it in a basket. I was very little; it was before I'd started school. He peeped over the edge of the basket and when Carry lifted him out, I held him. He was squishy and shivery. Black and white. I loved him. I stayed in the kitchen with Carry and we made balls out of newspaper and rolled them across the floor for him to chase.

I said to Mother afterwards, I've got a kitten and I helded him. She smiled and said, No, you didn't helded him. I did, I said. Carry gave him to me and I helded him. You held him, she said. Yes, I did. I helded him and I played paper balls with him.

She laughed and stroked my hair in the same way as I stroked the kitten. I didn't know at the time why she laughed. I suppose she must have known that the kitten was coming. I played with him in the kitchen and I went to say goodnight to him before I went to bed. I did that for a few days, then one evening I went into the kitchen and I couldn't find him. I said to Carry, Where is he? Where's Rollo? And she said in a choky voice that she didn't know and Mother came in and was trying to take me off to bed but I wanted to keep on searching. We'd got into the hall and I wanted to rootle under the hallstand and Mother was saying that she'd explain when we got upstairs, when Father came out of his study and told me to desist from making that infernal racket. The cat's gone, he said. Nobody asked my permission. I don't keep pets.

Mother said, as I was crying in bed, that she was certain he'd gone to a good home where he'd be loved. I knew no one could love him as I had.

And Tom hadn't seen him. I'd wanted to give Tom a surprise when he came from school for the weekend, but the kitten had both been and gone in the time Tom was away. It had happened, the whole thing, while he wasn't there. I told him when he came back and he said we should hunt in the garden because cats didn't like to move to a new home. Tom and I combed the garden on our hands and knees. I remember looking up and seeing Mother in the drawing room window, watching.

We're in Holly Hideout when Tom says, Let's rescue him from his new family. We could find out where they live and kidnap him back. You could say things like that in Holly Hideout. That's why we went there, to be safe and comforted. It was at the bottom of the garden, in the corner by the wall. Some holly trees had grown together so they seemed impenetrable, but if you knew what to do, which no one but Tom and I did, you went round it and pulled on one crucial branch and a whole section moved out enough for you to squeeze between it and the wall and when you got inside, it was hollow. You were in a green room that you could easily stand up in. You had to beware of the prickly leaves – the dry brown ones on the floor were the sharpest and we used to sweep them out every so often with one of my hairbrushes. Carry had given us an old kitchen towel without asking what it was for – she was tactful – and we had it on the floor like a carpet. When it got damp and buggy, we flapped it around and it did the job. Nobody knew, because it was hidden from the house by the other shrubs down there. That part of the garden was left to its own devices, although Mother painted there sometimes. Not even she knew about Holly Hideout. We kept liquorice water there in a jam jar and Tom had some glow-worms in an old Oxo tin.

We never did rescue the kitten. We didn't know where he was, Tom and I. You couldn't ask Father. He was the one who knew, but you couldn't ask him. You couldn't risk it. He didn't expect to be crossed, that's what he'd say. You couldn't risk it.

Carry got married. Not at the time of the kitten – it was after Mother died. Father was furious. What does she think she's doing? Why should she leave a good position like the one she's got here? And after all this time! For marrying! She's too old for that malarkey.

I don't know how old she was. Somewhere in her thirties, I should imagine. She had a white wedding, despite its being wartime, with a bridesmaid, in the Catholic church. She borrowed the dress from her sister, who had married before the war. They cut off the train and the bottom of the dress to make a frock for the bridesmaid. With Tom being away in Hull, I went to the wedding on my own. Father didn't go. He said she was a deserter. Her husband was a plumber before he joined up. After the wedding, she went to live with her sister and I don't know what happened to her. Father said he wasn't getting anyone else in after being let down like that. It was to be my responsibility, apart from the heavy cleaning. He said no daughter of his was cleaning, so we did get a string of women in for that. Trimble went on doing the garden, digging for victory. He was too old to be called up, like Father. Tom didn't pass the board because of his chest. That was the worst part, when he was away at the aircraft factory. My word yes. The worst part of all. At long last the war was over and Tom came back.

Tom and I and Father. The ones left. Tom and Father running the business. Me running the house. Father running Tom and me.

We had lions on the gateposts to the drive at the front of the house. Big cats. It was a little cat I'd wanted.

Later on, we found out that Tom was allergic to them. We didn't know it at the time. That wasn't the reason. I don't keep pets. That was the reason. Mother died, and Carry got married, and Tom and I were left with Father.

After Mother died, when I took over the housekeeping, Father made me enter all the domestic expenses in an accounts book with a marbled cover. I had to submit them to him each week. He'd audit every item and afterwards he'd say, What munificence eh? And I'd have to say, Yes Father, you're extraordinarily generous, or something like that. If I didn't, he'd say, Eh? Eh? What's that? until I did.

It was the same for Tom. Father didn't pay him directly into a bank account, nor into private envelopes like the employees got. He paid him personally, at home. He would call Tom into the study and make him fetch a chequebook from the bureau where he kept his documents. He'd say, I presume you expect an allowance, eh? Tom would have to say, Yes please, or the ritual wouldn't go any further. Father would put the chequebook on the table by his big chair and move himself forwards in the chair with a grunt. He'd open up the chequebook and run his finger down the spine. He'd get out his fountain pen from his inner pocket and hold it poised above the cheque. Date? Tom would have to tell it to him. And how much was it? Tom would have to tell him the amount. As much as that, eh? That's when Tom would have to give his panegyric about generosity. Father would grunt again and write out the cheque slowly in beautiful handwriting. He would admire the proof of his liberality until the ink dried, tear the cheque out and put it on the table. Tom had to return the chequebook to the bureau, and wait for Father to replace the pen into his pocket. Finally, Father would pick up the cheque and hand it to Tom, saying, That's a lot of money.

It wasn't. My allowance came along with the housekeeping, and that wasn't a lot either.

I never saw Tom being paid. Tom told me about it. He said he writhed, writhed, each time, and had to grit his teeth to get the words out. You had to say them, or no money.

Why didn't we escape?

We did. Didn't we?

Eventually.

Big lions on the front gateposts. A gravel drive to the front door, painted black like ivy berries. Parquet floor in the hall. Curved staircase with brass rods. Quite a substantial house.

A corridor from the hall that led to the kitchen. A green baize curtain hanging in front of the kitchen door. That curtain was a nuisance, but Father wouldn't consent to its removal. He'd never tried to carry a loaded tray past it. If he had, he'd know. You had to be careful or everything would get knocked off.

He'd know.

He'd know it all.

You have to be careful they don't know.

Keep quiet, that's the main thing. Keep yourself to yourself.

We managed.

CHAPTER XI
Lucy and Beth

'Why does Grandma keep saying that she's got to go to London?' asked Lucy, as Beth drove them away from the nursing home.

'Your guess is as good as mine,' said Beth. 'Though it might just be because she didn't come from London originally. She was born in the Midlands.'

'Was Grandpa from up there too?'

'Yes. Couldn't you tell? They both spoke with short a's, not like Londoners.'

'Did they meet here or in the Midlands?'

'Do you know, I'm not sure. I've always assumed that they came here together after they were married, but I could be wrong. I suppose they could have met here. I was born here. That I do know.'

'Why did they come to London?'

'Probably to work. A lot of people do.'

'There must have been art shops in the Midlands.'

'I don't know. I took things as they were when I was a child. Children do. To a child the world is ready-made the way they know it. And I never knew my grandparents on either side.

They were dead before I was born, so there wasn't any context there. Why this sudden interest in your ancestry, Luce?'

This was a question that needed to be answered carefully, without raising any suspicion or anxiety, whether or not her mother was in on a family secret. Lucy thought for a moment, then, 'It's because, like you said, when you're a child you take everything for granted. And I've come to realise that I don't know enough about our family's past. Grandma and Grandpa were in my life when I was a child, but that's all I know about them – who they were in relation to me. It's as if there's a whole chunk of their previous life history that's going to disappear because I don't know what it was and Grandma can't tell me.'

'I'm not much help, I'm afraid.'

Beth pulled up at traffic lights. Lucy thought again for a moment, then said, 'What about photos? Hasn't she any photos?'

'You know she has, Lucy. Didn't you find an album at Grandma's today? Grandpa used to take lovely ones of you children – and of me too, and Grandma.'

'I mean from earlier than that. Their wedding, for example. I've never seen any of their wedding photographs.'

'Neither have I.'

'I've seen yours.'

'All innocent optimism.'

Lucy ignored this. 'Where can Grandma's be?'

'She may not have had any. People didn't take as many photos in those days.'

'Even of a wedding?'

'It would be not long after the war, Lucy. Things would be rationed. They wouldn't have had any fancy do.'

The lights changed and Beth pulled away.

'They don't mean anything,' she added.

'What?'

'Weddings. When it comes to yours, Lucy, what you want is a financial contract, not a silly big frock and photos.'

Lucy didn't reply, and after a moment Beth said, 'You're worried about her, aren't you?'

'Not worried.' She said it speedily, to deflect any further questioning along that line. 'I'd just like to know more. When she says things that seem to be nonsense, I often get the impression that they aren't really nonsense at all. It's because she's not where we are, she's elsewhere. If I knew more about her, I might be able to recognise where she was and understand what she was talking about. She mixes up the outside world and the world inside her head, and the world inside her head is more vivid. That's what makes it incomprehensible to us.'

'What's truly incomprehensible is how the rest of us do manage to tell the difference between what's going on inside our head and what's going on outside. It's the normal state of affairs that's incomprehensible to me, not the breakdown of it. The breakdown's utterly comprehensible.'

Lucy pondered this one. She had had the experience, especially when she was at school, of the alarm clock ringing in the morning, of clambering out of bed, going to the bathroom, washing, dressing, picking up her bag and being ready. Surprisingly, the alarm would ring again, and as she reached to stop it, she would realise wearily that she wasn't ready. Everything had to be redone, but was more of a chore since she felt as if she'd already been through it. She had sometimes visualised a variant of hell in which you were trapped in a cycle of ringing alarm clocks and getting ready, only to find it was a dream when the alarm rang again, and having to drag through more getting ready, only to find that was a dream too as the alarm went off again and again, ad infinitum. You were repeatedly getting ready, never going anywhere, like reincarnation without getting either better or worse.

When you get dressed in your early morning dream, you believe you have done it. How do you know, when you do it the second time, that this one is the reality? How can you know?

Merrily, merrily, merrily, merrily,

Life is but a dream.

'Not necessarily merrily, though,' she said out loud.

'What isn't?' asked Beth.

'I was thinking about Emma. Her world isn't very merry.'

'No. She's better off waiting for non-existent taxis than when she glimpses what her life is really like.'

'Grandma thought Dan was Grandpa.'

'Dan has always had the look of his grandfather. I imagine that Dan's quite similar to Grandpa at the same age.'

'Would Grandma have known Grandpa when he was as young as that?'

'She might have. People do sometimes marry people they've known since their school days. Particularly in the past, when people didn't travel around as much. They wouldn't meet many alternatives.'

Lucy made a final probe. 'Did Grandma's parents have a shop?'

'Oh, Lucy, I genuinely don't know these things. They could have. There used to be a lot more family shops around, but I don't know.'

Lucy had pursued this too long.

'They were modest people, your grandma and grandpa. They rarely talked about themselves. I expect they thought it wasn't polite.'

Lucy enquired no more. Patently, her mother knew less than she did, which was something to be thankful for. If Lucy was shaken and troubled by what the portraits revealed, what would it do to her mother to be aware that she was the product of brother-and-sister parentage? A parentage that was illegal, immoral, taboo and dangerous. How could Lucy's staid grandparents have been in such a relationship? What circumstances had led to this?

On the other hand, there could be a simpler explanation: Grandma might have married someone with the same name as her brother. That was plausible.

Or the husband Tom might not be her brother but be, for example, a cousin called Tom. Not ideal, but legal.

In that case, what had happened to brother Tom? Grandma couldn't have eliminated him from her life.

Perhaps she could. Lucy didn't often talk about Daniel to her friends, and Adam scarcely impinged on her consciousness since he'd become a wearer of suits. All the same, it was unimaginable that she would be able to live till old age without her own children being aware of Adam's and Daniel's existence, with no evidence that they had ever lived.

I'm going to crack this, resolved Lucy. I'm having a wasted year, with nothing happening. At least let me find an explanation. I want to know.

CHAPTER XII
Lucy and Beth

Lucy sat cross-legged on her bedroom floor, the photograph album brought from her grandparents' house on her lap. In the sitting room across the hall, her mother was lying on the sofa reading the Sunday paper, feet towards the posher dining table that they hardly ever used. Daniel was not yet back from Neal's. Propped on the carpet against Lucy's chest of drawers were the two portraits of Tom and Mary. At their side, on top of the newspaper and tissue padding in the green leather box, she had placed the open locket. Now that she had the photos in the album to compare with the photo in the locket, she could see that the woman's features were also there in the young husband, Grandpa Tom. Was this Grandpa's mother, and the person who had painted the portraits? If she was Grandpa's mother, she was Grandma's mother too, which would explain why the locket had been kept hidden away. Lucy was glad now that she'd not had the chance to show it to Beth.

She slowly turned the pages of the album on her lap. There it was. Her grandparents' life in pictures – or rather, her grandparents' life after Beth in pictures. Nothing from before. There was baby Beth sitting on Mary's knee next to an older woman whom Lucy didn't recognise. There was baby Beth sitting on Mary's knee next to Tom against the same unrevealing scenery – a door, a house wall, an oblong of window. Had the unknown woman taken that? There was a toddling Beth holding on to a dog on wheels. Beth in a crinkly bathing costume building a sandcastle. An older Beth in dirndl skirt, bolero and startlingly white socks. Tom leaning on his spade in the garden of the house Lucy knew so intimately. Beth with Lucy's father, Tony, sitting side by side on the sofa. Tony's shirt collar was deep, his tie wide, his hair luxuriantly long. Beth, all leg, looked as if she could barely contain her euphoria. Then Tony and Beth radiating pride over a tiny crumpled Adam. An older Adam gazing curiously at another bundle that he held gingerly in his arms – Lucy herself. The trickle of Adam and Lucy photos became a flood. Lucy knew why there were suddenly many more: Daniel had been born and her mother was ill; Lucy and Adam had gone to live with their grandparents. She remembered having *Rainbow* read to her and hot chocolate at bedtime in a Peter Rabbit mug that had belonged to her mother. She remembered Grandpa bringing home drawing paper and packets of wax crayons for them. Or did she? Was she mixing up her memories of that time with the photographs, and were those memories mixed up too with those of a later time, a time again indicated by an increase in photos, these ones including Daniel? This had been the time of the bust-up; the time after which Dad no longer lived with them; the time of changes in life's daily characteristics, unpredictable switches of mood, and ordinary behaviour taking on a significance beyond its own mere actions.

He was throwing Daniel up towards the kitchen ceiling. Daniel screamed with excitement, and Lucy jumped up and down by her father's side, hoping to be thrown too.

'He can't throw you, Lucy,' said Adam, with an elder's rationality. 'You're too big.'

'Oh please.'

Tony caught Daniel, burrowing his head into the child's tummy as Daniel squirmed and giggled helplessly. Daniel encircled Tony's neck and bounced against him, shouting 'More! More!'

'My go,' said Lucy, from below Tony's elbow. 'Me next.'

'Poor old Dad,' said Adam sympathetically.

Still holding Daniel, Tony turned to Beth, and Lucy saw his gloating satisfaction. She left Tony's side and went to stand by her mother. Beth put an arm round Lucy.

Tony set Daniel down.

'Come on, Lucy. I'll try one.'

Lucy shook her head. She did not want to be part of a triumph.

'Come on.'

'I will. I will,' said Daniel, arms up ready to be lifted again.

'Sure, Lucy?'

'Yes.'

'She's too big.'

'Me! Me!'

Daniel was tossed up for the last time. Slowly, slowly, it seemed to Lucy, he rose in the air and hung there, arms outstretched like wings, before descending languidly towards Tony's grasp and his upturned, revelling face.

'More!' shouted Daniel, bouncing. 'More!'

Tony removed him.

'No,' he said curtly. 'I've had enough of this,' and walked out, Daniel running after him in bewilderment to the closing door.

Such was the pumped-up merriment that hinted at functions other than fun, and which could equally explode into irritation or deflate into indifference. Such was the withdrawal that could change to sudden tight hugs. There were increasingly long intervals when the family was not together in the same place. Sometimes the children were at their grandparents' house, sometimes at home in the flat. When they were with Beth in the flat, their father usually wasn't. In the middle of it, Adam told Lucy that Uncle Stefan had died. The children hadn't seen Stefan recently, but Lucy remembered a patient, elderly man with silver hair who spoke to them in a funny accent.

Adam said, 'Grandpa will have to work on his own.'

And Lucy felt everything to be shifting, changing, moving apart.

Except for her grandparents themselves. Except for Mary and Tom.

Who now were shifting too.

Lucy laid the portraits in the box as she had originally found them, and nestled the locket between the top two layers of padding. She replaced the box in her chest of drawers, then, taking the photograph album with her, she went into the sitting room.

'Mum,' she said, 'do you know where our birth certificates are?'

Beth put down the Sunday colour magazine.

'Should I let my hair go grey and be done with it?' she said.

'No. Not yet.'

'It says here that your skin tone gets lighter as you get older, so dark hair is difficult to hang on to and appear natural because it can make too harsh a contrast with your face. That's what it says here. I don't want to look like Olive Oyl.'

'Oh, Mum, you look lovely.'

'You're very chivalrous, my darling. So I don't give up?'

'You don't give up.'

'Thank you. What was that about birth certificates?'

Lucy repeated the question.

'Yes. They're in a big old envelope in the bottom drawer of the cabinet. Why?'

'Just curious. It's what I was saying in the car on the way back from Grandma – that I don't like to know so little about her. I've been going through the photo album from her house. It's got our babyhoods in it.' She passed the album over to her mother and opened it at the photograph of Mary with Beth and the stranger. 'Who's that woman?'

Beth inspected the photograph.

'It could be Mrs Jessop,' she said finally.

'Who's Mrs Jessop?'

'She was a friend of your grandmother's. A neighbour from where they lived before.'

Lucy's ears pricked up. 'Where did they live before?'

'Over by Battersea Bridge. I've no memories of being there. Grandma pointed it out to me once a long time ago when we were on a bus. The whole site was being cleared and they were building an estate of flats. There had been a lot of bomb damage in the war.'

'What happened to Mrs Jessop?'

'She went to Australia. Grandma used to write to her.' She

turned the pages. 'Why does the album make you want the birth certificates? I don't mind. It's just that I can't see the connection.'

Lucy was already riffling through the pile of things in the cabinet drawer. A demolished house near Battersea Bridge wasn't going to enlighten her, nor an emigrant to Australia who in all likelihood was no longer alive. By the time she had found the relevant envelope and returned to the sofa with it, her mother had swung her feet to the floor and was engrossed in the album. Elbow on the sofa arm, head propped on her hand, she was staring at the photograph of her young self with Tony.

'Newly engaged,' she said in a tone that Lucy recognised as mingling rancour and regret. 'A souvenir snap.'

'Amazing tie,' said Lucy, sitting down by her side and pulling the certificates out of the envelope. There were Adam's, her own and Daniel's: large, comprehensive certificates with the name of the hospital where they were born; their own names; their father's full name – Anthony Stuart Kinnon; his place of birth – Croydon; his occupation – insurance broker; Beth's full name and place of birth, given as Battersea, London; her maiden name – Pearson; her address.

Next were three more certificates, again one each for Adam, Lucy and Daniel, but much briefer, giving name, sex, date of birth and where they were registered.

Lucy felt in the envelope again. This was Beth's birth certificate. Elizabeth Frances Pearson, it said, and the same items of sex, birthdate and registration. There was nothing else in the envelope.

'Is this everything?' asked Lucy.

Beth dragged her eyes from the album. 'Why? Aren't they all there?'

'There are two for each of us, a large one and a short version. But there isn't a large version of yours. Shouldn't you have one too?'

'Not that I know of,' said Beth, holding out her hand to take the certificate. 'I've only ever seen this one.'

'Why haven't you got a big one too?'

'I don't know,' said Beth again. 'I think you have to pay for one of them – the larger one, I suppose. I'm not sure. I can't remember if you pay for the shorter one or not. But it would be cheaper to have the short one. Possibly they were on a tight budget at that time.'

'Mmmm,' said Lucy.

'The short one's enough. That was what we sent in for your passport and mine's always done me on the rare occasions I've needed it.'

'We haven't got Grandma's either.'

'That must be in her house, though you'd have thought we'd have found it as we were going through. And your grandfather's. That must be there too. Were you wanting to see where she was born? Tracing your roots?'

'Sort of.'

'You can find out, you know. Birth, death and marriage records used to be kept at Somerset House. They've moved. I don't know where, but you could find out. There'll be a record of her. Of all of us, in fact.'

'I might do that,' said Lucy lightly, her heart leaping. That could be the first step. She could see who were registered as father and mother of both her grandparents; that would solve the nature of their relationship, and she could get further evidence from who were given as the parents for her own mother's birth registration.

Was this unethical, was it squalid? Investigating the background to her mother's birth when her mother had no notion that it might be questionable? Barging into her grandmother's silent past when her grandmother was no longer capable of defending it from intruders? But Lucy did want to know. Not to use it against anyone, not to hurt or agitate. No one else would know what she found out. But she did want to know.

'I'll put these away,' she said, folding the certificates and sliding them inside the envelope.

'Thanks.' Beth was immersed in the album again.

Lucy put the envelope of certificates back in the cabinet drawer and went to her room, picking up the telephone directory as she crossed the hall.

She tried S for Somerset House, which repetitively said: 'For Registration of Births, Deaths & Marriages see under Registration of Births, Deaths & Marriages.'

R for Registration – and there it was: General Enquiries, Smedley Hydro in Southport.

They wouldn't be open on a Sunday for her to telephone them straight away, and she was working all week. If she rang from the shop, she might be overheard and Maya would give her the third degree. She'd have to go out to a phone box, which she could but didn't want to for something so intimate and potentially complicated. In any case, they might not be able to tell her over the telephone and she'd have to write.

She composed a letter:

Dear Sir or Madam
I would like to apply for copies of the full birth certificates of three members of the Pearson family. I know their

names and dates of birth. I also have the place of birth registration of one of the people, but unfortunately not the other two, although it is possible that they were born in the Midlands. Here are the details—

'Lucy! Lucy! Are you happy to have a takeaway tonight? I haven't enough oomph left to cook. We can order a delivery when Dan gets in.'

'Yes, that's OK by me,' said Lucy. She would subtly find out Tom and Mary's other names over dinner and get the letter in the post on her way to work in the morning.

CHAPTER XIII
Mary and Tom

Tom came into the kitchen of their father's house as Mary was cooking the evening meal and said, almost inaudibly, 'I need to talk to you, Mary. Where we won't be interrupted.'

'In Holly Hideout?'

'Yes. You go first and I'll be with you in a jiffy. I'll say I'm going to get a breath of fresh air before dinner.'

Mary took the pan of potatoes off the heat and made her way down the garden to the dense evergreen bushes in the secluded part. It was nearly dark already, and chilly in the autumn air. Mary wrapped her cardigan, also her arms, round herself as she waited for Tom to make his excuse and come outside.

'What is it, Tom?' she said as his shape arrived under the branches of the holly.

'I've been deliberating. And I think that what we should do is leave – go away.'

'Go away where?'

'London.'

'London!'

'Yes. I think we've got to go to London.'

Mary gaped into the darkness of the holly bush.

'Tom! What will Father say?'

'We won't hear what he says. We'll be gone.'

'You mean, we go, pack up and go, without saying anything?'

'That's it.'

She stared at Tom's shape, utterly discombobulated. How could they just leave everything and disappear like that?

'But where will we go in London? We don't know anyone and nobody knows us.'

'That's the point. He'll never trace us there. We start a new life as new people. We live our own lives our way.'

'What about the business, Tom? It will be yours in the future. You'd lose that.'

'Good riddance. I never wanted it.'

'You may say that, but how would we live? What would we live on?' She pulled at the neck of her cardigan in agitation.

'I've got some money saved. Not a large amount, enough to start us off until I get a job. There must be jobs in London. Office jobs, shop jobs. I could work in a factory again at a pinch, like I did in the war.'

'That was in a different world.'

'Not entirely.'

'Where would we live? We don't know London. Oh, Tom, it's too big a risk.'

Tom reached out both hands to find her shoulders. 'What will life be like here if we don't? Think about that one, Mary. You know jolly well what it'll be like. Isn't it worth a modicum of risk to get away from that?'

Mary thought about it. She thought about it through dinner, as her father instructed Tom in how he should have handled some commercial transaction that he had carried out in an entirely inappropriate manner. She thought about it while she was doing the washing up, during which her father stormed into the kitchen in anger because the knob on the wireless set had been moved during the day and had thus spoiled his tuning. She thought of it in the town, where girls wafted along in make-up, smelling of Californian Poppy. When she walked past the cinema, which she had never been into. And when she analysed the behaviour of the assistants in her father's stores, and knew they felt sorry for her. She thought of her life as it had been, especially in recent years. Before the war, with her mother alive, there had been crannies of love and comfort when her father was out of the house. Winter teas after school of scrambled egg and bacon on toast, eaten, if she liked, in front of the fire, with the lights out so that the walls were lustrous with reflection and shadows leapt around. Trimmings of biscuit pastry left for her to dangle into her mouth, head back, tongue licking the yellow ribbons in.

These could occur only during the week, and before her father returned home. Once he was in the house, rigidity ruled, and it was better to keep out of his way than be reviled. At the weekend he was unavoidable, for the family ate together, Tom too, home from school until Sunday night. Tight-lipped, straight-backed mealtimes. Her father ate slowly, methodically allocating the appropriate quantity of each food item per forkful to keep the proportions exact to the completion of his plate. Everyone waited till he was ready. No one could progress to the next course till he did. No one could leave the table early. Everything had to be eaten. Mary grew adept at palming morsels of food that she didn't want while her father was examining his own serving. She hid them on the ledge under the table and tried to smuggle them out at a safer time.

On Sundays they went to church. Church, lunch, church, tea. After tea, one of the men from the shops took Tom to the station. Sunday nights were a jumble of emotions – relief that the weekend with Father was over, dejection that Tom was off again and to the school he loathed, philosophical acceptance of her own school life, anticipation of forthcoming cosy moments with Mother.

Then Mother died. Tom had been taken into the business by this time and was living at home. It became increasingly problematic to find inlets away from their father's control. Tom hated the daily life of commerce, Mary was tied to domestic management. They had minimal chance to go out and minimal money to go out with, for their father's prosperity, far from making him generous, had emphasised to him the importance of thrift. The regime endured through the war and beyond, austerity having long been a virtue in their household. Tom's remuneration was to be thought of not in terms of his pay but in the value of the experience he was gaining and the strength of his inheritance. Dreary. Dreary. Dreary.

And in the future? Her father was robust and gave no sign of ceding power in any department of his life. Without some extreme action, Tom would be stuck as he was indefinitely. As for herself – it hardly bore thinking about. She must go.

'Yes,' she said to Tom. And as the country organised the election that would return Churchill to power, Tom organised their departure.

They left on the night of the Worshipful Master's dinner. Tom, who was usually compelled to attend the dinner too, had coughed and wheezed throughout the day, his lungs, affected by childhood pleurisy, ostensibly causing him trouble again and forcing him to rest at home rather than accompany his father.

Mary had been packed ready for some time. She didn't care which clothes she took since she didn't like any of them, but had been distressed by having to choose the practicable few mementos of her mother to take.

Tom had ordered a taxi, not from a local firm. It was to collect them from two roads away, by the overgrown site where the stray bomb had dropped. Tom took the cases up one by one as it became dark, and hid them between the ruined wall and the buddleia. Any playing children had been called indoors, and he took the cases individually to be less conspicuous and so that he could skirt round more deftly into the shadows if there were passers-by. There were not many. It was drizzling and windy and the few people who were out hurried with heads bent, umbrellas up and no interest in the attributes of other pedestrians. Tom was wet, the cases were wet, and the concealing buddleia showered him further, but he was not recognised.

Tom choreographed the getaway. He left the house first on his own and went to the bomb site to wait for the car. As it drove up, Tom retrieved the cases from under the buddleia, soaking coat sleeve and shoulder, and put them in the boot. By this time Mary had arrived, hidden under her umbrella, and got into the back. Tom climbed in after. The driver was half-turned in his seat, observing dryly.

'Gretna Green?' he enquired.

They arrived at Euston late at night. Mary stood on the station concourse, gazing out into the city. Nobody here knows us, she thought. All these buildings, all these people, and we are nameless among them. We can be whatever we become. She felt both exhilarated and fearful at braving the crowding possibilities. To Tom she said, 'Where do we go?'

'A hotel for the night,' said Tom. 'There are bound to be some close to a railway station. Tomorrow we'll look for a place to live.'

There were several cheap hotels in the nearby streets. They chose at random from those that had the vacancies sign displayed in the front door. Tom booked two rooms and carried their cases upstairs himself while the shirt-sleeved owner eyed them from his boxed-in cubby hole.

Do we look suspect? wondered Mary. She was becoming too tired to care.

It was cold in her room. There was a gas fire without any matches, so she got into bed and lay without moving to encourage the air beneath the sheets to heat up. She thought of her father coming back from the dinner to an empty house. Did he realise that it was an empty house? Would his suspicions be aroused by the fact that she was not there, waiting up in case he wanted a hot drink before retiring? Or would he assume that she had already gone to bed? He could be annoyed by that alone. And when he realised that they'd gone – what would he do? He couldn't know that they had gone to London. Gone to seek their fortune. She smiled. Like Dick Whittington and his cat.

Breakfast was in the basement. She could see the lower part of people's legs through the window as they walked past on the pavement outside. She had never been in a basement before.

'What we'll do,' Tom said, 'is put the cases in the left luggage at the station so we can explore. We should do our best to find digs today, but although they can't be expensive, we want them to be in a respectable part. I expect some can be rough and I wouldn't want to land you up in one of those.'

They paid the bill, left the cases at the station and went down into the Underground. The distant rumble from the black tunnel, the sudden gust of warm stale air, the roar as the train shot out, lights blazing, like a mythical beast pouncing with eyes a-glare from its lair. That exciting fusty smell again, and the way the doors slid automatically open. Once the train stopped in the tunnel between stations for quite a long time. Mary, peeking out of the window to discover what was happening, could see nothing but her own darkened reflection, and behind it the swags of wires and pipes fastened along the tunnel wall. No one else in the carriage was reacting to the halt. Tom had bought an early edition of the *Evening News* and was scouring the situations columns. The newspaper gave him the air of belonging to London, thought Mary with satisfaction, so she must do too, by contiguity. The train moved off again.

They would emerge from the Underground, walk the surrounding streets to, as Tom said, get a feel for the neighbourhood, or what was left of it, and search the cards stuck in the windows of the corner shops and post offices to see if any rooms were available and at what price. Having carried out their recce, they would take the tube again to another station. In some places, cards stated who was and who was not acceptable – 'No Blacks, No Irish Need Apply'. People, thought Mary, judged and rejected for being themselves. Tom kept notes on what they had seen and read them out to her as they snacked at an ABC café.

Mary began to feel drained. They were displaced, not wanting to return to what they had left, but without a base in a way she did not want to protract. While Tom was utilising the public convenience at Shepherd's Bush, which was not at all as its name implied, she approached a loitering policeman. Casting away a ridiculous foreboding that her father might already have a network of officers on the lookout for them, she spoke in as dignified a manner as she could muster.

'We're new to London, and we're trying to find lodgings. Could you recommend an inexpensive district that's reasonably pleasant?'

The policeman rocked on his toes.

'Madam,' he said, 'I'm a Battersea boy myself, and I'd recommend going south of the river. It's more cheaper. There's plenty of open spaces, and you can get up the West End easy if you want a night out. You couldn't do better, I'd say.'

So Tom and Mary caught a bus, which went past bomb sites and craters and shored-up buildings, through fashionable shopping localities, through museum-land and over the river to the south side, where they got off at the first stop and walked into damaged streets of houses and prefabs, punctuated by wastelands and partially overgrown gaps between buildings, legacy of the cataclysmic years. They found a postcard in the window of a corner shop, and found the house itself in the middle of a terrace of identical houses, with a railingless low wall at the front and steps edged white with scouring stone. Tom knocked. Mary stood torn between the need to be accepted and the need to find acceptable.

The door was opened by a middle-aged woman with a shrewd grey face, wearing a wrap-round floral pinafore in green.

'Yes?'

Tom spoke formally.

'Good afternoon. We're hoping to find accommodation in the area and we saw your advertisement in the shop window. Is the flat available?'

The woman folded her arms and scrutinised them both.

'It is,' she said. 'Yes, it's not been let.'

'Would you allow us to view it?'

The woman's head rose. 'Yes, I would, dear,' she said decisively. 'Come in and see. Come in.'

She opened the door wider and extended the other arm in invitation to let them through. They entered a narrow hall with brown linoleum up the stairs and *The Light of the World* on the wall. The woman closed the door, smiling at them now in a welcoming way.

'It's no picnic trying to find somewhere to live,' she said. 'Let's hope we suit each other. What name is it, dear?'

'Pearson,' said Tom.

'Pleased to meet you, Mr and Mrs Pearson. I'm Mrs Jessop. I'll show you the flat, if you'll follow me. It's upstairs. Mrs Pearson, you look done in, dear. I'll make you a cup of tea in a minute. Just follow me.'

CHAPTER XIV
Mary and Tom

Mary kept her glove on her left hand while she drank Mrs Jessop's cup of tea. She felt self-conscious and anxious knowing that she was deliberately concealing the part of her where a real Mrs Pearson would have been wearing a wedding ring. When she had opened her mouth to contradict Mrs Jessop's assumptions, to explain that she and Tom were brother and sister not husband and wife, Tom had surreptitiously shaken his head at her, so she'd controlled herself and meekly climbed the stairs with Mrs Jessop to see the flat.

The term 'flat' glamorised the unconverted accommodation. It consisted of two rooms, with furniture that included a double gas ring and enamel washing-up bowl, and access to the bathroom from where the water for cooking also came. The bathroom was a rare advantage, according to Mrs Jessop, one of a handful in the street. And she was on the lucky side of the street, the side that had suffered less bomb damage. The rooms were clean and cheap and would do as a temporary measure, thought Mary, unable to concentrate on further details as the future implications of the deceit accosted her. Didn't Tom realise? If Mrs Jessop were not put straight without delay, the deception would have to be maintained throughout the time they lived there, and probably afterwards too. How could they do that?

Tom was unperturbed. He discussed gas and electricity, deposits, inventories, advance payments and procedures for paying rent. He sought and received approval from Mary, and asked when they could move in. 'Whenever you like,' was the answer. They agreed to the following day and Mrs Jessop took them downstairs for the promised cup of tea. Fortunately, Mrs Jessop's parlour was on the chilly side, which enabled Mary merely to loosen her coat and remove her scarf. Keeping her coat and hat on made it acceptable to keep one glove on as well.

Mrs Jessop was a widow. Her husband, Norman, had been in Burma. He had survived, was recovering from the horror, only to succumb to a heart attack the previous year. She showed his photograph. Had Tom been in the forces? Tom explained how he had worked in the aircraft factory after his weak lungs caused him to fail the medical. Take heed of the fogs then, said Mrs Jessop. Why had they come to London? For work, said Tom. He thought there would be better prospects in the capital. Yes, acknowledged Mrs Jessop, you had to make a living. That was why she let out half her house. With her sons having married away, she didn't take up as much space and letting gave her an income. The problem was that there were folks of every shape and form around in search of an abode, so much housing having been lost, and to be honest it was a relief to find a genteel couple such as they were to share her roof.

'I trust you'll find us good tenants,' said Tom primly.

Mrs Jessop said she was confident they would not disappoint, and arrangements were finalised for the moving-in.

'Tom! Tom!' said Mary as they walked away down the street.

'We've found rooms! We've made a start, Mary!'

'But Tom – Mr and Mrs Pearson? We'd have to keep that pretence up. How can we?'

'We just do.'

'It's an untruth.'

'It's an assumption, an understandable assumption, which we didn't rectify. That's all.'

'It's scandalous, Tom.'

'It's convenient, Mary. Weigh up the situation. It will make things easier to go along this way. And it can't be scandalous when we're the only ones who know.'

'What if you meet someone and want to get married really?'

'I'm happy enough just to have got away and to be here with you like this.'

'You might feel differently in the future. If you did meet someone, could you pretend to divorce me?'

'I dare say I could, if necessary.' He smiled at her affectionately and raised his brows for her reply.

Mary capitulated. 'All right. I suppose it might be better for us to be married,' she said.

'I'm sure it is. Come on, cheer up, Mary. We've made it to London. We've got a home. I'll get a job. We've escaped! Let's enjoy ourselves.'

After supper at a Lyons Corner House, they went to see *An American in Paris* at the Empire. It was Mary's first visit to a cinema and she was exhilarated by its zest and cosmopolitan glamour. They stayed another night at the hotel with the taciturn proprietor and in the morning, bound for Mrs Jessop's with their bags, they bought Mary a wedding ring.

They lived in Mrs Jessop's flat for two years. Tom took a job in the local department store, and at first Mary worked part-time in the corner shop. It was handy and enabled them to save a little money. She got to know many of the local people and liked being part of an increasingly familiar community, especially with her new status as married woman.

It was a glorious freedom, to make your own choices and not have to be grateful or pandering. Together, Tom and Mary saw the sights of London. The Festival of Britain had finished, but they toured the landmarks, the museums, galleries, theatres and cinemas. They became a married couple, and then became a family.

Baby Beth had the features of their mother, inherited by Tom. They named her Elizabeth after their mother. Elizabeth Frances Pearson. Mary was bowled over by the violence of the love she felt, a dark primeval surge of protective energy encompassing the infant. She didn't want to be separated from the baby for a moment. Mrs Jessop gladly put herself forward as babysitter so that Mary could go with Tom to the pictures or a show, but although she was entertained by these outings, Mary felt severed, cold and aching at the absence of her baby, temporary as it was, and was happier to be at home, making clothes and soft toys for Beth to the accompaniment of a radio programme. Tom would sit reading or sketching or have a night out with his colleagues. Sometimes Mary thought of what they had left in the Midlands. She imagined their father coming into the house to find them gone, with no explanation. What did he do? Did he contact the police? Would they do anything if two adults vacated their home, unexpectedly, with no sign of foul play? Was he wrathful?

Embarrassed before his employees? Lonely? Mary could only speculate, for there was no way they could make contact with him from their new way of life. 'Would you want to?' asked Tom. 'Would you want any of that back?' It was a question that did not require an answer.

By the time Beth was walking sturdily, though, several factors were changing. One was that a mobile Beth took up more room. Mrs Jessop had given them the run of her yard, and on a sunny day she and Mary would sit out together while Beth pushed her wheely dog or scrambled her wooden building bricks. Mary waited for the impetus to come from Mrs Jessop, despite the open invitation. She didn't want to encroach; moreover, she felt it politic to keep up a tinge of formality in order to distance Mrs Jessop from the possibility of discovering the truth about her tenants' family life. It would be less arduous to have their own outdoor space, with a kitchen and living room on the ground floor so that Beth could run in and out as she liked when she got older.

Then Mrs Jessop had to make a big decision. One of her sons had emigrated to Australia and was writing letters so brimful of enthusiasm about the opportunities there that her other son was talking of doing the same. They had both asked Mrs Jessop to take the plunge too. She discussed the ins and outs of it with Tom and Mary, her reluctance to uproot at her stage of life contrasted with the allure of this warm colourful continent; the demands of resettling and finding a niche for herself against the pain of being permanently separated from her sons and missing seeing the potential grandchildren growing up; apprehension about what would happen to Tom and Mary if she did go.

However, Tom had the possibility of another job. He had met a man who owned an art shop in Wimbledon and who was after an assistant both for sales and for the picture framing that was part of its remit. He would train Tom in this, and the offer had the advantage of combining what Tom already knew about – shops – with what he was interested in – art. Stefan Szczepanski was a cultured man with graceful, East European manners. It would be a pleasure to work with him.

Everest had been conquered, the new queen had been crowned, and in the autumn, Tom and Mary moved out of Mrs Jessop's flat to rent a small house a bus ride from Mr Szczepanski's art shop. Mrs Jessop left her own house and went to Canberra. Mary wrote to her, sending photographs of Beth as she grew up. In return came postcards: postcards with descriptions of the climate and the family and none of herself. Mary never knew whether she had adjusted.

Tom continued working at Mr Szczepanski's, who was his employer but also his friend, Stefan. Stefan had no family and he subsequently bequeathed the business to Tom. When Tom reluctantly sold up on retirement, he bought their house from the landlord.

Mary lived simply, keeping herself to herself. She was amiable without being forthcoming. Neighbours and the parents of Beth's school friends considered her to be shy. What had started out as deliberate policy with Mrs Jessop became a habit: she was maintaining a distance so as to keep enquiries and intimacies at bay, to safeguard herself and her life from exposing that they were not like other families. There must be no occasion for comment or suspicion. All must be clean, quiet, tidy and unexceptional. No more irregularity. They must be like everyone else.

Yet incomparable treasures mingled with the lurking fear of being found out: Beth's arms in squeezing cuddles round her neck; the dainty dresses and cardigans; the certain love; Tom carrying Beth to show her a bird's nest in the garden, their dark curly heads pressed together; Tom's unwavering devotion; the uncensorious routines of everyday domestic life.

And it worked out. Mr and Mrs Pearson, that's who they were. Conventional, decorous Mr and Mrs Pearson. Mr and Mrs Pearson with their pretty, demure daughter, Elizabeth. It worked out. They managed it. No regrets.

CHAPTER XV
The Family

Adam said, 'You ought to find something better to do, Lucy. You'll have wasted an entire year. I thought you were intending to go abroad.'

Adam was pleased with how his career was progressing. He had a good degree, experience in marketing with a company in Manchester – a steep learning curve but he'd climbed it, and now he had been not exactly head-hunted, but he could describe it that way, by the Singapore branch of a multinational. Flying out tomorrow. Not bad for starters. On this balmy May night, with the window open, and the sound of the flight path to endorse him, he occupied the big armchair in his mother's sitting room and tried to teach his younger siblings what's what in the real world.

'I was going abroad,' said Lucy from one end of the sofa. 'It fell through.'

'Fell through! That's a feeble excuse, isn't it? You should have found something else.'

'It didn't fall through, Adam,' clarified Beth from the other end of the sofa. 'That's Lucy's modest way of putting it. She gave it up because Grandma was in a particularly bad way at that time. She gave it up of her own accord, unselfishly, because she thought she could be of benefit here.'

'That was good of you, Luce,' said Adam. 'But not a priority any more, is it? The frame of reference has changed. Grandma's being cared for in the Home so you can forget about that.'

'We're hardly going to forget about her, Adam,' said Lucy.

'I didn't say forget about *her*. Come on, what do you think I am? I'm saying that it's someone else's responsibility to care for her, and I mean *physically* care for her. That frees you up to get on with your own lives. Which Lucy above all should be doing or it will be lost time, which you'll regret in the future.'

Lucy saw Beth's worried expression.

'I am getting on with my life, Adam. And I want to see Grandma regularly. I want to.'

'It's commendable of you, Luce, but face the facts. She doesn't know where she is or who her visitors are. She called me Father when I went to see her this afternoon. She's in her own world and it makes no odds whether you personally are there with her or not. You should shift your attention onto your own projects.'

Actually, Adam, thought Lucy, I already have a project that would astound you if you knew about it. Outwardly, she merely said, 'It's a bit late.'

'It's certainly slipping away. This year's not going to be a very impressive entry on your CV if all you've done is work in a shop. It's a jungle out there, you know. You have to go for anything you can to give you the edge. Your minimum objective now should be to get at least one significant thing out of the time you've got left.'

'Like what?'

'I can't tell you. You'll have to think it through for yourself. You should find something applicable to your future career pathway. Employers expect you to be just about plug-and-play nowadays.'

'I haven't got a career pathway yet.'

'You should have. Frankly, Luce, you've got to get more focused. You too, Daniel. It's never too early to plan for your future.'

'Daniel's got plenty of time,' interposed Beth.

'He should make use of it. Listen, Grandma's condition is what lies ahead for most of us – except maybe Dan and me, who'll probably die before we get to that stage, being male. Either way, there's no time to hang about. That's why I'm going to Singapore. You've got to make your opportunities and take them.'

'God, Adam, you're tiring,' said Daniel from the floor between Beth and Lucy.

'You'll learn, laddie. You'll learn.'

There was a pause. Beth stretched.

'If no one objects, I'll go to bed. I haven't got your stamina. Goodnight.'

They chorused a responding goodnight. When Beth had left the room, Lucy confronted Adam.

'You should have told her,' she said. 'You should have told her earlier about Singapore.'

Adam's smooth, fresh complexion flushed.

'It wasn't deliberate, Luce. I've been busy. I didn't get round to it.'

Lucy didn't answer.

'Anyway, she couldn't have been put in the know much earlier,' he went on. 'Clearly, Dad told her pretty quickly.'

'It would have been better for her to hear it from you. It felt as if you two were sidelining her.'

'Oh, come on, Luce. Don't make a conspiracy out of it. It was Dad who told me about the job. He was central from the start. And he told her about the outcome.' Adam jutted his jaw. 'He told it all, he told it fast, he told it truthfully. That's what you're supposed to do. Good PR technique.'

'You're supposed to tell it yourself,' cut in Daniel, moving onto the sofa. 'Who wants to hear it from him? No one.'

Adam leaned forwards.

'Listen, Daniel. It's time you grew out of these knee-jerk reactions and thought about things more maturely.'

'I have thought about it. He's the jerk.'

'You don't know that.'

'Yes, I do.'

'Danny, a lot of marriages break up. I've got friends who've already split and they're not much older than me. The faults are usually six of one and half a dozen of the other. There's no point in taking sides. It's one thing for Mum to hold a grudge against him, that's normal, but you ought to make more effort to be civil about him and to him. He's kept up contact with you, and not everybody does that, you know. Some fathers disappear.'

'I wish he'd disappear.'

'You wouldn't like his financial contribution to disappear, though, would you? You'd notice fast enough if he packed that in. Not every absent father is so reliable.'

'Come off it, Adam. He's not reliable. I expect he's forced to pay some money by law. That doesn't mean he gives a toss. He does it because he has to.'

'It's still his money and it's still reliable.'

'Reliable?' scoffed Daniel. 'He's so reliable that he barges in out of the blue at his convenience, not ours, and wants everything to revolve round him. He's so reliable that if he's said he'll see you and then decides he can't be bothered, he doesn't. He's so reliable that he can't be bothered with any explanation either. That's the type of reliable he is. You can totally trust that type.'

'When did this happen, Luce?' asked Adam.

'All the time,' said Daniel. 'You know it, Adam. It's happened to all of us. Why are you pretending?'

Adam spoke slowly, with deliberate emphasis.

'That was when we were children, Daniel. Even you aren't a child any more. A lot of men aren't good with small children, but you can't hold it against them for ever, and it doesn't mean that they can't be any good later on. Look how he's helped me. I wouldn't have got a job like this without him. Not so soon.'

'Wacko.'

'You're being a fool to yourself, Daniel, if you don't get over this. Consider it from his point of view. It can't have been easy for him either over the years.'

'You're trying to justify yourself.'

'Think about it, Daniel. And grow up.'

'Yes, *mein Führer*. At the double.'

Next morning was subdued. Adam was up early, his weekend necessities stowed, his cases lined up in the hall. He sat at the kitchen table, flicking through *Marketing Week*, his foot jiggling against the floor. Daniel hunched blearily over a bowl of Coco Pops. Beth put her emotions into tidying up.

The door buzzed.

'I'll go,' called Lucy, coming out of her bedroom. There were the stilted sounds of a voice through the entryphone, then she came hotfoot into the kitchen, eyes wide, mouthing and gesturing over her shoulder.

'Here we are again!' Tony's beam pursued her. 'And everyone together this time. Hello, Adam. How's it going? All ready?'

'Yes, just about,' said Adam, jumping up with alacrity and shaking hands. 'I didn't know you were coming.'

'I couldn't let my son and heir travel to the further reaches of the globe without saying Godspeed. And you'll need a hand with the luggage. I've got a big boot so it won't be any problem.'

'We're taking him, Tony,' said Beth firmly. 'Thank you.'

'In your car? No, no, Beth. It couldn't stand the strain. We'll go in mine. There's plenty of room for everyone and the cases. No problem.'

'I don't want to go with him,' said Daniel. 'Nobody invited him. He can go on his own.'

'It's more comfortable in my car, Daniel.'

'You think?'

'We do have it arranged, Tony,' said Beth. 'I can easily take Adam and the others.'

'What for, Beth? There's no sense in it when my car's outside, which is infinitely more suitable.'

'I don't want to go with him,' repeated Daniel.

'Don't go then,' said Tony.

'Thank you very much,' said Daniel and walked out.

'Bloody hell,' said Adam. 'Would you credit it? What a fuss over nothing.'

'It's not nothing,' said Beth. 'Why did you make him feel unwanted, Tony? He can do without that.'

'I'll go to him,' said Lucy, and went after Daniel.

'Dear God,' said Tony. 'All I'm doing is bringing my larger car to take my son, his luggage and the rest of the family to the airport. It's a perfectly simple procedure and it gets blown up into a Balkan crisis. I bet you'll be glad to get away, Adam.'

Beth flinched. 'It was already arranged, Tony.'

'And I've got a better arrangement, haven't I? Anybody can see that. Adam, are we going to allow ourselves to be late for the flight because of these shenanigans?'

'I would hope not,' said Adam grimly.

'Let's go. Are you coming, Beth, or not? Is Lucy? Daniel can suit himself.'

'He wanted to come,' said Beth.

'Nobody's preventing him.'

Beth took a deep breath. 'I know what. You and Adam go in your car with the luggage. I'll bring Lucy and Daniel in mine.'

'Lucy might prefer to come in mine.'

'We'll keep it as it is, thanks.'

'Let's go, Adam. We'll see you there, Beth, whenever you make it, with whoever you make it with. Ha.'

'Bye, Mum,' said Adam. 'I'll be at the check-in queue.'

'Yes, you go on,' said Beth. 'We'll see you there. Daniel does want to come, you know. He'd be disappointed to miss seeing you off.'

'I know. You round them up and I'll meet you at the check-in.'

The flat door closed behind Tony, Adam and the cases. Beth knocked on the door of Daniel's room. He was lying, twisted away, on his bed, Lucy sitting at the foot. Burlington Bertie, in a cardboard frame, hung on the wall. Adam's bed was neither made nor stripped.

'They've gone,' said Beth

Lucy was aghast. 'Aren't you going?'

'Yes,' said Beth. 'The three of us are. We're going on our own in our car.'

Daniel rolled over. 'Why did he have to muck everything up?'

Too true, thought Beth. She said, 'It's fixed. But we'll have to get moving.'

'It'll be too late. Thanks to him.'

'No. We'll get there. Come on, though.'

Lucy stood. 'Come on, Dan. It's not fair to Mum. You'll make her miss saying goodbye.'

Daniel got up.

They drove to the airport in Pollyanna state, Beth playing the game of determined cheerfulness, Lucy collaborating. There was heavy traffic on the motorway. By the time they had arrived and parked and pounded to the terminal, Adam had checked in his luggage and was standing in deep discussion with Tony.

'That took you some time,' said Tony. 'I told you you'd be better off in my car. You decided to come after all, did you, Daniel?'

'There was a tailback,' said Beth. 'We've got here, that's what matters. Adam, you'll let us know that you've arrived safely, won't you?'

'Yes. Don't worry.'

'You haven't always kept us up to date.'

'I know, I know. I'll email directly I get there and I'll send you a postcard. With lanterns on it.'

Beth gave a watery smile.

'I don't go for protracted leave-takings.' Tony took Adam by the arm. 'When it's time to go, go – that's my maxim.'

'I agree,' said Adam. 'It's better not to draw it out. Let's go to passport control.'

He heaved his flight bag onto his shoulder and went with the ushering Tony. Beth, Lucy and Daniel trailed behind. At passport control, he took his passport and boarding card from the zipped side panel, put them in his jacket pocket and dropped the bag to the floor.

'So,' he said. 'This is it.'

He hugged Beth and Lucy, shook hands with Daniel and Tony.

'I won't forget the postcard,' he said to Beth. 'And I'll email to let you know I've arrived.'

He turned to Tony. 'And Dad – thank you, Dad. I appreciate it.'

'A pleasure, my son. Any time.' He clapped Adam on the shoulder.

Adam picked up his bag and went through, raising a hand to wave before he was lost to their sight.

'Off into his new life,' said Tony as they walked back past the check-in queues. 'Tomorrow belongs to him. Next, it'll be you, Lucy, in the autumn, even if you're not going as far. And before we know it, Daniel, it'll be you. All flown.'

'We won't be going completely,' protested Lucy, glancing uneasily at her mother.

'You'll change,' said Tony. 'You'll be bound up in your own life. Don't feel bad about it, Lucy. It's a natural progression. All the birds leave the nest and have to wing their way. Ah, yes.' He stopped walking. 'That reminds me. My forthcoming winging – to LA. Make sure you get your skating order in before I go, Dan. Give me a ring and let me know. Here you are.' He felt in his inside pocket and brought out a card, which he gave to Daniel. 'Where to contact me.' He cursorily included Beth: 'New number, Beth. It's on the card. And,' he put an arm round Lucy, bending his head close to her face, 'I've had a brilliant idea, lovely Lucy.'

'Mmmm?' said Lucy awkwardly.

Beth stood stiffly by Daniel, who was chafing Tony's card against his palm.

'Mmmm, yes indeed,' pronounced Tony. 'And this is what it is. Why, Lucy, why don't you come on this trip to LA with me? You can drop that little shop job and you can be my personal assistant instead. We could extend the trip if you came – drive up the Californian coast, have a few days in San Francisco. You've got a passport, haven't you? And another time for you, Daniel. When you're older.'

'Oh, I don't know,' Lucy hedged. 'I—'

'Take your opportunities,' interrupted Tony. 'Look at Adam. Seized his chance with both hands.' He began to walk again, his arm draped over Lucy, who kept her own arms at her sides. Beth came after with Daniel. 'Don't be held back, Lucy,' Tony was saying. 'Do what's good for you. Will you come?'

'I'm not sure.'

'You're not sure. Accepted. Lady's prerogative. Maybe you'll become sure when you mull it over. You will think about it, won't you Lucy? Promise me that.'

'I will think about it.'

'That's my girl.' He gave her a squeeze. 'It would be silly not to, wouldn't it?'

He looked at her quizzically. Lucy nodded briefly.

'Good.' They had reached the outside of the terminal and he dropped his arm. 'I'll leave you to find your own way. I've got to go pronto. Cheers!'

He made off quickly towards the car park.

Beth, Lucy and Daniel took the same direction slowly, in silence.

CHAPTER XVI
Beth

The silence continued unabated on the drive home. Lucy sat in the front, and gazed forwards. Daniel had flung himself in a back corner.

Beth experienced considerable turbulence as a tangle of emotions punched out from inside her. She extracted each emotion from the inner bag in sequence, held it with tongs at a distance, and inspected it to see what it was and what events were attached to it.

First, sadness drooped from the tip of the tongs, limply attached to Adam's departure. The corny platitude was borne out: it seemed no time at all since he was that blond, rosy baby gazing up at her in absolute trust. Beth had been blissful. This was what she had achieved: a son, a home, a husband. An image flashed of Adam as a toddler, hair darkening to become like Tony's, shrieking with glee as he scampered in and out of the garden sprinkler one summer day at her parents'. And here he was, firmly and decisively moving to the other side of the world for how long? Two years? Three years? Ever? With no ostensible qualms or fears on his part, no tugs on his heartstrings. Yes, he'd been away from home for the past four years, at university and in his first job. But not so terribly far away.

And it had been an effort, this weekend, keeping her sense of loss under control while doing what she could to maintain a tranquil atmosphere for Adam's final hours with them. And then Tony arrived, with his ability to slide the knife between the intercostals: 'I bet you'll be glad to get away, Adam.' Perverting the leave-taking into a getaway, making her and her family group into something to escape from. When it was Tony himself who was the instigator of the ruckus.

Resentment flew to the tip of the tongs, impaling itself there and smothering sadness. Resentment at usurping Tony commandeering her precious hours with Adam. Resentment at the connivance that had preceded it. At the weaselling up to Adam, insinuating himself into Adam's ambitions. That the Singapore project had been engineered without her knowledge or consultation. That they had left her out – doubtless deliberately in Tony's case, although in Adam's case it was obvious that she just had not entered his head.

Slight jabbed into the resentment. The resentment bucked and reared.

And Adam was so grateful to Tony for his role in the opportunity. Although – and her scepticism momentarily quelled the resentment – how great an influence had Tony really exerted? He had a long history as a walking bag of bullshit, which could easily have hoodwinked Adam, who appeared to lack any detection system. What about the role she had played in the success story? The more subtle, long-term role, which Adam similarly appeared unable to detect. The years of holding the family together. The slog she'd put in, supervising his homework, prodding him to revise, testing him from his exercise books, coddling him through exam time. Wasn't this more enduring than the one-off exploitation of a business contact?

And now Tony was circling round, wooing both Daniel and Lucy. Resentment was joined by anxiety, taut and skittish, and soon after by guilt, recoiling. She ought to be pleased that Tony was mindful of his children, giving them opportunities that were outside her power. Buying them, sneered resentment. Colonising them. Surely, quivered anxiety, he couldn't take them over so easily. Surely, they could receive the perks he supplied and hang on to their independence too. Couldn't they?

It was the Los Angeles proposal that was the most troubling. Adam had been acquiring a hard-edged entrepreneurial zeal in any case; Daniel loathed his father, and a pack of fast wheels, no matter how desirable, wouldn't convert him. The LA trip was a different kettle of fish and Beth didn't want Lucy to go. Granted, it might not come to anything, like many of Tony's promises; yet the Singapore job had materialised for Adam, and if the LA trip were real too Lucy did deserve it. Adam had a point, for all that his style of delivery was tactless – the situation had changed and there was no reason for Lucy's selflessness to persist. She deserved to have a glamorous holiday abroad. She must want to go and Beth mustn't stand in her way. Beth knew it was allowing her strain over Mary to show that had led to Lucy cancelling her au pair placement. Beth was responsible for that.

It had happened the previous summer. Daniel was at school, Lucy was sitting her exams. Beth was up to her neck in work, organising stationery, checking invigilation rotas, overseeing candidates with clashes, sending off scripts. She was in the middle of a nightmare day, heavy with examinations and exacerbated by the large number of candidates sitting a range of subjects at rescheduled times. At this butt end of the summer session she was worn out by the demands of her job, not to mention her vicarious stress for Lucy and keeping some attention left over for Daniel and wondering how Adam was getting on. And helping Mary to wash and dress and go to the lavatory.

Desree came to get her as she was pinning up the 'Silence' and 'Warning about Cheating' notices in a late-starting exam room. Mary's attendant, Mrs Abbott, had rung from the flat to say that she had found Mary lying on the kitchen floor saying that Tom hadn't had his breakfast. Mrs Abbott had telephoned for an ambulance. Beth should return home urgently.

Beth slumped. Desree took the notices out of her hand. 'Go,' she said. 'I'll take care of everything here. Go.'

Beth returned to the exams unit to collect her bag. Colm Murphy, the office manager, was standing by her desk. 'I know,' he said as she approached. 'I'm so sorry.'

'I shall have to go home,' said Beth dully.

'Of course.'

'It means leaving you all to pick up today's nightmare on top of your own work.'

'Don't worry about it.'

'When you're desperately busy.'

'We'll get by.'

She drove home with tears standing in her eyes from fatigue and her colleagues' unselfishness. No one was in the flat. A note on the kitchen table said that the ambulance had already been and that Mrs Abbott had accompanied Mary to hospital. Beth wrote another note for Lucy and Daniel and drove to the Accidents and Emergency department, where she found Mary lying on a trolley, bewildered, Mrs Abbott at her side. Beth gave Mrs Abbott the money for a taxi and took her place. Mary said that her leg hurt, and her hand. There was some gravel in it, she said. They could wash it out at the fountain.

It was mid-evening before Mary was X-rayed and plastered up. A wrist fracture, a sprained leg and a bump on the head. She would be kept in hospital for a few days but would have to wait on the trolley until a bed was available. Mary dozed. Beth drove to the flat, where Lucy and Daniel had made dinner and saved her share. She packed Mary's nightdress and toiletries and went back to the hospital. Mary hadn't been moved from the trolley. She tried to change position and caught her breath in pain. She said, 'Tom, Tom. Is that you, Tom?' She said, 'He died.' She wept, fat tears cascading down her gaunt cheeks.

Beth wiped Mary's tears, holding the undamaged hand, crooning. Eventually, a bed was found. Beth stayed until Mary fell asleep again, driving home through predawn suburbia. She crept into the flat, where Lucy had been waiting up for her. Beth went to bed for an hour, then got up to see Daniel off to school. Leaving Lucy asleep, she went into work. She updated Desree, and gazed at her screen, striving to penetrate the meaningless symbols. Desree left her desk and minutes later Colm put his hand on Beth's shoulder.

'Go home, Beth,' he said.

'I can't take more time off.'

'Yes, you can. Go home and recuperate.'

'Obey,' said Desree.

Beth obeyed.

She drove home, working out the logistics. A nap if it could be fitted in, back to the hospital, home for dinner – what had she planned to eat? What food had they got in? The jaws of her consciousness kept biting on the mundane knowledge of everyday routine, but the thin detail slid away. She pulled in at a supermarket, took a basket and tried to pin down her thoughts. What to buy? Mary wouldn't know where she was when she woke up. She would be frightened.

The supermarket was full of elderly people, chiefly women, whom a free bus service collected once a week to shop at an off-peak period. Beth made for the chill counter. Any food, provided it was quick. She must go into college as normal tomorrow. It was an imposition to land the others with her responsibilities at such a hectic time. Desree would have had to work late to get everything done. How could Beth repay her? And Colm had stepped in too despite his own workload. Beth would have to do overtime to catch up. When would she fit in visiting Mary? When would Mary leave hospital? Would Mrs Abbott be willing to increase her hours? Did they need some vegetables?

'That's it – knock me over.'

Beth stared in amazement at the skinny white-haired woman who was standing angrily in front of her.

'Barging around,' ranted the aged one. 'No respect for us senior citizens.'

'No, they're not bothered.' Another old woman entered the fray, leaning on her mini-trolley and raking Beth with a belligerent gaze. 'Dashing about with their minds on themselves, that's all they do. No consideration. Couldn't care less about the old 'uns. It's all Self.'

Beth dropped her basket and ran. And that was what Lucy saw as her mother entered the flat: Beth, wet with tears, trembling and exhausted. Beth overextended, incoherent with sobs.

She shouldn't have let Lucy see it, thought Beth. It had been her worst moment and she shouldn't have let Lucy see it. Some days after that, when Mary was returned to the flat, patched, bruised but recovering, Lucy casually mentioned that she had decided not to take up the au pair post. It was no problem. The agency had found someone else to replace her. She'd realised that she'd prefer not to go abroad at the moment.

Beth's fault, although Lucy was adamant that it was her own independent decision. Beth was contrite. She deeply regretted her lack of self-control and resolved to hide her dislike of the Los Angeles proposition now. Too much had been spoiled for Lucy already.

Lucy would go to California and afterwards to university. Before long, it would be Daniel. Adam already in Singapore. One by one, like the green bottles. That was what else lurked in the writhing bag – fear of a future alone. Thank you, Tony, yet again, for pointing that out. All flown. Off into new lives, leaving her with the shards of the old one. The one in which home and family and work and ailing mother had left virtually no room for anything else. The one in which, by and by, nothing but home and work would be left. And in time nothing but home.

Beth shuddered. She had better do something about that prospect too. More to attend to. More to sort out. Why did life require such unremitting effort?

And there wasn't a parking space left. People had parked leaving ample room in front of themselves to get out easily, not ample enough to let another car in. Beth cruised the road, searching for the largest gap, which might afford a possibility. There. Sharp-angled reverse. Not tight enough. Out. Line up again. Sharper angle. About to scrape the wing? Slowly, slowly. Touched it, not more. Wheel round. Forwards. Reverse nudge bumper. Forwards nudge bumper. Reverse a fraction. Done it.

'Neat parking,' observed Daniel from the back seat.

'Yes, pretty good, Mum,' said Lucy.

Beth jumped.

Engrossed in her thoughts, she had forgotten anyone else was there.

CHAPTER XVII
Daniel

'He's a sad old bastard, but he'll do,' said Neal.

'Never seen him.'

'He went off to America when I was a baby. He sends me money though. A lot of money. Penance, my mum says. I get a lot of stuff off of his money that I wouldn't have otherwise, clothes and that. And my phone. So I'm not vex.'

'He's safe.'

'He's not bad. He tries.'

Daniel ran through in his head the comments he had heard his friends make about their fathers. He recognised that in general he'd hear more complaints than praise or tolerance because you tend to talk about people you can criticise more than those you accept. Despite that, his friends did seem to accept their father and the way he was, even if the way he was, was to be non-existent. Nobody revealed the same aversion that he felt. Several positively liked their dad, despite attempting to disguise it for the sake of detachment. His skating friend, Matthew, enjoyed the weekends he spent at his father's. They did things together that were fun. He got better marks in his homework those weekends because his dad explained it to him.

Not like the Git.

But the Git had helped Adam.

'*Et toi, Daniel?*' asked Mademoiselle Dodin. '*Qu'est ce que tu voudrais?*'

Mademoiselle Dodin's question jerked Daniel back to the part of the world he was supposed to be inhabiting at the moment: school in a French lesson, the last class of the afternoon. Mademoiselle repeated her question, more slowly.

'*Qu'est ce que tu voudrais, Daniel?*'

Daniel gaped. What was she on about?

'*Oho, Daniel. Tu n'écoutais pas.*' Mademoiselle tilted her head morosely. 'You were not paying attention.'

'Yes, I was,' said Daniel. 'I'm thinking about it.'

He creased his forehead and cast around wildly for clues. There was a sprinkling of sniggers, subdued by a frown from Mademoiselle.

'*En français, Daniel. En français.*'

'*Je, errrr, je cherche dans ma tête pour un répondre.*'

'*Une réponse,*' corrected Mademoiselle. '*Très bien. Et qu'est ce que tu y trouves? Qu'est ce que tu voudrais?*'

Ade, sitting in front of him, turned round and said huskily. 'Lotto.'

Lotto? Whaaat?

'*Tais-toi, Ade, s'il te plaît,*' said Mademoiselle.

Lotto? Wasn't that an old-fashioned name for bingo? Hadn't Grandma had a box of it, which she used to play with their mother, she said, when she was a girl? Cardboard squares with numbers on that you pulled out of a bag to see if they matched any on your scorecard. Did Mademoiselle think he played bingo, or what?

One table over, Penny surreptitiously held up a scrap of paper. Daniel squinted at it beneath his furrowed brow. It said: WHAT WOULD YOU DO IF YOU WON THE LOTTERY?

Daniel coughed and readied himself.

'*Oui, Daniel. Qu'est ce que tu voudrais?*'

'*Je voudrais un skate-park.*'

'*Un skate-park? Qu'est ce que c'est, un skate-park?*'

God, why hadn't he said that he'd buy a big house or something?

'*Um, c'est un parc et on peut skate vite et, um, jump et les choses comme ça.*'

'*Tu aimes patiner, Daniel? Patiner.*' She mimed skating.

'*Oui.*'

'*Oui, j'aime...*'

'*Oui, j'aime patiner.*'

'*Bon.* And who can tell me what is "to jump"?'

Quite a few people could, including Penny, but Mademoiselle asked someone else and the heat was off their corner.

'Thanks,' mouthed Daniel. Penny was safe. She was clever but didn't act up to it. She helped people.

The Git had helped Adam, so Adam said. Adam said that some men who weren't any good with small children got better.

Daniel hadn't noticed the Git getting any better, though. Adam said it was because Daniel didn't give him a chance. Daniel was being a fool to himself, Adam said. He'd had a big go at Lucy too. Adam could be a dirge at times.

Mademoiselle was hopping questions about holidays around the class and Daniel heaved his brain into the topic. What country would they visit if they won the lottery, and why? The various countries of the world were cited and hackneyed reasons trotted out. America for New York; Australia for its beaches; Greece for its old history; Iceland for its hot water; America for—

No, Mademoiselle wouldn't accept America again. It had to be a different country.

Daniel had been going to say America if he was picked. He'd rehearsed it. *Je voudrais visiter les États Unis pour voir Alcatraz.* Sod.

'*Et toi, Daniel?*'

'*Je voudrais visiter Singapore.*'

'*Singapour? Très interessant! Et pourquoi, Daniel?*'

He didn't particularly want to visit Singapore. It was what had popped up as an emergency measure. He didn't know anything about the place, other than Adam had said something about lanterns.

'*Parceque...*'

'*Je voudrais visiter Singapour parceque...*'

'*Je voudrais visiter Singapore parceque mon frère est, est, est là.*'

'*Vraiment? Qu'est ce qu'il fait a Singapour, ton frère?*'

'*Il travaille.*'

'*Est ce qu'il aime Singapour?*'

'*Oui, mon frère aime Singapour.*'

Daniel hadn't the foggiest what Adam thought about Singapore, but it had to be *oui* or *non*, and *oui* was safer because if he said *non* Mademoiselle would ask why and he'd have to come up with something else to say. With Mademoiselle, *oui* sounded more like the completion of a conversation.

It worked. She transferred to Penny, who wanted to go to India to see the Taj Mahal.

The bell rang and Mademoiselle left, tracked by those who didn't want to be on the school premises a moment longer than necessary. Daniel grabbed his bag, cramming in his books as he ran out of the room, walked briskly along the corridor and, with Neal behind, belted out of the building and down the back path to the main road. If you legged it you could catch the early bus, which gave you a longer evening.

A bus was already at the stop, the tail of the queue climbing on board. Daniel arrived panting and stood waiting for Neal to catch up. The lady in front paid her fare and moved off down the aisle towards an empty seat. Neal charged up, Daniel put a foot on the bus step, the driver smirked at him and shut the door.

'Hey!' shouted Neal. 'Let us on!'

The driver showed his teeth and wagged his finger at them. The school group had swollen. One of them danced in front of the bus, giving the driver a different finger. He tooted the horn and began to move off, making both Daniel and the gesticulator leap for the pavement. Rows of disapproving faces glided by behind the bus windows.

Neal cursed.

'Anybody'd think they got paid for the number of people they leave behind.'

By the time the next bus came, a large crowd jostled and complained. Neal and Daniel, holding pole position with difficulty, hurtled upstairs and along to the back seat.

'Look,' said Neal, ignoring the hullabaloo from outside. He pulled a magazine from his bag. 'Look at these.'

It was a skating magazine and Daniel looked. 'Ayay! Boom skates.'

'Boom.'

'The price of them though! Who can afford that?'

'Nah.' Neal thumbed through the magazine. 'It's skank. They're cheaper in the States. A lot cheaper.'

'Are they? How do you know?'

'A kid told me. Round our way. His uncle went over and says that things over there are nuff cheap. Everything. Things here are waaay more expensive.'

'Why? Why do we have to pay more for the same stuff?'

Neal shrugged. 'My mum says they fix prices for as much as they can get out of you.'

'Why should they get more out of us?'

'They en't getting nuffin out of us, are they, cos we can't afford skates like these. Answer – go to America, my boy.'

'Fat chance.'

But Daniel did know someone else who was going. Someone who had specifically offered to buy him something there.

'Get in your order,' he'd said.

Only 'he' was the Git.

If he did ask the Git and the Git agreed, that might put him in the Git's power. A favour granted meaning a favour could be extorted in return. He might lose his separateness.

He pondered the ramifications as he left Neal on the bus to travel a further two stops, and walked along the road home.

'You're being a fool to yourself,' Adam had said. And that was without the issue of the skates being thrown in. Maybe there was something in what Adam said. Maybe the Git could be OK, given a chance, now they were older. Maybe it was Daniel's own fault, at least partly. He knew he was never remotely civil to his dad. Maybe it was he, Daniel, who was preventing himself from having the advantages of a father.

It wasn't about skates. He wouldn't have asked for the ones in the magazine. Even with American prices they must be expensive, and he couldn't push it to that extent. It wasn't about skates. It was about something else.

He opened the main door of the block and climbed the stairs to the first floor. Once inside their own flat, he dropped his bag on the hall floor and drew himself up with resolution. Yup. Now. In the empty flat, before he lost his bottle. He scrabbled around in the clutter on his desk to find Tony's business card and returned to the telephone in the hall. Now.

He dialled.

'Johnson and Grimshaw,' chirruped a female voice. 'Mr Kinnon's office. How can I help you?'

'Er, hello,' faltered Daniel. 'Could I speak to Mr Kinnon please?'

'I'm afraid Mr Kinnon is unavailable at the moment,' said the secretary. 'Would you like to leave a message?'

'Oh no. No. It doesn't matter,' said Daniel, crushed. He hadn't thought of that possibility.

'May I ask who is speaking?'

'Er, it's Daniel. I'm his son Daniel.'

'Daniel!' The secretary's voice lost its affected efficiency and flowed into genial familiarity. 'Hello, Daniel. I didn't realise it was you. How are you?'

'OK,' said Daniel, bemused.

'He's having a day off. Didn't he say? I doubt he'll be there but you could give him a bell at home. Or on the mobile – if he's taken it with him. Sometimes you want to get away from everything for an hour or two, don't you? Where are you? Ringing from school?'

'No, home.'

'There's nothing wrong, is there? You sound a bit – I don't know – a bit something.'

'No. Nothing's wrong. I'm cool.'

'Can I do anything for you?'

'I don't think so. Unless,' he suddenly thought, 'could you give me his number?'

'Give you his number?' She sounded surprised. 'Oh, you mean his mobile! Did he never give you his mobile number?'

'No, he didn't.'

'He's a dizzy one, isn't he? Here you are. Got a pen ready?'

Daniel knelt down and pulled a biro out of his school bag, writing the number on his forearm as she dictated it. They rang off with good wishes for each other. Daniel was filled with cheer. She knew who he was. The Git must have talked about him. She was friendly and concerned because he was his father's son. He must be valued.

He dialled the mobile number with greater confidence.

'Hello,' said a voice.

'Hello. Could I speak to Tony Kinnon?'

'He's out. Sorry.'

'Isn't this his mobile?'

'Yeh. He left it behind.'

'Do you know when he'll be back?'

'No. I've only just got in. They left a note to say they've gone shopping. It didn't say for how long.'

'They?'

'Him and Mum. Who are you anyway?'

'Who are you?'

'Me? I'm Daniel. Who are you?'

'Daniel!'

'What's wrong with that?'

'Nothing.'

'Who are you?'

'It doesn't matter.'

Daniel rang off.

He was still sitting on the hall floor when Lucy returned. Her key clicked in the lock and there was a hiss of annoyance as the door pushed against Daniel's school bag, hindering it from opening fully.

'Daniel,' she called through the gap. 'Move it, whatever it is. I can't get in.'

Daniel reached over, plucked up the bag and hurled it at the wall. When it fell off, he booted it towards the corner.

Lucy stood in the doorway, astonished.

'What on earth's that for?'

Daniel kicked the bag again with the flat of his foot.

'Are you going to Los Angeles?'

'What?'

'Are you going to Los Angeles?'

Lucy shut the door. 'I don't know. I haven't decided.'

'If you do, you might find you've got a companion.'

'I know I would. I'd be going with Dad.'

'Another companion. Or two.'

'What are you on about? What other companion?'

'Daniel.'

'Has Dad asked you to go, after all? When did that happen?'

'Daniel and his mum.'

'Mum too? The three of us? Will she want to go with Dad? How do you know this?'

'Because,' Daniel kicked the bag again, 'I rang him.'

'You rang Dad? Why? You've never rung him before.'

'Neither have you.'

'No.'

'Because we didn't want any more to do with him than we had to.' He kicked again.

'Stop that kicking. So why did you ring him?'

'To be nice. To give him a chance. Adam says I should be nice. Everyone says I should be nice. I was going to be nice. And ask, nicely, for some stuff from LA.' He withdrew his foot for a further attack on the bag, but left off and put it to the ground, eyeing Lucy.

'And he asked you to LA?'

'Nope.'

Lucy swung her own bag from her shoulder, took off her jacket and hung it with the bag on a peg. She had enough on her mind already without playing games.

'I have no idea what you're talking about, Daniel. I've done a day's work. I'm tired, and if you can't tell it sensibly, don't tell it at all.'

'I won't,' said Daniel. He went into his room and slammed the door.

Lucy sighed and went into the kitchen to make a mug of coffee and some toast.

CHAPTER XVIII
Mary

Tom's back from school for the weekend. We're having our dinner, the four of us round the table. Sitting on eggshells as usual. Well, three of us are. Tom summons up courage: 'I want to do art,' he says.

I'd told him before. Try it, I'd said. It might work. Mother will be on your side. You never know, I said. It might work. Try it.

It didn't work.

'No,' said Father.

I was willing Tom to have another go. Usually he was the one giving the support; this time it was the other way round.

Tom says, 'I would like to.'

'Definitely not.'

Mother says, 'He is good at art. Mr Smithers says he's exceptionally talented.'

'Mr Smithers?' My father could pack a sneer into his voice when he wanted to. 'Who cares what Mr Smithers says? A scarcely weaned whippersnapper of a teacher whose experience of the world is a boys' boarding school! What does he know about anything that signifies?'

'He'd be doing other subjects too,' says Mother. 'Art would give him a broader outlook.'

'A broader outlook!' He banged his fist on the table and pushed his head out towards Tom. The cutlery leapt and jingled. Mother was looking apprehensive and I sat unmoving, with my hands under the table so as not to do anything to add to his anger. 'An outlook for feeble lemon-scented fellows and silly wet women with nothing better to do!'

His head snapped round to the side as he said this, to stab it at Mother, who went pink but sat mute. For the same reason as me, I suspect.

'I'll tell you what the outlook is, young fellow-me-lad. You get that School Certificate, and you enter the world of business, a real man's world. And you thank your lucky stars that you've got that waiting for you. Because there's many a boy of your age already bringing home a wage from factories and from mines and from works where the outlook,' he banged the table again, 'isn't so broad.'

'You, my boy,' he says, pompous and haughty, 'have a business empire to attend to. Don't you forget that – a business empire.'

He said it slowly and emphatically, as they did on *Twenty Questions* later. They used to say, 'And the next item, ladies and gentlemen, is a dah de dahdah.' They'd say it again with greater articulation in case you hadn't caught it the first time. 'A dah de dahdah.'

Animal, vegetable or mineral. He was mineral. Obdurate.

I went down the corridor to Tom's room after everyone had gone to bed, to console him about the art. We'd done that for years, since we were small, if something particularly oppressive had happened. Our childhood refuge Holly Hideout in the day, under the bedclothes in Downland at night. You could be cuddled up together, snug and comforted, and it made something congenial when nothing else was, especially after Mother died, and there was only Tom and I for Tom and me. Even Carry left to get married.

You didn't have to wait long for everyone to be in bed. Father made us go early.

'Early to bed, early to rise, makes a man healthy and wealthy and wise,' he says. 'I'm living proof of that maxim.'

He wanted the electricity off, that's why. He was perpetually switching off lights.

'Who's been using my electricity?' he'd say if he found a light left on, or a single lamp more than he deemed necessary. There would be an inquisition of each of us, one after the other, raining questions and recrimination. I don't know why Carry put up with it. Probably because of Mother.

Rain, rain, go away,

Come again another day.

Except don't.

We left the rain.

We were the ones to go away.

Away! Away! Tender is the night.

I was frightened when I was a child of going upstairs in the dark so I'd plan to go up before dark and leave the landing light on ready for bedtime.

'Who's been using my electricity?'

Switched off.

Mother would go up before me if she could or with me in the dark. Or Tom would be with me. Weekends and holidays. He was only there weekends and holidays.

'Who's been using my electricity?'

Who's been sleeping in my bed?

Ssh. Ssh. You've got to keep quiet. No one must know.

No one knows.

Nobody knows the trouble I've seen

Nobody knows my sorrow.

Maybe.

Maybe. Maybe. Maybe.

It works out.

It all works out in the end.

In the end.

You don't like him, but you wonder. You can't keep yourself from it. You wonder, you can't keep from wondering what happened. When he came back from the Masons. What happened when he came back? What did he do?

He wouldn't know at first. They don't necessarily. They don't know. People don't know what's been happening. Keep it quiet. Keep it quiet. Let it happen. Keep quiet. What the eye doesn't see, the heart doesn't grieve over.

Does it?

What the heart doesn't know...

What the heart doesn't find out...

Animal, vegetable or mineral.

He'd come home. He'd assume we were in our beds. He'd go to bed. He might be grumbling: Why isn't Mary up to make me a hot drink?

If he wanted one. He might not. He might directly go to

bed. It would be in the morning when there was no breakfast. That's when.

Does he shout? Does he stand in the hall and shout? On the parquet? Mary! Tom! What the blazes are you playing at?

Boys and girls come out to play.

On the stairs. By the bend. What's got into you? Don't you know what time it is?

Mr Wolf.

Time and tide wait for no man.

We haven't waited. Not any more. Beds not slept in. Not Tom's, not mine. Some clothes gone. Our birth certificates from Father's bureau. Our ration books. We haven't taken much else. A few precious things – not valuable, but precious. Reminders. Not that I needed reminding but I didn't want to leave anything like that with him.

I burned Mother's painting things. After he'd gone, while Tom was ferrying the cases, I took them out of hiding. I was a successful concealer of what I wanted to protect. Nowhere too inaccessible: behind and under things on the wardrobe's top shelves. I took out her paintbrushes, her tubes of colour, her pictures, and I took them downstairs into the kitchen and I burned them on the kitchen fire. I'd told Tom. He too thought it was the right thing to do.

It was a blue enamel range, and the coals were smouldering. The tubes swelled up and burst as they got hot because I hadn't taken the caps off before I threw them on. The bristles went up instantly but the handles took some time to catch. I thought of the metal collars of the brushes and the silver globules from the molten tubes that would be left in the cold grate. What would he make of them? If he saw them. It wasn't likely.

Mother's paintings, one by one. Not too quickly – they catch easily and the flames flare up high, if fleetingly, for each one, and I don't want to set the chimney alight. The fire burns with blue, green, purple spurting into the yellow and red. A draught holds the garden, flat against the firestone like a frieze till it chars with the heat from behind; another draught sucks up a sketch of a corner of the drawing room; I catch it with the poker and drag it down to the fire grate, to the coals. The lions by the front gate, the trees, Carry hanging out washing, sparrows picking at crumbs. Tom and I, and again Tom and I.

After each painting or sketch has gone, I mash up the chars with the poker and manoeuvre the rippled fragments into the gaps between the coals. I've got to be vigilant that they don't smother the fire. My face is burning and wet like my eyes, and drops fall onto my hand when I lean over the poker. She'd understand why I was doing this. We can't take her with us, and she mustn't be left behind with Father. She must be kept safe.

The last one is of me. I watch myself blaze, then I beat the scraps into ashes. Finished. Completed. I clamber up from my knees, ungainly, but in reality arising like the phoenix from an incinerated past. Ready to start again.

Artful dodger.

Phoenix.

On with my coat. A handbag – Tom's taken the cases already – and an umbrella. It's a wet night. Across the parquet, out of the door, crunching the gravel, past the lions. Tom. Tom. To London. With Tom.

Goodbye-ee. Goodbye-ee.

Mother used to sing that.

Not when Father was there. She didn't sing when Father was there.

Nah-poo. Toodle-oo. Goodbye-ee.

We won't be seeing him again.

Never.

Nowhere.

Never again.

There are Tom and I alone with each other.

Tom and I and then Beth.

That's what matters.

Try to sit still. Try to sit still, Beth. Snuggle up to me and we'll be safe. The waves have been tossing us, but keep by me and you won't see them. This is a good boat, provided we're careful. We'll make it. We'll make it if we're careful. We must be careful and sit still. Don't rock the boat. Keep quiet and steady. See how comfortable we can be. I'll wrap this rug round you. We aren't getting wet. We're not even damp. We'll be safe. We'll manage it. Tom's at the oars and we're safe. We've got to keep steady, move carefully. That's what's important. We'll manage it.

It'll all work out. It all works out in the end.

We managed it.

Carefully.

No regrets.

Tom and I and Beth.

Hush little baby don't say a word

Mamma's going to buy you a mockingbird.

Beth, darling Beth.

It was too wet for Holly Hideout, so I went along to Tom's

room after bedtime to tell him. Holly Hideout! Two adults using Holly Hideout! How silly! There must have been other places that we could have found to be private but it's the power of tradition. Holly Hideout and under the bedclothes in Downland. Both traditions hung on.

Of all the trees that are in the wood

The holly bears the crown.

Traditions. Routines. Solace. Protection.

That's something I should have known more about.

Father slept at the front of the house. I could hear him snoring and I could open doors inaudibly. Both Tom and I could.

Tom was sitting up in bed reading. He turned back the bedding as usual for me to get in, but I went on standing up because although I'd been rehearsing, I still didn't know how to say it.

He climbs out of bed and comes over to me, draws me close. Kisses my forehead. That does it. I can't help it. I'm crying now. Arms round each other as so often before. Dear, dear Tom. At last I say it,

'I'm pregnant, Tom. I'm going to have a baby.'

When the bough breaks, the cradle will fall.

Down will come baby and cradle and all.

I'm going to have a baby.

CHAPTER XIX
Mary

'My goodness! That would surprise us, Mary!' said the care assistant, putting the spouted beaker of tea into her hand. 'Here are a couple of biscuits, lovey. They're on this plate. Here lovey – on your table. That's it.'

'He doesn't know what to say. He doesn't know what to say.'

'None of us would know what to say. You'd be headline news all over the world.'

'No, no. We've got to be quiet. No one else must know. We've got to talk about it between ourselves. No one else must know.'

Mary was shaking her head vehemently, her whole body trembling in agitation. The care assistant perched on the chair and put her arm round her, securing the beaker, which was in danger of being tipped over, and returning the scattered biscuits to the plate.

'Nobody else will know. We can talk about it between ourselves. Have a sip of tea and we can talk about it.'

Mary sucked at the spout, her fingers crushing the biscuits. She gave up suddenly, the spout sliding off her chin.

'Such a beautiful baby.'

'Beautiful. A lovely baby. Is it a boy or a girl?'

'I don't know.' Mary was puzzled. 'Do I? I haven't had the baby yet. How can I know?'

'They give you tests nowadays. The tests might have told you.'

'Tests? I'm not sitting any tests. I'm not at school, you know.'

'Fair enough. You're not.' The carer got up from Mary's chair arm and came round to the front to continue the conversation.

'Although I didn't mind tests when I was at school. I quite liked them. It's satisfying – taking what's inside your head and putting it outside your head. Arranging it. Making it neat. I used to be quite good at it.'

'You were a clever little girl, were you, Mary? Lucky you! I wish I was.'

'Tom didn't like school.'

'I can sympathise with him there. I can't say I liked it either.'

'Boys' schools, you know. They can be rough. Tom wasn't rough. He didn't like rough things. He wasn't competitive either. He didn't like tests.'

'Nor me. They scared the living daylights out of me.'

'You can't always do it, though.'

'You can't always do what?'

'Take things out of your head. The things you know. You can't always do it.'

'Most of us forget things now and then.' She put Mary's relinquished beaker within reach on her table. 'Do you know what I did yesterday? I put the milk in the oven instead of the fridge and thought we hadn't any left.'

'You can't always take them out. They have to stay there because no one else must know. Keep quiet. Ssh. Ssh.'

'Don't fret, lovey. No one will know anything.'

'He'll find a way. He'll know what to do.'

'He will. I'm sure he will.'

'Ooo! There's a man! There's a man!' called Sadie from her chair, in horrified indignation. 'What are you doing in here?'

One of the few men who were cared for by the Home had entered the room. Usually Arthur kept to the rear of the building, where the more lucid residents were gathered to interact, but sporadically he strolled through to the front areas, immaculately dressed in brown suit, rust tie and polished shoes. He wore a trilby in the corridors, taking it off and holding it flat to his chest when he entered a room.

'Madam, I am a guest,' said Arthur, approaching resolutely.

'He's coming for me!' shrieked Sadie. 'Get him off me! Get him off me! He's after me!'

'Nothing so fortunate for you, dear lady,' replied Arthur. He disposed himself in a chair, sitting with his knees together beneath the hat, the fingertips of his two hands touching before his chin.

'Don't you dear lady me,' retaliated Sadie. 'I'm not your dear lady.'

'Indeed not.'

'You're no gentleman. You wouldn't come in here if you were. You're no gentleman at all.'

'You, madam, would be incapable of recognising a gentleman if one were to rise up and strike you,' said Arthur loftily.

Sadie screamed and put up an arm as if to protect her head.

'Don't, don't, please don't,' she whimpered.

The care assistant left her conversational post by Mary's chair and hurried over. Hearing the scream, another came quickly into the room. Between them they reassured Sadie and deterred Arthur.

'It's all right, lovey. He won't hurt you.'

'You mustn't say things like that, Arthur.'

'Why?'

'Sadie was frightened. She thought you were going to hit her.'

'Hit her? I wouldn't dream of it.' Arthur was offended. 'If that's your opinion, good day to you.'

He stalked slowly out, followed by one of the carers.

'Good day,' said Mary. 'Good day. Goodbye. We're going to London.'

Arthur stuck his hatted head back into the room.

'I bid you a pleasant journey, madam.' He doffed the trilby and moved away, the hat and his hand, lastly the hat alone, hanging disembodied for a few moments, before vanishing round the jamb.

'Goodbye!' called Mary. She relocated the beaker and plate from the table to her lap.

'Nasty old man!' shouted Sadie, recovering with gusto. 'Dirty old man. Always at it. You can't get them off you. Filth. Cut it off, I say. That'd learn them.'

'Ssh-ssh, Sadie,' said the remaining care assistant. 'He was just having a walk. He wasn't going to do any harm.'

'Walk! What's he walking in here for? Eh? He's after me, that's why. Keep him out. Dirty old man. They're all the same. Keep him out.'

'He doesn't come in here often, Sadie. He can if he wants to, you know. He lives here.'

'Lives here! He shouldn't be allowed. He's a man. A nasty dirty man. Keep him out.'

'You're safe here, Sadie. Don't worry.'

'Yes,' said Mary. 'Yes. You can worry and worry. But it can work out. You can manage it. If you're careful. You do have to be careful.'

Her hand smoothed over the material of her skirt.

'There you are,' said the care assistant, rescuing Mary's plate and beaker before they got pushed off. 'Mary agrees with me. It's better not to worry.'

'Mary? Who's she?'

'This is Mary.'

'What's she know about it? What does anybody know? He's got to get out. Out, out, out.' Her voice crescendoed as the words were flung towards the entrance to the room.

'Help me. Help me. Someone please help me.'

'Oh my. You've woken Hilda up.'

'Have I? Woken her up? I don't give a monkey's.'

Hilda grimaced wildly, snorted and flumped back. Sadie's pizzazz forsook her. Her chin fell onto her chest and she worked her mouth, gazing downwards. The care assistant went round collecting plates and varieties of cup, piling them onto a trolley.

Again, a man's face peered through the doorway. Not Arthur's. An ageing tremulous face, its eyes sweeping round the room, over the drooping white heads, the slumped bodies, pausing to scrutinise one or two, panic rising in its expression.

It stepped unhappily into the room, wearing a pale blue V-neck sweater with diamond patterning down the front.

'Excuse me,' he said to the care assistant. 'Do you know where I might find Mrs Morgan?'

'Mrs Morgan?' The carer thought for a moment.

'She came in yesterday,' said the man. 'I brought her in, but I can't find her.'

'Oh, Annie,' said the care assistant. 'Yes, she's here. There in the corner, fast asleep.'

'Has she…' He swallowed. 'Has she settled?'

'She's settled in well,' said the carer reassuringly. 'She had a peaceful night and she's enjoyed her food. I'll get you a chair.'

He stood in the middle of the room, shoulders bowed and arms hanging, while she fetched a chair from the hall and set it down in front of the relevant dormant old lady.

'There you are.'

'Thank you,' he said blankly.

The carer pushed the tea trolley out of the room. The man dropped into the chair and sat, hands dangling between knees, speaking at the unconscious figure before him.

'I didn't recognise you,' he said. 'Oh Mother, how could I? I didn't recognise you.'

He bent over, his hand covering his eyes. Then he sniffed and braced himself.

'I wouldn't have done it, Mother. I didn't want to do it. It was because it was better for you. I wasn't looking after you properly any more. I tried. I did try. They advised me. For your sake. Oh, I'm sorry, Mother, I'm sorry. I had to do it.'

He broke down again. His mother dozed on.

'You can only do what you judge to be best,' said Mary clearly. She was regarding him from one eye.

'Yes,' said the man heavily, not turning round. 'You're right.'

'Could be right, could be wrong. You never know. Time will tell. What time? It may be right one time, it may be wrong another time. May be right another time. Who can tell? Time goes on. Life goes on. You can only do what you judge best in the circumstances.'

The man rotated in astonishment, caught Mary's one eye and spoke to it.

'That's what I did. I did what I thought best in the circumstances. It's not easy. It feels wrong.'

'Wrong things can be right. Right things can be wrong.'

'I know. It's hard to tell. It's hard to decide what you should do.'

'We decided.'

'Did you?' The man was uncertain about this apparent change in direction of the conversation.

'We're going to London.'

'You are?'

'Tom's arranging it. He knows what's best to do.'

'Yes. I expect so.'

'Not to Australia like Mrs Jessop. That's too taxing.'

'Yes. It's a long way.'

'He died you know.'

'I'm sorry.'

Mary's eyelid dropped.

'That's the best thing to do. In the circumstances. Go to London.'

The man turned back to his mother.

CHAPTER XX
Daniel and Lucy

Early June. Beth with Colm in a senior administrators' planning meeting at college. Lucy in pyjamas at one end of the kitchen table, eating a bowl of muesli. Daniel covering the remainder of the kitchen table with wheels, bolts, frames, screwdrivers and Allen keys.

Lucy was wondering how much longer it would take for the birth certificates of her grandparents and mother to arrive. Her first request had been answered by a friendly letter accompanying three application forms and several booklets about tracing family records. Lucy had filled out the forms as best she could. On none could she give everything they asked for. She didn't know where her grandparents had been born, nor who their parents were, and she hoped she wasn't prejudicing the upshot by putting the father's surname for each of them as Pearson. Despite having more knowledge about Beth, she had felt a similar uncertainty about stating Beth's mother's maiden surname as Pearson. Her brain had been knotted by the time she had sent off the form and fee. One of the booklets had been about the Family Records Centre in Islington, and she reflected that if she had made the wrong decisions on the application form, she would be able to go to the centre and do the search herself. But from neither method could she subtract a niggling scruple that she was doing something underhand and dishonourable in this secret investigation of her mother's parentage. Sometimes she wished she had never come across the little leather box. Then there would have been no disruption, no calling into question the past behaviour of someone she loved so much. No fears about its repercussions. No guilt about concealment. Except what if her mother had found and opened the box instead? If nothing else, Beth had been shielded from that.

Daniel said, 'Got any nail varnish?'

'Nail varnish? What do you want nail varnish for?'

'To paint over the screws. It makes them hold firmer.'

'OK.' Lucy put down her spoon and swung her legs round. 'Colour?'

'Optional. I'll get it, Luce, if you'll tell me where it is.'

'That sounds gallant, but I'd rather you didn't go rummaging through my drawers.'

'Ha ha.'

'Ha ha.' Lucy went to her room for the nail varnish.

'So,' she said, returning and handing the bottle to Daniel. 'Why aren't you at school today?'

'Half-term,' said Daniel, wrestling with the screw-on top. 'Forgotten these things already, have you Luce? And why,' he succeeded with a brief fanfare, 'aren't you at work?'

'Time off in lieu,' said Lucy. 'I'm owed a day for doing extra. Don't bend that brush, will you.'

'I won't.' He painted the screw.

'Or cross-thread the top.'

'That neither.'

'Let's see.'

'Satisfied?'

'Mmm.' Lucy ate the last of her muesli. 'Are you upgrading those skates?'

'As far as I can. That's not very far.'

'Well, with luck you'll have the ones you really want from America.' She put her bowl and mug in the sink and got going with the washing-up sponge.

'No, I won't.'

'What do you mean? Has Dad gone back on it?'

'Nope. Not yet.'

'Are you asking for something else?'

'Nope.'

'Nothing?'

'Nope.'

'What do you mean "nope"? Why? What's happened?' She put the crockery in the drainer and turned to look at him.

Daniel lifted an upturned skate to eye level and squinted along the length of the frames.

'I've told you what happened.'

'No, you haven't.'

'Yes, I did. You wouldn't listen. If you don't know about it, that's why.'

'Know about what?' Lucy strode to the table, exasperated.

'Dad's other family,' said Daniel calmly.

'What?'

'Dad's other family.' Daniel rolled the wheels, checking the alignment. Lucy caught his hand and stilled the wheel-rolling.

'What,' she said, 'other family?'

'He's got one,' said Daniel.

Lucy let go and sat down, arms folded on the table.

'Tell me,' she said.

'I said – I've already told you.' He began work on the second skate.

'When?'

'I told you as soon as I found out. If only you'd listen to what I say instead of worrying about a kick to a school bag.'

'You knew then? How?'

Daniel puffed out his cheeks.

'Dan, I'm sorry. I didn't realise at the time what you were going on about. Truly I didn't. Tell me. Please?'

Daniel deflated his cheeks.

'Well, he definitely is a git,' he stated in a matter-of-fact voice. 'Adam tried to make out he isn't, but he is. He's actually a worse git than we thought.'

Lucy pulled out a chair for Daniel. He took no notice, continuing in phlegmatic tones as he varnished a screw.

'Adam kept on saying I wasn't being fair to him and that it was different when you were older, so I thought I'd give him a chance and I rang the number on that card he gave me. And a woman answered.'

'Oh, that's nothing, Daniel.' Lucy leaned back. 'It was his business card. She'd be the secretary.'

'That's not the point, Luce. I know she was the secretary.'

'Sorry. I'm listening. Go on.' She leaned in again.

'The woman was official at first, till she asked me who I was, and when I told her she changed completely. She became matey and behaved as if she knew about me. She gave me another number to ring. I rang it and a boy answered. A boy called Daniel with a mother who was out shopping with Dad. They'd left a note to tell Daniel where they were. Wasn't that considerate of them?'

'Perhaps,' tried Lucy, thrown, 'Dad just knows them. Perhaps they're neighbours or something.'

'The secretary thought I was that Daniel, didn't she? Why should she know a neighbour's kid? Where Dad just happened to have left behind his mobile? Anyway, I'd already told her I was his son. And that Daniel called them "they". Come on, Lucy, that's his other family. Or rather that *is* his family. I'm not.'

'Did that Daniel know who you were?'

'No.'

Lucy was thinking. Daniel went steadily on. 'We didn't know about them. They don't know about us. He's a double git, an infinity git. And I don't want anything that he's had anything to do with. Not even skates.'

'I wonder if Mum knows,' said Lucy.

'She'd have said, Luce. She'd have told you. And she hasn't, has she?'

'No, she hasn't.'

'Then my guess is she doesn't know.'

'She might have known but thought it better if we didn't know,' said Lucy, well acquainted with unpalatable information being kept quiet. 'In case we felt bad about it.'

'I don't feel anything about it now.'

'You did. All that bag-kicking.'

'It was because I'd been trying to be nice to him. I won't be trying that again. I can't be bothered with him any more. What about you? You going to America?'

'You must be joking.'

'Not many jokes in this.'

'No.'

Lucy watched Daniel checking alignments again, then:

'I doubt Mum does know. But if we both know and she doesn't know, it's sort of deceitful. Like lying by omission.' As she already was, she thought, not sure that her conscience could deal with more concealment.

Daniel stopped rolling the wheels.

'We can't tell her, Luce. She might be upset.'

'I'd feel wrong not to.'

'It's not us who're the wrong ones here. Better to get him totally out of our lives.'

'We have to put up with him off and on, Dan. He's our father. That's an undeniable fact.'

'Father! I could be a father that way. Come on – you know what I mean. Being a real father's what you do afterwards. And he hasn't done it, no matter what Adam says. If Adam likes him, good luck to Adam. The rest of us don't need to waste any brainpower on him. He's not worth it.'

Lucy ran her finger pensively along the edge of the table, pushed back her chair and stood up

'I'm going for a bath,' she said, leaving the kitchen.

'I'll probably have gone by the time you've finished.'

'Gone where?'

'Ade's.'

'Are you skating?'

'Should be.'

'OK. Have fun.'

'And don't say anything to her, Luce, or I'll wish I hadn't told you.'

Lucy went into the bathroom. Daniel put on his skates, clomped down the stairs, and skated off to Ade's.

CHAPTER XXI
Daniel

Ade lived in a new development of small red-brick houses, each garden separated from its neighbour by a low flat-topped bunker for the dustbins and meters. Ade was putting out a rubbish bag as Daniel swooped up to the gate.

'Good boy,' said Daniel. 'Very house-proud. You ready?'

Ade was resigned.

'I can't come.'

'What? Why?'

'Oban was sick in the night. He can't go to Club so I'm stuck here to look after him.'

'He would choose today, wouldn't he?'

'Tell me about it. Do you want to come in?'

Daniel followed Ade into the hall, pausing to take off his skates – after all, it was someone else's house. Ade led him to the sitting room, where young Oban was ensconced on the sofa in his Sonic pyjamas, watching television and eating a bag of crisps.

'Definitely ill,' said Daniel.

'I was.' Oban defended himself stoutly. 'I was sick over my bed. There's a big green patch on the carpet as well. Shall I show you?'

'No thanks. I'll believe you.'

'Do you want some crisps?' asked Ade.

'OK.' They left Oban with his programme about in vitro fertilisation and went into the kitchen. Ade rummaged in a cupboard and produced two bags of spicy tomato flavour, the squashed runts of the pack.

'That's all there is. He's been going through them like there was no tomorrow.'

'Whatever.'

Ade levered himself onto the units and opened his crisps. The telephone rang. Ade jumped down and, accompanied by Daniel, went to the sitting room, where Oban was already handling the call.

'Would that be deep pan or stuffed crust?' he was asking solicitously. 'Any extra toppings?'

'Give it here,' said Ade.

'Side orders? Garlic bread? Coke?'

'I said, give it here.'

'Oh, a cab. I'm sooo sorry. I thought you were ordering pizzas. Yes, I can get a driver to you in about twenty minutes. What address is it?'

Ade leapt on Oban and grabbed the telephone from him.

'Ow,' said Oban. 'That's my arm, you know.'

'Stupid. Stupid,' said Ade. 'No, not you,' into the receiver. 'Who? Oh, hi, Neal. You know who that was.' Oban chortled on the sofa. 'Claims to be sick. I know he doesn't—'

'I was!' shouted from the sofa.

'I can't. I'm stuck here with him. Want to come over? Dan's here. Later.'

He put the telephone down. 'Neal's coming round,' he said. 'And you, you're lucky to be alive, never mind sick. Budge up.'

He sat by Oban on the sofa, and Daniel sat in an armchair. They ate their crisps and watched the human-interest stories of IVF and surrogate motherhood, followed by the start of a rerun of *Lassie Come Home*, until Neal simultaneously hit the door and rang the bell. Tall for his age and lanky, he was down the length of the hall in a single glide.

'Come on, children,' he said. 'There's no way that one's sick. You going to let that blagger keep you in?'

'I can't leave him on his own,' said Ade. 'I said I wouldn't.'

'I'll come with you.' Oban bounced to the door, eyes sparkling.

'No.' In unison.

'Go on.'

'No.'

'Pretty please.'

'No.'

'Come on, Ade,' said Neal. 'He'll survive on his own.'

'I won't.'

'I can't. I promised to stay. You two go. I'll have to give it a miss.'

'If you say so.' Neal wheeled round on his blades. Ade looked anxiously at the marks left on the carpet. 'Coming, Dan?'

Daniel felt sorry for Ade.

'Look,' he said. 'Why don't we skate outside here, for today?'

'Yeah, that would be thrilling,' said Neal sarcastically.

'You don't have to if you don't want to.'

'You going for that, Ade?'

'You wouldn't have left Oban on his own, but you'd get some skating all the same. We could grind the kerb.'

'It's better than being stuck inside.'

'Can I come?'

'No.'

'You going to hang around then, Neal?'

'Could do.'

Neal went out to wax the kerb, leaving the gate open. Daniel put his skates on by the door and joined Neal. Ade walked up the hall, rubbing the carpet with his toe to erase Neal's tracks, on his way upstairs for his skates. Oban sat resentfully on the doorstep and made himself a wilful obstruction for Ade to get past.

Neal waxed the kerb with finesse and tested it with a Soul.

'Lousy,' said a voice from the doorstep.

'You're so good, are you?'

'At least I don't put it on.'

'Nothing to put on, boy.'

Ade went next.

'Looks like you wet yourself,' said the doorstep.

'I'll make you wet yourself in a minute.'

Daniel's turn. Silence. The doorstep was empty. Neal again. Ade.

'Ow!' Ade grabbed his bare arm. 'What was that?'

'Hey!' Neal rubbed his neck.

A sharp sting hit Daniel's cheek. 'What the…?'

Up in the bedroom window, Oban giggled. He held his BB gun to an open slit at the bottom and fired again. A yellow plastic ball bearing clipped Ade's ear at speed.

'Oban! That's dangerous. You've been told about shooting at people.'

Another plastic ball, green this time, skimmed Daniel's nose.

'Oban! Stop it!'

'I'll fix him.' Neal stomped into the house. Oban vanished

from the window. There were muffled shouts, then Neal was at the door brandishing the gun, Oban jumping up around him like a terrier pup.

'Give it back. It's mine.'

'You're too young for it.'

'It's mine. Give it to me.'

'You're too young.'

'It is his,' said Ade. 'But you shouldn't shoot at people, Oban. You shoot targets.'

'Hey, that's good,' said Neal. 'Got a target, Oban?'

'Paper ones.'

'Go on. Get some.'

'Why should I?'

'I'll challenge you. Go on. This is good. Got any empty tins, Ade?'

'In with the rubbish.'

'Where?'

'In the rubbish bag in the dustbin.'

'Yuk. Manky.'

'I just put them there.'

Wrinkling his nose, Neal opened up the nearest dustbin in its bunker, untied the topmost bag and fished out two tins. He put these on the edge of the path, leaving the bag untied and the dustbin open. Ade retied the bag and replaced the dustbin lid. Oban came out with two card targets, which Neal propped against the tins.

'Now.' He took off his skates and climbed on top of the bunker. 'Come on, Oban. First to reach a thousand.' He hauled Oban up to crouch beside him, Oban gleeful at finally being part of the action.

Ade and Daniel ground the kerb a few more times, then took a break to watch the BB match. Oban was good. He'd had plenty of practice with this gun on these targets and he shot the plastic bearings accurately. But Neal was catching up. He had honed his skills on countless hours of computer games and had swiftly adapted to reality. He was going to win.

Ade and Daniel watched until the outcome was inevitable. Bored with it, Ade said, 'Want a drink, Dan?' They walked across the firing range, against a howl of protest from Oban, to the house.

'Want a drink, Neal?'

'In a minute. I've almost won. Take my skates in with you, will you?'

Ade and Daniel took theirs off inside the door and went in their socks to the kitchen. Neal shot his winning bearings and sprang up, punching the air and whooping in triumph. Oban hung his head. It would have been gratifying to have vanquished Neal.

'Neffer mind,' said Neal, adopting a cod sinister tone. 'You did vell, my boy. Not vell enough to beat the Master, but that vas to be expected. Now you are under my command.' He stuck the BB gun in Oban's back. 'Ve go inside for a trink. Go slowly. Do not make any sudden movement.'

They slid off the roof of the bunker and marched into the house.

'Now,' said Neal to Ade, 'give this boy a trink or I vill shoot him. And one for the Master too.'

'We've only got squash,' said Ade, pouring some.

'It'll do.' Neal put the gun down and reverted to himself. 'That was good, you know. You're a good shot, Oban.'

Oban was elated. 'I've got more targets upstairs. I stick them onto the cupboard door. Want to have a go?'

'Yeah.'

Oban picked up his BB and took Neal off to his bedroom.

'Want some Frosties?'

'OK.'

Ade and Daniel ate a bowl of Frosties each. Shouts and whoops came from upstairs. They put the bowls and spoons and empty milk bottle in the sink.

'I'm dying for a whizz.'

'Do I have to know?'

Ade went upstairs to the bathroom and Daniel rearranged the fridge magnets until he heard the lavatory flush.

'Want to go outside again?' asked Ade from the hall.

'All right.'

They opened the door to make room for putting their skates on. In front of them, on the path, was a man in full body protection, pointing a gun. Crouched behind the gate was another, and another's headgear was visible over the wall.

'Sweet Jesus,' said Ade.

'Police,' said the man on the path. 'Put your hands up.'

Ade and Daniel put their skates down and their hands up. Another armed officer raced up the path, spreadeagled Ade and Daniel and began frisking them.

'What's happening?' said Daniel.

'What's happening,' said the first officer, keeping them covered, 'is that we have received information that an armed man is in this house, possibly with a hostage.'

'It's a BB.'

'What?'

'It's Neal. Him and my kid brother have been shooting targets from the bunker. You can see, the targets are there.'

The first officer waved his arm and another raced up. 'Sounds like a false alarm, but have a butcher's inside.'

The third man went into the house. Daniel, facing forwards again, noticed that the position by the gate had been taken up by another one of them. It seemed a long time until Neal and Oban and the third officer came out. Oban was rigid with terror.

'Yup, it's a toy one,' said the third officer. He handed the BB gun over to the first, who inspected it, lowering his real gun.

'We're only shooting at targets,' said Neal resentfully, sticking his chin up. 'You can't do us for that.'

'And less attitude from you, Sunny Jim,' said the first officer.

'They were,' confirmed the third. 'That's what they were doing upstairs. There's no one else in the house.'

The first officer exhaled loudly.

'Obviously a false alarm,' he said. 'It is,' he handed the gun to Neal. Oban watched wide-eyed. 'It is extremely foolish to play around with any gun, even though it is a toy gun, in public. People have got killed by doing that. Understand?'

The boys mumbled compliance.

'Good. Don't do it again. Go indoors and play there. Go.'

The boys went.

'What a load of wankers,' said Neal, safely out of hearing inside the house. 'All that for a BB gun. Tossers.'

'You probably can't tell from a distance,' said Daniel.

'Some neighbour must have reported it,' said Ade worriedly.

'They would have noticed the targets, wouldn't they?'

'They might not have been able to see them from where they were.'

'Have you got a half-blind neighbour?'

'I hope they don't tell Mum.'

'It could have been somebody passing in a car,' said Daniel. 'They wouldn't know you.'

'God, I hope so.'

'But when I opened the door and saw him there...!' said Daniel, with a snortle.

'Aiming at us!'

'In body protection!'

'And those two upstairs popping ball bearings as innocent as pie!'

'Hey, ours had his gun ready on us too,' said Neal. 'Didn't he, Oban? It was scary, my boy. Scary.'

'Scary,' said Oban.

'It's a good story though, isn't it,' said Daniel. 'How we got rushed by the AFOs! Wait till Matthew hears. He'll laugh himself silly.'

'My mum won't laugh herself silly,' said Ade. 'She'd better not find out.'

'Don't tell her,' said Neal.

'I'm not going to. Oban, not a word – you hear? Not a single word.'

Oban swelled his chest. Power at last.

'Shall we have a go on the computer?' said Ade.

'I suppose we'd better.'

'Can I play?' asked Oban.

'Yes.'

Oban led the way.

CHAPTER XXII
Lucy

While Daniel was skating, Lucy lay in the bath, her mind churning. Another part of life hit by an uncovered secret. Another clash between protecting her mother's well-being and the consequent discomfort of sham ignorance. How might her mother react if she learnt about the unknown family? What did Lucy think about it? Tony's secret, although clearly momentous at first for Daniel, seemed minor when put alongside Grandma's secret and it also involved a lesser sort of person as perpetrator. The horrifying implication of the portraits had not changed the fact that Lucy dearly loved her grandmother, that consoling presence throughout childhood who had done everything within her power to support Beth and the family through hard times. Whereas the children had never known much about their father's life away from them, mainly because his visits were erratic and he invaded their lives as opposed to taking them into his. Beth rarely referred to him between times. They had married and it had not worked out, as Beth termed it, tight-lipped. Lucy could remember what that meant: sharp voices, tears, bluff callousness.

The children spent placid weeks with Grandma and Grandpa, when they were spoken to especially lovingly but when she would sometimes see her grandparents exchanging worried glances. She was making pastry with Grandma, rubbing in fat with her fingertips and lifting the flour high above the bowl so that it descended in a shower of white specks like snow falling on the Alpine scene inside a plastic dome that she'd won at school for spelling. Grandpa came into the kitchen and as Lucy turned to demonstrate her prowess, she caught sight of his eyebrows raised in query and Grandma's almost imperceptible shake of the head in response. Lucy and Grandma were scraping new potatoes for dinner. On the kitchen table lay sprigs of mint, picked from the garden by Lucy, the clean green scent rinsing her nostrils. Outside the window, Grandpa and Adam kicked a ball to Daniel. Grandma broke off, gazing down into the silty brown water, breathed heavily and resumed the task. When Lucy wet the bed in her own home, Beth burst into tears. When Lucy wet the bed at her grandparents, Grandma said, 'Don't worry, Lucy. It doesn't matter,' and didn't mention it again. The bed felt different when Lucy got into it after that, which she knew was because of a layer of rubber covering the mattress, although there came a time before long when it could be removed. She also knew that when her mother cried it wasn't simply because of the smelly wet bedding.

By the time Grandpa stopped working, they were living permanently in their own flat. Yet Daniel and Lucy often went to Grandma's after school until their mother collected them after work. Grandpa watched children's television with them and drew the cartoon characters with Daniel. Her grandparents went to the school concerts. Her father, the author of the upheaval, had no further consistent input. Was he really being a father in another family? As far as Daniel was concerned, the revelation appeared to have liberated him now from the anger and truculence that had long kept him emotionally tethered to his father. As for herself, the initial impact having worn off, to what extent did it affect her one way or another?

Lucy wriggled her toes under the tap and found that in all honesty it didn't make much difference. It was just another aspect of the unsatisfactory-father factor. His deception of two families simultaneously, though definitely unsavoury, couldn't further worsen relationships that were already so defective. It was neither here nor there and, despite Daniel's fears, she suspected that her mother would be past caring much what Tony got up to outside her own family. But Daniel was concerned about upsetting their mother, so she wouldn't say anything. Better to continue living their own lives, keep their father out as far as practicable and make sure that they didn't weaken under any temptations – Los Angeles, for example.

So, she said to herself, standing up and reaching for a towel. The year wears on and I won't have done anything with it beyond snooping around in Grandma's past, worrying about it and feeling guilty. A great list for that CV Adam's so keen on. No au pairing, no America, not much at all. Adam patently thinks I lack initiative. I should probably be more like Maya.

She pulled out the plug, swilling away lingering foam with the shower hose. She had a day to spend at whim as she liked. She could browse the shops, though that lost its allure once you were stuck in one each working day. She could marvel as people shouted abuse at each other before ecstatic audiences on daytime television. She could write to Rebecca, whose letters from France implied she was beginning to entertain misgivings about the extent of Serge's commitment. Some people went to the cinema on their own in the afternoons, but Lucy didn't feel up to that. It gave the impression that you hadn't any friends. It was better to wait and go after work with either Maya or Niomi if they felt like it.

Lucy opened the bathroom window to let out the steam and went to her bedroom to dress. She felt like a driftwood twig floating in the water of an inlet, moving this way and that as other objects generated flux and pull, not progressing in any direction. A trip to Los Angeles would have meant that she hadn't been wishy-washing about for the entire year; she would have accomplished the one significant thing Adam had gone on about. Oh, forget it. With her father's record of unreliability there was absolutely no guarantee that he'd stick to his offer. And if he did, it would have meant putting up with him for longer than ever before. She usually managed to keep reasonably polite and unconfrontational with him because early on she'd realised that he came and went and it was better to assume so and not really engage with him, even with hostility. She could keep that up for short stints but it would have been tougher for an extended period, particularly now. And he might have used it to make her feel obligated to him. And her mother couldn't have been happy for her to go.

No, no. Too complicated. Too sensitive. Ignore the whole lot – everything to do with her father – and carry on as before.

She wandered into the kitchen, groaning when she saw the debris left over from Daniel's skate-improvements. She gathered it up and dumped it in his room on Adam's old bed, then went downstairs to see if the mail had come.

Some junk mail. A postcard picturing Chinese lanterns said, 'Lanterns as promised. None of these in my office. Cutting-edge technology here. It's good. Adam'. Quite quick, for him. There were some bills for her mother and two letters for herself, one from France – so soon? She hadn't replied to Rebecca's previous letter yet. The other was in a large envelope, printed in blue at the top left-hand corner with a silhouette of the British Isles, a crown and the words 'Office for National Statistics'.

Aha. What she'd been waiting for. Would they have been able to trace the certificates on the basis of the incomplete set of facts that was all she had been able to come up with? Lucy ran upstairs with the letters, dropped the wodge of junk mail in the bin, put the bills and postcard on the kitchen table and sat down to find out what she had been sent.

She had been sent a compliments slip and copies of three birth certificates. First out of the envelope came her grandmother's. Mary Isobelle. Mary's father's name was Charles Albert Pearson, tradesman (master). Her mother, Elizabeth Anne, formerly Mortimer. The given address was a Lion Lodge in Fordham, Leicestershire.

Lucy unfolded the second certificate – Thomas William. The date of birth came three years before Mary's; the father, mother and address were identical.

So that was that. She swallowed a sick stone in her throat. It was incest. A breached taboo from which her mother seemed lucky to have swerved the genetic penalty. To which her father's sole undeniable service lay in contributing genes from outside and thus making his children's chances pretty much like other average people. But Grandma and Grandpa in such an illicit relationship! What in the world?

Lucy put the birth certificates side by side on the table. Her baby grandparents. Time reversed and looped as she looked back with her present knowledge to the time before it had happened. Tom unaware of the future Mary. Both unaware of the future Beth, the Adam, Lucy and Daniel to follow in the past and present that were the future then. All was concentrated in the birth certificates. The future that awaited those babies had been held compressed, until it was released and became their present and then their past with her, Lucy, scrutinising it in dismay. She was looking at the beginning in the birth certificates: she was part of the temporary, ever-moving finale. What had happened in between? The irregularity of her grandparents' relationship was confirmed, but was still unaccountable.

The third certificate. Elizabeth Frances, born at a Battersea address. Informant and Mother – Mary Isobelle Pearson with the same Battersea address and Pearson as her maiden name. Father – Frank Lawton. Occupation – garage mechanic.

Lucy stared: What? Father – Frank Lawton? Not Thomas William Pearson? Frank Lawton! This was her biological grandfather. Not the grandfather she had known, easy-going, artistic Tom. There was no incest, no breached taboo, no genetic threat. Her real grandfather was a stranger. Tom had been pretending. Mary had been pretending. It was a cover-up. Lucy threw her head back and gasped in relief.

Thank goodness for Frank Lawton, garage mechanic!

Well, kind of thank goodness. There must have been some shame. Grandma couldn't have married Frank, because her name was given as Pearson on the birth certificate. Lucy's sweet, well-spoken, seemly grandmother had had an intimate, unmarried relationship with a garage mechanic. In those days.

And the result was Beth, apparently adopted by Tom as his own child so successfully that Beth had no idea that he was not her real father, even less that he was her mother's brother.

Why had it been made obvious on the birth certificate? If Tom was going to pretend to be the father, why wasn't he named there?

Perhaps that really would have felt too much like incest. Or someone in the registry knew they were brother and sister. In that case, why hadn't they left the real father's name off the certificate, rather than make overt a truth that was intended to be concealed?

Perhaps you weren't allowed to. Perhaps you had to name the name. And perhaps Tom didn't start pretending till later on. Maybe Frank Lawton, garage mechanic, was with Mary Isobelle Pearson at the time the birth was registered.

What a tangle of unknowns and possibilities. Her grandparents had seemed unchanging and conventional with their self-sufficient orderly life. Behind that facade, what? No, it wasn't a facade. It was what they were. But they stretched further than Lucy could ever have guessed.

CHAPTER XXIII

Lucy

Lucy spent a fitful night turning over the changed situation. Her relief and happiness at finding her first supposition to be incorrect were mingled with yet another set of unanswered questions. Again she knew something that her mother didn't know, and her feelings of guilt continued to mix with her feelings of protectiveness. Not that this new information was in the same league as before. If her mother did ever see her full birth certificate, it would be a shock, but couldn't be anywhere near as devastating as Lucy had previously dreaded.

She crawled into work, braced to cope with Maya's comments on the bags under her eyes and what she should have done to make them less noticeable. Maya's preoccupations today, however, were not with eyebags, lashes, nails or any other aspect of personal grooming. She disentangled the hangers energetically, jubilation spilling from every pore as she sang along to the music playing: the song, the riffs, and the session singers' parts, in seamless sequence. Niomi, emptying bags of cash into the till, smiled indulgently. Lucy regarded Maya gingerly.

'She's had good news,' said Niomi.

'Oh yes I have, oh yes I have.' Maya sashayed forwards, swinging her arms across her body in the rhythm of her words. 'Guess what, Lucy – I've got a job for when I finish the course.'

'Have you? Where?'

'And it's better paid than here.'

'Not a drawback.'

'And it's a promotion from here.'

'Congratulations.'

'And there's a career structure. With advanced training opportunities.'

'It sounds terrific.'

'Don't be sorry about leaving us or anything, Maya, will you,' said Niomi, clinking coins.

'Oh, you know I will be when it comes to it. But I only got the letter this morning and it hasn't had time to sink in.'

'You'll be my only experienced staff, Lucy, when Maya goes back to her course.'

'Not much of it left. One assignment for after the placement.'

'Goes and never returns because she's gone to an incredibly superior job.'

'Oh, leave off.'

'We'll have to get someone else in to do Maya's tatty old job. If anyone can bear to do it.' Niomi closed the till drawer with a grin.

'Come on. You can't blame me for being pleased.'

'No, I don't. I'm happy for you. I'll have to interview for a replacement, though. I'd part-thought that you might stay on afterwards.'

Maya clucked her tongue and drew away from that aspect of the situation.

'Lucy won't be here much longer either, will you Lucy?' she said.

'A little bit.'

'Not after the summer. Where do you go to uni?'

'Bristol.'

'You're not going to be commuting from Bristol to do your hours here, are you?'

'I shouldn't imagine so.'

'Everyone's moving on,' said Niomi plaintively. 'Everyone apart from me.'

'Get a new job,' said Maya. 'Get a new man.'

'I'm already trying for half of that.'

'Try for the other half too.'

Strange, thought Lucy as she travelled home later, how Niomi felt that everyone was moving on apart from herself. Lucy had been entertaining a similar view of her school friends most of the past year but as Maya spoke, she had begun to get a sense of her own future life, of the changes to come.

She entered the flat, shouted hello to Daniel and as usual went to the kitchen. A sports catalogue addressed to Daniel lay on the table along with a couple of letters for Beth and, at the side, Rebecca's letter from the previous day, still unopened. Disoriented by the arrival of the birth certificates, Lucy had forgotten about it till now.

Dear Lucy

When you've read this letter, destroy it. Please. I'm telling you because I want to say it. Hardly anyone else knows. Don't tell anyone, Lucy. Burn this letter afterwards. Burn it so nothing will have happened so nobody will talk about it.

It's not been easy to discuss things with Serge recently because he's been working hard so I haven't seen him as often and when I do, he doesn't feel like making plans. I've been upset about that, which was bad enough, but then I didn't come on. At first, I hoped I was just late, but nothing happened and nothing happened, and when nothing went on happening I went to a pharmacy and bought a kit (embarrassing). I didn't know the word in French and I couldn't see one in any pharmacy to point to so I had to describe it with the other people in the shop listening in and knowing. I got one and oh yes, there it was, the blue line that means you're preggers. I could have died. Madame heard me crying and came into my room – she's been understanding about Serge and she thought it was to do with him. Which it was, but differently. I didn't tell her at first what it was but she saw the carton of the testing kit on the floor and realised. Oh Lucy, she's been so supportive. We talked about it and she went to the doctors with me and to the hospital. I'm not pregnant any more and nobody knows beyond Madame and you and the medical people and Monsieur he might and I'm never going to talk about it again after this so it won't have happened and it won't make any difference to my life it would have been catastrophic except that it would have been a baby and a part of Serge and now it isn't. Serge doesn't know. I didn't want him to. I'm only telling you, Luce. Please please don't tell anyone else.

Cyrille and JoJo keep cuddling me. They're such poppets. I want to have children.

And now you know why I want you to destroy this letter. You will, won't you? Burn it. Please.

Lots of love

Becca

Poor Becca. Poor, poor Becca. Lucy carried the letter across the kitchen and reached for the box of matches by the cooker. She dropped the letter in the sink and set fire to it. Becca's secret flared, went amber, shrivelled and was obliterated in dark flakes. Lucy washed them down the plughole and went into her bedroom. Taking her grandmother's leather box from the chest of drawers, she removed the wadding, the locket and the two pictures. She propped the pictures against the box on her bed and spread the birth certificates out in front of them. Poor little girl. Self-sacrificial little boy. What a trusting, protective relationship there must have been between them. Becca didn't want anyone to know what had happened to her, not her parents, not anyone. How vastly more difficult it must have been all those years ago for Grandma Mary.

Mary Isobelle Pearson. Thomas William Pearson. Fordham. In Leicestershire. Traceable on a road map or an atlas of Great Britain. Traceable and therefore visitable. That's what she would do. First, she would write to Rebecca. Afterwards she would plan an expedition to Fordham on her day off to find out whatever she could. She repacked the pictures and the locket and folded the birth certificates into their envelope.

'Hello,' came Beth's voice from the hall. 'Anybody home?'

'Coming,' called Lucy. She replaced the box and envelope in her chest of drawers and went out to greet her mother, back from work.

CHAPTER XXIV
Lucy

Lucy came out of the station at Fordham and set off up the road. It had to lead to the town – the station was in a cul-de-sac – and Lucy told herself that if she strode up the road purposefully enough, some unambiguous strategy might enter her brain too. For as the train got nearer and nearer to Fordham, Lucy had found her programme for the day becoming more and more indistinct. Finding Fordham on a map of Leicestershire, arranging the journey, taking a day off work – that had been a sequence of practical activities each with its own precise aim, the fulfilment of which gave her a pleasing impression of achieving something. They fell into place as a necessary prelude to the main event, but what the main event itself consisted of was yet to be seen. The road crossed a waterway with the Railway Tavern on one side and a mail order headquarters on the other. It passed a bowling alley, car salesrooms, a DIY megastore, a multiscreen cinema complex. They were solid functional buildings, a contrast to the shimmering amorphousness of her intentions. All she had were the names and address on the birth certificates.

She went up to one of the infrequent pedestrians and held out the notelet to which she had transferred the address. Yes, he did know where it was, quite a step. She had better take a 49 bus. It came up from the station. You got on outside Tesco.

Lucy stood in the queue outside Tesco and followed some pensioners aboard the single-decker bus. She showed the address to the driver and sat down at the front to be told where to get off. The bus laboured up the road, past a housing estate, and along a procession of shops until it deposited four of the pensioners and a mother with two children at the entrance to a hospital. The shops and flats became a row of modern houses, followed by a development of Tudorbethan, after which the bus swung into Victorian terraces. 'This is the nearest,' called the driver. 'One of those on the left further up.'

The one on the left further up was a broad tree-lined road. Apart from the chugging of the departing bus and the whirr of a few cars, there was no noise. At first, the banks of doorbells on the detached and semi-detached houses indicated that the majority of them had been converted into flats; subsequently they became single-occupancy households, with thickly lined curtains at the windows and front gardens laid out to designer plan. A row of tall railings, spearheaded and gleaming black, led to a wide gateway flanked by two stone pillars, each with a lion squatting on top. Lion Lodge. This must be it.

The house was detached, set back behind the railings. Between the house and the railings, the forecourt was paved in York stone with large Italian urns of overflowing plants at each side of the doorway. The heavy four-panelled door, painted dark green, had stained-glass side windows and fanlight. The knocker was large and brass, the letter box was large and brass, the doorknob was large and brass, the circular bell-push was large and brass. Everything gleamed, untarnished. Parked diagonally at the left side of the house was a new registration four-wheel drive. Lucy could see the jazzy pattern of a child seat fixed in the rear. Round the other side of the house, the prop of a swing was visible in the garden. Obviously the abode of an affluent young family, it must have counted as an impressive residence in her grandparents' childhood too, incomparably grander than the terraced cottage in south London that Lucy had known as their home.

She'd found where they came from – but where did that take her? She had acted upon her sole clue, and although the result was fairly satisfying, there were no further leads. She balked at knocking on the door to see if the owners were in, and besides they were unlikely to know what had gone on there fifty and more years before.

Lucy stared at the sash windows of the meticulously groomed house, hoping for inspiration or epiphany. Neither occurred. Growing aware that her intensive lurking could arouse suspicion, she turned and retrod her steps along the way she had come. When she reached the corner, a bus that said 'Town Centre' was approaching. Lucy ran towards the stop holding out her hand, and managed to catch it. The bus took the same route initially as the 49 had, past the Victorian roads to the Tudorbethans, but changed direction before it arrived at the hospital and almost immediately was in shopping streets. Lucy got off when the remaining passengers on the bus left, outside a shopping centre. It had been a short journey. Lucy could easily have walked, had she known how to get there.

Although labelled 'Church Mall', it was more like an arcade tunnelling through the surrounding office buildings, its shops at ground level as if it had originally been a minor street. There was a health food shop, a card shop, a children's clothes shop, a jewellery shop with nothing in it that Lucy liked. She came out into a road running across the top, overshadowed by a stern building containing a bank and insurance company. Church Road. Lucy could see a large church blocking the road some way up on the right, so she went left. She crossed the end of a street parallel to the one that the bus had driven down, and continued past the corner building. Here, Church Road dog-legged into a wider section, practically a piazza, filled with sunshine and high street stores. Vehicles were prohibited, and the sparse midweek shoppers ambled freely across the uniform paving stones.

Lucy was wondering where to go from there when her heart jumped. Pearson's! The name leapt out at her, written over the windows of a shop situated in the corner with tables and chairs outside. It was a coffee shop, with a basket of baguettes and trays of pastries in the window. Lucy went in. A couple of people sat at tables inside, and two young men with butchers' aprons tied at the front stood behind the counter before a blackboard with sandwich fillings chalked up on it. Lucy ordered a tuna baguette and cappuccino and was told it would be brought to her. She sat in the sunshine and resigned herself to acting in a way that might come over as stupid.

One of the young men brought out her order with a flourish. Lucy said, somewhat embarrassed, 'Could I ask you something?'

He folded his arms, crossed his legs and tilted his head. 'Anything personal?'

'Not very.'

'Never mind. Ask away, ducky.'

'I wanted to ask you – are you called Pearson?'

'No. Not at all.'

'So why is it called Pearson's?'

'We wanted a name for our new venture. Neither of us comes from Fordham so we thought we'd have a solid name that was already familiar here. Get ourselves linked in. You know, benefit from novelty and continuity at the same time. That sort of thing.'

'It wasn't called Pearson's before?'

'No. It was a charity shop before we took over.'

'Why Pearson's? Why that name, rather than any other?'

'You're not from round here, are you?'

'No. I'm from London.'

'Lucky lady. What are you doing up here when you could be in Covent Garden?'

'Visiting.'

'Okey-dokey.' Taking her arm and walking her a little way along, he pointed up to the wall above a Galt toyshop. There an old street sign said, 'Pearson's Corner'.

'That's what this area's called. We took the name from the sign.'

'Who is the Pearson person?' asked Lucy as they returned to her table.

He spread his hands. 'Search me.'

'It's some Pearsons I'm hoping to find out about, you see. That's why I came over to your shop.'

'Ah – *dommage*. Not because of our lovely baguettes.'

'That too.' Lucy sat down again.

'You could try the telephone directory, I guess.' He began to go inside. 'If that coffee's gone cold, I'll bring you another.'

'It'll be fine, thanks.'

Before long, he brought out another cup anyway.

'Michael – that's Michael inside – Michael says why don't you ask at the library. They might have town records or something. If Pearson were the builder, say, or, I don't know, a mayor or what have you. The library's up there.' He pointed to the road leading out at the opposite side of the pedestrian precinct.

Pearson's was filling by the time Lucy paid her bill. Her table was promptly nabbed when she stood up, and a queue had formed out of the door for takeaways. Lucy crossed her fingers that the most knowledgeable librarian wouldn't be at lunch.

The library was a red-brick Victorian building. A modern glass swivel door led into a tessellated hall and more incongruous glass went through to a lending library. In the corner of the hall, a wrought-iron staircase curved round to an upper floor, and a notice attached to the wall pointed to the reference library. Lucy climbed the stairs, went through more glass doors into a room of books and tables and computers. She approached the information desk, behind which a middle-aged man was hunched wearily over a screen.

'Do you need assistance?' he asked without enthusiasm.

'It's a question about local history,' Lucy explained. 'I'm investigating how Pearson's Corner got its name. I was told there might be town records in the library that would tell me.'

'I can tell you that myself,' said the man. 'It's because when I was a boy that part of town was a series of shops, all called Pearson's. There was a grocers, a bakery, I think there was a hardware shop, a drapers definitely – my mother bought my shirts there. It was like a department store, but in a parade of shops along the street. Later it was split up and each shop went into individual ownership, and today, as you can see, it's largely chain stores. When I was a lad, though, the corner was literally Pearson's. Does that fit the bill?'

'Yes, it does,' said Lucy. 'It's a Mr Pearson I'm wanting to find out about. And I know that he was a tradesman here.'

'Then Pearson's Corner Pearson is a strong candidate for being your fellow,' said the librarian in a more sprightly fashion. 'Why are you interested in him?'

'Oh, local history,' said Lucy. She thought it better not to be too precise. 'My grandparents came from around here, and I'm trying to put them in context.'

'Aha! Family research!' said the librarian, livening up further. 'That's what I've got planned for my retirement. My name is Dollond, which is a Huguenot name. There isn't known to have been a Huguenot community here, so what was he doing in this neck of the woods, on his ownio? If he was. Possibly one of his descendants carried the name here. That's what I want to find out. It'll take time. A thorough research project requires time.'

'It sounds intriguing,' said Lucy.

'Oh yes. Undoubtedly.'

'How can I find out about the Mr Pearson who owned the shops?'

'The county archives would have documents about how the town was developed,' said Mr Dollond, 'and we – no – I know what might be a better lead. In the paper recently there was an article about an old lady who used to work at Pearson's as a young woman. She was in the same Home that my mother was in for a short time, God rest her soul. It was the old lady's birthday, and her family had travelled from the corners of the Earth to celebrate it with her – that's why there was the report on it. Let's get it up and see – hang on a minute.'

He withdrew into a room behind his desk and came out after some time carrying a black box.

'I wasn't sure whether it had been put on film yet,' he said, 'but here we are. Let's have a shufty.'

Lucy tagged after him down the length of the library, past one or two solitary sloggers to a heavy door labelled 'Microfilm Room'. Here, he switched on one of three readers, threaded in the film, adjusted the focus and began to scroll the newspaper projection across the horizontal screen.

'No, no, mm, no – here she is!' He arrived at the relevant page. 'Looks good for her age, doesn't she?' He squinted at the screen, enthused by the unanticipated task. '"Beatrice Smollett, known as Beatty..." Where is it? – "After leaving school she first..." tra la la, "but" – here we are, this is it – "can recall the pride she felt on gaining a position in one of Pearson's stores, which in those days dominated the town centre. 'It was considered to be a superior job,' said Beatty, still neat and spry. 'You were someone if you worked at Pearson's.' Mrs Smollett remained at Pearson's until her marriage to childhood sweetheart, Alfred..." Tra la. That's all it says about Pearson's. She should be able to tell you something.' He unbent himself. 'She's at the Park Rest Home. Why don't you go over?'

'Would I be let in? They don't know me.'

'We can ring up the Home and see.'

'It's good of you to do this,' said Lucy, swept along.

'It's more engaging than what I spend the bulk of my days doing,' he said grimly. 'There comes a time in your working life when – oh, pay no heed – that's another tale. You're young and starting out. Let's see what we can do.'

By the time she left the library, Lucy had heard her mission explained by Mr Dollond to someone at the Home, had spoken a few words to them herself, had directions written down by Mr Dollond, including the bus route and where to board, and had received his blessings on her research. He was a changed person from the one who had been hunched drearily over the monitor when she entered.

CHAPTER XXV
Lucy

The Park Rest Home was on Park Road, both so called because they were up by the park. The Home was in two semi-detached Edwardian villas made into one. The garden walls had been taken down and a tarmac forecourt led from the pavement to the front doors. In the glass of the first was a handwritten notice 'Please use other door. Thank U'.

Clutching the bunch of flowers she had bought on the way, Lucy rang at the second door, saw a shape approaching through the stippled glass, and heard the familiar rasp of bolts being drawn. Through the large bay windows she could see this Home's equivalent of her own grandmother's setting: rows of armchairs holding frail somnolent bodies.

The door opened to a cheerful middle-aged woman.

'You must be the young lady the library rang up about. You want to talk to Beatty, don't you? She'll like that. I'll take you down to her. And by the way, she does prefer to be called Mrs Smollett until you're firmly in her favour.'

'My grandmother was the same,' said Lucy, with a sudden pang of guilt for the murderous past tense.

'In that case, you'll know all about it.'

They went down a short corridor, passing rooms whose partially opened doors revealed in each an occupied bed. Lucy averted her gaze, alert to presumption. The corridor led to a conservatory lined with more chairs, the people in which were awake, reading or chatting, and whose curiosity was piqued for a moment or two by Lucy's arrival.

'Beatty, you've got a visitor,' said the care worker. 'This young lady's come from London to see you. She's bought you these flowers. Sit down, ducky. I'll put them in water for her. Would you like a cup of tea?'

Lucy declined the tea and braved Beatty. She was an upright old lady. She wore an oatmeal-coloured blouse with lace around the collar, a pale pink cardigan and a pleated skirt with a pink and oatmeal pattern on it. Her white hair was waved. She sat feet together, head erect.

'Thank you for letting me visit you, Mrs Smollett,' Lucy began cautiously.

Beatty inclined her head.

'Thank you for coming, young lady,' she said, 'with your bouquet. And I must say it's reassuring to meet a young person with manners. You can't take it for granted in this day and age. In fact, it's unusual. The same standards don't apply. What can I do for you?'

Lucy tried to behave like a young person with manners and high standards. She spoke decorously.

'I was told that you used to work in Pearson's.'

'That I did.'

'I'm interested in those times, Mrs Smollett. Would you be willing to tell me about them?'

Lucy hoped she was treading the path between politeness

and grovelling. It wasn't easy to be natural when you were being explicitly judged, and she felt relieved when a happy pride crept over Mrs Smollett's challenging features.

'Oh, that was a good job, a respected job. It was quite something if you obtained a position at Pearson's, you know. Mr Pearson owned those shops, a long frontage of them, round Pearson's Corner. They were high-class establishments. That's what it said over the doorway: "High Class Baker and Confectioner". And over the shoe shop it said, "High Class Boots and Shoes". And there was "High Class Grocer and Provisioner" and so on. And they were, you know. If you were selected to have a position there, it was an achievement. They didn't give employment to any Tom, Dick or Harry who wanted it. You had to be a certain type. You felt the prestige of it.'

'And Mr Pearson – did you like him?'

'Liking didn't come into it. It wasn't my place to like or dislike, nor anyone else's. It wasn't the way it is today. You respected someone for their station. You knew what your own station was and what your duties were. And you had to do them in the correct way. You had to mind your p's and q's. Mr Pearson used to come into the shop unexpectedly from time to time to ensure that everything was as it should be. The senior staff had an eye on you, because nobody knew when he would come in and they didn't want him playing hamlet with them if something was amiss.'

'It sounds as if it was run rather strictly,' suggested Lucy.

'To the highest standard in every way,' said Beatty staunchly. Then she pursed her lips and her eyes twinkled briefly. 'I must confess he was a bit of a tartar,' she conceded. 'You were a Pearson's person irrespective of whether it was a work day or not, and you were required to behave in a manner suited to a

Pearson's person. One gentleman – not a gentleman as it tran-spired – he was dismissed because he was heard using language at a football match. You wouldn't find that happening now, would you?'

'No, I don't expect you would.'

'In my view, served him right. There's some words shouldn't be used. They don't care about it any more. In my time there was words no lady would use and no man would utter in front of a female or a child. I suppose a few would. You always get some. I'm talking about in general. It was the rough ones who had that brand of talk. Modern folk – girls, children, people with education – they feel no shame in it.'

She drew breath. Lucy put on a sober face but didn't have to say anything as Beatty was in her stride.

'I mean we was working class. No two ways about it. My father was a labourer and we lived in the back-to-backs that were condemned and pulled down in the end. But we were brought up with standards. I never heard my father use language, nor my brothers. They wouldn't have done it before my mother or us girls. We were taught decent behaviour, respect, right from wrong. And that's why I was given employment at Pearson's. I wouldn't have been engaged otherwise. My mother was made up by my appointment, you know. She'd had a hard life, people did in those days, and it was like recognition for her.'

'Did Mr Pearson have any family?'

'His wife passed away not long before I left. He ceased trading for the day of her funeral and we all attended. We wore black armbands, both male and female employees – supplied by Mr Pearson, mark you. We didn't have to buy them.'

'Were there any children?'

'Yes. His son joined the business. We used to collect our wages from him, and he'd exchange a cordial word or two. He was an unassuming young man, different from his father. Not that I'm speaking against Mr Pearson senior. We respected him and we earned good wages for the time. We were aware that there were many people less fortunate than ourselves. We were grateful.'

'What was his son's name?'

'We called him Mr Thomas. There was a daughter too. We didn't see a lot of her. She came in for shopping sometimes, but normally an order was sent up to the house.'

'Do you know what the daughter was called?'

Beatty cogitated, her mouth pursing up again.

'I'm not sure I ever did know. We referred to her as Miss Pearson. And that's something else I concur with. They get too personal too fast today. I had a home help before I came in here – I'm not clever with walking or I'd never have given up my home – and when she first came she commenced calling me by my Christian name. We'd never met, and there she was, a slip of a girl, talking as if I was a friend her own age. I thought – you could profit from a spell in Pearson's, my girl, though unfortunately Pearson's had long since gone and she wouldn't have been given a job there in any event. An aimable girl, but not suitable, I'm afraid, for Pearson's.'

'I wonder why Pearson's closed,' said Lucy. 'Why didn't Mr Thomas take over running it? What happened to him and Miss Pearson?'

'When I left, Mr Pearson senior was in charge,' said Beatty. 'I got married and left. However,' she measured her words, 'I did hear that Mr Thomas suddenly departed from the business. After the war, you know.'

'Why would he do that?'

'I don't know. Some said there had been a spot of bother between him and his father. It's true he didn't take over. It was sold off in separate parts and,' she dropped her voice, 'I heard that when Mr Pearson died, he left his money to the Masons.' She resumed her normal level of speaking. 'Maybe that was gossip. He must have seen Miss Pearson right. I never heard that she'd married – and it would have been a big do if she had, so I doubt that she did.'

'Do you think – if there was conflict between Mr Thomas and his father – Miss Pearson could have sided with her brother?'

'I don't know. I never heard. I was fully occupied with my own family by that time. They used to say, when I was employed there, that Mr Thomas was fond of his sister, and I do know that Miss Pearson never had a happy comportment on the occasions I did see her.'

'Might they have kept together?'

'They might. I don't know. If there was any conflict – and I'm not saying there was – I don't know – if there was anything, it would have been kept private. Mr Pearson wouldn't brook any Tom, Dick or Harry being conversant with his family affairs. And I don't believe we should. It was their province. People are entitled to run their affairs as they see fit. People with standards, that is.'

Lucy felt things were getting prickly. She abandoned that line of questioning and made a closing bid.

'Mrs Smollett, did you hear of someone called Frank Lawton at about the same time?'

'Frank Lawton? No. That doesn't ring any bells. Why? Is he someone I ought to know?'

'It was a name I came across. I was curious about his connection with Pearson's. Like – did they own a garage too? I mean, as part of the general enterprise?'

'No. No garage that I know of. They were shops.'

'The name doesn't ring any bells?'

'You didn't know everybody.'

'No, no.'

'You're from London, are you?'

'Yes.'

'They know about Pearson's in London, do they?'

'That's where I heard of Pearson's, in a general way,' said Lucy truthfully. 'When I came to Fordham to find out more, it was the librarian who said that you were the person who would know.'

'I'm famous, am I?'

'I would say so.'

'My, my.' She tapped the chair arm with the pads of her fingers. 'Mother would have been thrilled.'

'This has been fascinating for me, Mrs Smollett,' said Lucy, minding her p's and q's. 'I hope you haven't felt that I was prying.'

Mrs Smollett directed her hawkish mien towards Lucy and softened it with a fleeting smile.

'No, ducky, no.' She dismissed the notion. 'I've appreciated your company. I had a big birthday not long ago and it was grand. I had a lot of family here. They came from as far as Australia. It was a lovely do. But, you know, there's the other days too. Everybody here's obliging and I've got friends, as you can see, to converse with about this and that. But it's gratifying to talk about your past life too occasionally. The things that you used to do. I don't recognise the modern world. It's a different place from the one I knew, and I don't feel part of it.

When you can talk about how life used to be, to someone who listens – and you're an attentive listener – it makes you feel that it has been your own life, that you did do things and know things. It makes you feel that you own something. It makes you feel you're a proper person.'

Lucy kept schtum. Mrs Smollett was such a proper person that Lucy feared she might be accounted rude if she said so.

'I was married for fifty-two years,' Beatty continued. 'And I'd known him since childhood. We were at school together so it was nigh on all our lives. He said to me one day, "It's about time we set up house, isn't it?" That was a marriage proposal – none of this living in sin they go in for nowadays. We got married. Not a romantic proposal, you might say, but I never had a better friend. We knew each other and we had no secrets from each other. Fifty-two years of marriage. I miss him every day.'

Lucy reflected on this statement as she crossed the road to the ice cream van in front of the park gates. While Mrs Smollett might not have had any secrets from her husband, there was no guarantee that her husband had had no secrets from Mrs Smollett. You didn't know about secrets until you found them out. Or came across something that didn't fit in with what you already knew or thought you knew about someone.

What could you ever really know? She bit into the chocolate flake as she walked the gravel paths of the park, past a pond, a fountain, a flower clock with moving hands, up to a red pagoda. Lucy snapped the point off the cone wafer and sat on a bench. She sucked the last of the ice cream down through the cone funnel, a technique she hadn't used since she was a child. Good thing no one could see her.

The pagoda was surrounded by wire fencing, attached to which was a large notice: 'Danger. Unstable structure. Keep out.'

What did she know? She knew that her grandparents were brother and sister who had left behind them a prosperous environment in a small Midlands town to come to London and pretend to be husband and wife, living a discreet, ordinary life together, bringing up a daughter whose father was in fact a Frank Lawton. Someone who mattered enough to be commemorated in his daughter's middle name Frances. But she was no further on with discovering who Frank could be. He might be from Fordham. He might be from London. He might be from a completely different town or city. Although the county archives and records that the librarian had spoken of might tell about the buying and selling of the Pearson property, they were unlikely to contain information about Frank, or about family rows.

She crunched the ice cream cone and laid her head on the top slat of the bench towards the sunshine. It was as if a door opened onto a door that opened onto a door. She was in a square atrium, a door in front, behind, to left and right. Doors of different-coloured woods, different grains, different sizes, with different handles. All opening onto another door, which opened onto another atrium with other doors.

And all those people, the owners of the new Pearson's, the librarian, the ones in the conservatory of the rest home, or in the slumped crumpled bodies seen through the bay windows or with Grandma Mary. All had stories, stories within stories. Stories behind stories. Doors behind doors. All the stories somewhere. None fully known.

The long day caught up with her and she felt exhausted. Time to go home. Time to find a bus to take her to the station and return her to her family, each with their own undisclosed world. Beth had worked assiduously to keep the family together and give them a reasonable life. And unknown to her, in her own parents' past, was the hefty sum of money that went to the Masons. Mary and Tom must have been desperate to leave.

CHAPTER XXVI
Mary and Tom

Tom kept his arms round Mary as they stood together in his bedroom, but nevertheless drew back a little in shock at her disclosure.

'Oh my good night, Mary,' he said. 'A baby!'

'It was once. Just the once. And Frank was so remorseful, Tom, so apologetic. Don't despise him.' She began to cry again. 'Or me.'

'Mary, would I? But that's neither here nor there. What to do, that's the thing. What to do.'

'I don't know. I don't know what to do.' This came out amidst a fresh burst of tears. 'There's nothing I can do, is there? I'm beyond remedy.'

'Oh Mary, please don't cry. I'll look after you. You know I will. I'll always look after you.'

It was the next day that they met in Holly Hideout and Tom put forward his proposal:

'I think that what we should do is leave – go away.'

'Go away where?'

'London.'

'London!'

'Yes. I think we've got to go to London.'

At first, snag after snag arose for Mary, but also, more vividly, the consequences of not going. How could she tell her father that she was pregnant? By someone socially beneath her whom it was impossible for her to marry. How could she not tell him? Hers was a condition that couldn't possibly be concealed for long. Might she not have to leave home regardless? Whatever her reservations, it was unarguably better to carry out Tom's plan. Tom himself was excited about it. It was his escape too, his escape from a life he had not chosen and did not want, one in which there was no recognition of the sort of person he was, no outlet for his real interests. Mary's pregnancy was a blessing in disguise, a catalyst to speed them both into another, inevitably preferable, state.

They went to London and, initiated by Mrs Jessop's useful false assumption, became Mr and Mrs Pearson. Despite Mary's initial objections, she could not deny that it was, as Tom said, convenient. It enabled Mary's pregnancy to be respectable and no one need ever know the truth. And who could be a better husband than Tom? Who could have been more caring, more loyal, a dearer companion? What fun they had in those early London days! Despite their slender financial means, the re-registering of ration books, the lack of a proper kitchen; despite the shortages, the bomb sites, the pea-soupers and the Great Smog; despite the fear hovering in Mary's heart that their father would track them down (though it was more likely that he would consider them beneath his contempt and wash his hands of them); and despite a greater fear that their relationship would be found out – and what would happen then? – despite all these, they had freedom and the zest of the capital city.

Beth was born at home, Tom sitting edgily with Mrs Jessop in her kitchen while upstairs Mary laboured.

'My goodness!' exclaimed Mrs Jessop when she first saw the new baby. 'The image of her daddy!'

'You must be bursting with pride,' she said to Tom.

'I am,' said Tom.

The baby's birth had to be registered. Mary worried about this. About what facts she would be obliged to give. Whether the deception would be revealed. Whether she would be censured and belittled. She wept secretly in the middle of the night as she nursed Beth. She was happy now, but not unassailably. Her happiness could be sullied, made sordid by the registration.

Tom enquired of his married colleagues at work what the procedure was and came home with reassurances.

'It shouldn't create any difficulty,' he said. 'You don't have to give any certificates for us – no birth certificates, no marriage certificate. They do ask the name of the father and the mother's maiden name, but you could give me as the father and invent a maiden name – use Mother's if you like. They write down whatever you say.'

'You didn't tell them. At work. Did you?' Mary's fear rose again.

'No, of course not. I said it was new to us and I was asking because we wanted to know what to expect. It was Bill I asked first, and he didn't know because his wife had done the registration by herself with her mother. He called Stan over and Stan knew about it. He should do – he's done it every other year since demob. He was only too willing to give his knowledge an airing. He didn't find anything suspicious about being asked.'

Mary laid her head against Beth, who was up by her shoulder, legs tucked under, humped like a little frog in total trust.

'Honestly, Mary, they write down whatever you say. And there are two versions of the birth certificate, a long version with the particulars that are on the register, and a short version that doesn't mention the parents. You can have both or just the short one. That's it. There's nothing to worry about. I can do it if you'd find it easier.'

Mary sat unconsciously rocking, her head resting against Beth.

'Think about it,' said Tom. 'It's got to be done within six weeks of the birth, so there's plenty of time.'

Mary did think about it. In the following days she thought about Tom, dear Tom. She thought of the registration and how the most face-saving way would be to let him do it, as he had offered. And she thought of Frank, Frank whom she had loved in a different way from Tom, Frank who would never know that he had a daughter, Frank whom that baby daughter did not even resemble. He was being excluded from his own family. He was owed some recognition.

Mary blew her nose, fed and changed Beth. She got herself ready and, with Beth in her arms, caught a bus to the town hall and the registry office.

The registrar spoke simply and courteously. Mary gave her own name as Pearson, said that it was her maiden name and that it would be the baby's surname. She gave the father's name as Frank Lawton. She found that she was holding her breath. The registrar did not pause in his writing, nor comment. Elizabeth Frances. Frank's child. Through the ordeal of this registration ceremony, she was presenting the baby to its father.

Mary took both versions of the birth certificate. At the flat, she put the shorter in the drawer with the ration books and Tom's payslips. She put Beth in the cot and hung up her own coat. She took the full version of the birth certificate into the bathroom, struck a match and, holding the certificate over the washbasin, set fire to it. The final corner flared as she dropped it onto the plughole. She scooped out the burnt flakes and washed away the black powder.

Another fire ceremony. As with her mother's paintings, it was an entrusting of important things to the protection of flames so they could continue to exist for her while being safe from people who might use them detrimentally. From this time on Tom would be the father. But Frank had been given his place.

'It was easier than I'd feared,' she said to Tom that night.

'And now we're established,' said Tom. 'It's working out, isn't it? We're a family.'

Mr and Mrs Pearson with Elizabeth Frances Pearson. Brother, sister, baby with unsanctioned father. Loved brother, loved sister, loved baby and loved Frank.

Mary had loved Frank for a long time. They first met after her mother died, when Mary was filled with such sorrow that she had almost lost her capacity to feel. She had been withdrawn from school to be with her sick mother. Her mother died and her father decided that there was no point in her returning to school. Her friends, none of whom lived near, would have gone up a year by then. She had never been permitted to take part in any out-of-school social life, and the contact she'd tried to maintain initially had dwindled to nothing. There was Tom. There was Carry. Otherwise there was a monotonous, heartless undermining day after day after day.

The sun was shining. New green leaves were shooting. An industrious bee nosed its way into the spring flowers.

'Why don't you go for a walk?' said Carry, suspending her dusting as she noticed Mary gazing through the window. 'It would do you good to go out, Miss Mary. You're getting peaky.'

Mary took a walk into town. Bypassing the centre where her father's empire predominated, she went along the roads of large houses, which gave way to smaller houses, which gave way to large houses again, until she came to the park. Ducklings swam on the pond, a light breeze wafted the scent of wallflowers, and Mary lost her footing on the gravel. She sat on the path in misery, not moving, staring at the chips of stone surrounding her, grey, sharp-edged, waiting to hurt.

'Are you all right?'

Mary gathered herself together. 'Yes, I am. Thank you.'

'Let me help you up.' A hand under her elbow steadied her. 'Are you sure you're all right?'

'Yes. Thank you.' And Mary burst into tears.

'You're hurt,' said the young man. 'There's gravel in your hand. We ought to wash that. Did you twist your ankle?'

'No.'

'You're shekken up. Let's sit you down a minute.'

He guided her to one of the benches around the pond. An old man on the adjacent bench leaned forwards on his stick, following the spectacle with interest.

'Hurt yoursen?' he called. Mary mumbled something neutral, blowing her nose. 'Her hurt hersen?' he enquired again.

The young man patted the air to indicate that the situation was under control, and gave his attention to Mary, who was shrinking with embarrassment.

'I'm being silly.'

'No, you're not. A fall can be nasty even if you don't hurt yourself. It stirs things up.'

'Yes.' Mary sat tightly. 'It wasn't the fall.' She chewed her finger, glancing sideways at him and away. 'My mother died.' A sob rose again and split her words. 'She died very recently.'

'Oh ma duck,' said Frank.

CHAPTER XXVII
Mary and Frank

People did say 'ma duck' in those parts. It denoted benevolence, a readiness to let social contacts roll smoothly along. You could say it to a stranger, you could say it to the opposite sex without impertinence. It could cross divisions of age, unfamiliarity, sex, but at that time not usually of social class.

'Oh ma duck.'

He sat with his knees apart, elbows set on his thighs, hunched forwards, observing her. Sandy hair, light blue eyes, pale lashes. Not a handsome face, but suffused with goodwill.

'What happened?' he said.

It was the first time Mary had been able to talk about her mother's death. Anyone she could talk to – Tom, Carry – had been there at the time. For people who hadn't been there, she had been required to behave with dignity and composure. Now she told it, from the fainting fits to the ferocious headaches to the final terrifying haemorrhage. The young man listened without interruption, at times clicking his tongue sympathetically.

'It's terrible,' he said as she finished. 'There can't be anything like it. I lost my mother a couple of years ago and I still feel it.'

He told Mary his story, while she listened and understood. He didn't hail from Fordham but Bowerby, thirty miles away. He was the youngest of three brothers, the other two of whom had married and left home by the time his mother unexpectedly died. He had continued to live with his father and they rubbed along together until his father took up with a new woman, and the son found he was in the way. He had an auntie in Fordham whose husband suffered from angina, so he had gone to lodge with them. His keep paid for a few extras and he could do the household jobs that his uncle was no longer capable of doing, and it gave him a home away from home.

'Shall we try a walk?' he asked. 'See if you're better?'

They walked slowly round the pond and down the park paths to the fountain, where they rinsed Mary's hand. They learned that they were called Frank and Mary. Frank told Mary about his job in the warehouse that would do for the present but not permanently. He wondered if there was going to be a war or whether the *Express* was correct and there wouldn't be any wars in the near future. They speculated about what might happen.

'I'll have to go,' said Frank. 'I've used up my dinnertime. Can I see you again?'

'Yes,' said Mary.

'Can I take you to the pictures?'

'Oh no,' said Mary hurriedly. 'It's not easy to go out.'

'We could just meet here in the park at my dinnertime, by that bench we sat on. Will that suit you?'

'Yes, it will.'

By the park gates, Frank did an unnerved double-take as he looked at his watch.

'I'm late,' he groaned. 'I'm going get an earful. I'll have to dash.' He moved off fast, then pulled up. 'By the way,' he called. 'My other name's Lawton. I'm Frank Lawton. What's your other name?'

'Pearson.' She said it charily.

Frank's head jerked.

'Mary *Pearson*?'

'Yes.'

'I work for your dad.'

'I thought so.'

He walked back towards her. 'Does it bother you? Do you want to see me again anyway?'

'Yes.'

'Yes, it does bother you, or yes, you want to see me again?'

'Yes, I'd like to see you again.'

Frank broke into a broad grin.

'Righty-oh. Till next week then, Mary.'

And he sprinted off down the road to her father's warehouse.

Next week he was waiting for her by the bench, and the week after that. They walked as they talked, that was all, and Mary found in Frank someone to whom she could talk as easily as she could to Tom, someone who would listen and forbear. When she spoke of her father's relentless rigidity and control over their lives at home, Frank didn't remind her that this was his employer, that he himself was even more subordinate; he merely said that he could see why it was a palaver for her to go out in the evening but it would be nice to take her to the pictures some time if she could find a way, when she could manage it, no great hurry.

'Tom,' said Mary after supper. 'I'm going for a stroll round the garden.'

'OK,' said Tom.

'I don't want to hear any American slang in this house, young man.'

'Sorry, Father.'

Tom met her in Holly Hideout.

'What is it, Mary? Is something wrong? I'd thought you'd seemed happier recently.'

'Tom,' said Mary. 'Do you know someone called Frank who works in the warehouse?'

'Frank? Frank Lawton? Sandy-haired chap? Yes, I know who you mean. Why?'

'I see him, Tom.'

'What do you mean, you see him? How?'

'I see him deliberately. We meet every week in the park. We talk. I wanted you to know.'

Tom was flabbergasted. 'Do you mean that you're, as they say, "walking out" with him?'

'Well, we do walk. Round and round the park. And he'd take me to the cinema if I could go. Do you mind?'

'Mind? Why should I mind? It explains why you've been happier.'

'He works in the warehouse, Tom.'

'I know.'

'Not good enough, is it?'

Tom sighed.

'No, Mary. It's not good enough. Does that matter to you?'

'No.'

'And he knows who you are?'

'He didn't at first. He does now.'

'Does it matter to him?'

'No.'

'Well then.'

'Does it matter to you, Tom?'

'No, it doesn't. I'm pleased for you, stuck here day after day. I only know Frank slightly, but I do know who he is and he comes over as an open, decent chap.'

'It would matter to Father.'

'It would.'

'But,' and they spoke together, 'Father doesn't know!'

'Yes. Another thing he doesn't know,' said Tom. 'Good luck to you, Mary. Get whatever fun you can, I say. You've got to have something to compensate for what you put up with. Let's work on getting you out to the cinema.'

'There's no chance of that.'

'We can but try.'

'I've told Tom,' said Mary to Frank that week by the park pond, 'about meeting you.'

'What did he say?'

'He said good luck to us.'

'And he won't tell your dad?'

'No, he won't. He says it's another thing my father doesn't know about.'

Frank gave her a peculiar look.

'What did he mean by that?'

'Oh, that it's safer to keep hidden from him things that would make him angry or scornful. As my mother did with her painting. She liked painting, you see, and she was good at it, but she painted in private to avoid being disparaged.'

'Uh-huh.'

'What do they say – What the eye doesn't see the heart doesn't grieve over. Or rage about, in his case.'

'I know your Tom from collecting my wages. People speak of him as a straightforward person, no side to him. Approachable.'

'He says similar things about you. You must be two of a kind.'

The corners of Frank's mouth twitched. 'Not quite, ma duck.'

For the rest of that spring and summer, while the government in far-off London prepared for war, Mary and Frank met in the park and talked companionably about their lives and what was happening in Europe, although Frank knew a lot more about it than Mary did, until one day a sudden fierce downpour sent them skipping and giggling into the Chinese pagoda for shelter. Mary stood in the sudden gloom, shaking the raindrops from her hair. Frank had stopped laughing and was watching her intently. Everything went quiet.

'Oh, Mary, I do like you. I really do like you.'

He leaned towards her and kissed her, lightly at first as she stood awkwardly, arms by her side, unsure of what to do. When she whispered, 'I really like you too, Frank,' he kissed her again less tentatively, and she twined round him responsively.

The rain cleared. They emerged from the pagoda still entwined, Frank's arm round her waist, Mary's head on his shoulder. Mary felt simultaneously peacefully at home and bursting with elation. They walked slowly, without speaking, almost drowsily, along the path to the flower clock, where a censorious voice pulled them up.

'Good afternoon, Miss Pearson. Good afternoon, Frank.'

He was wearing brown shoes, that was what Mary saw first, brown shoes, a mackintosh and a hat, which he touched out of respect to her.

It was Mr Hopkins, her father's senior clerk.

'Time you were getting back to work, Frank,' he said coldly. 'Miss Pearson.' He raised his hat fully, theatrically, as if to emphasise a point, swung round and walked off with heavy step.

Frank dropped his arm from Mary and they stood facing one another in consternation.

'What now?' said Frank.

Mary's father came home early, shouting out her name as he entered the hall. In his study, he paced, sneered and berated her. An utter disgrace, he knew all about it. A warehouse boy. An uneducated working boy. Aspiring to make good, was he? Climb up and join the Pearsons? Through impudence. Through insubordination. Through subversion. Counter-jumping? He hadn't so much as a counter to jump. Who did he think he was? What did she think she was? A common factory girl – eh? A two-up two-down slattern? How dare they.

His lip curled, his nostrils flared. He silenced Mary with increased vituperation each time she opened her mouth to reply.

Tom, when he came home, knew the other side. Mr Hopkins had gone post-haste to their father to inform him of the meeting in the park. Mr Hopkins had been bound to silence – the other staff must know nothing. Frank was instantly dismissed.

Mary was initially kept on house arrest. She had no means of contacting Frank and she received no word from him, neither immediately nor as the war years dragged on. Presumably he was called up. As she witnessed the departure of the iron railings from the front of the house to be used for munitions, or as she knitted thick grey socks for the forces, round and round on four two-ended needles, she wondered whether any of them might be used by Frank, and mentally attached a message for him, just in case.

Eventually the war was over. The men returned and took up their jobs again in factories, offices, warehouses. Mary's life became ever narrower during peacetime, a dull respectability against which the memories of her pre-war meetings with Frank shone, golden capsules of contentment. Had Frank fought? Had he come through? She thought about him constantly.

And then one day Mary was in town when she saw a group of people gathered outside a shop. It was an electrical shop with a television set in the window broadcasting a cricket match. Mary stood with the crowd until the man in front of her, stepping back to enable someone to leave, trod on her foot and spun round to apologise. It was Frank.

They stared at each other. Mary wished she looked prettier, hoped she wasn't too dowdy. Frank's contours were tauter, his bearing stiffer. She couldn't read his expression. He said, 'I wondered. I did wonder if I might bump into you.'

'You did bump into me.'

He smiled. 'How are you, Mary?'

'I'm well, thank you.' Formal, wary, her heart thumping beneath it. 'How are you? Were you in the war?'

Frank studied the pavement.

'I was, Mary.' He looked at her. 'I wrote and told you.'

'I never received any letter.'

'And I wrote before that. When there was the big to-do and I got the sack after Mr Hopkins saw us. I tried to see you and I wrote to you.'

'No letter reached me.'

'I put one through your door myself.'

'It didn't get to me.'

Frank groaned. 'I went back to Bowerby. It wasn't long though before I was called up. I wouldn't have left you, Mary, like that.'

'I know.'

'All these years, Mary. All these years.'

Mary was silent. She had fantasised and worried about him, yet while her sentiments were still bound to that patch of life, she was aware that his might have changed. Nevertheless, it was he who had brought up that past, and with the implication that it did matter to him. He was sounding her out. He also did not know whether he belonged to an outgrown previous existence.

'We need to find out what's happened to each other,' said Frank. They went to the park as they used to, to the bench by the duck pond. He was in Fordham for a few days, visiting the aunt he had lived with when he was working in Pearson's warehouse. He lived at Bowerby, not far from his father, because – er – because he did. He had been in the Royal Army Service Corps, where he had learnt about vehicle maintenance, so on demob he had got a job in a garage, which he liked. He was intending to get some qualifications in mechanical engineering. If that wasn't on the cards, he would aim to run his own garage.

It was a strange combination of so much having happened, and yet essentially being the same as their younger selves. They met in the park the next day and the next, laughing as they followed in their old footsteps, heaping invective on Mr Hopkins and his disastrous interference. Mary's heart began to sing again.

Until Frank told her he was married.

He was married to a girl who had lived round the corner from his father. He had known her from childhood, had re-met her when he was on leave and they'd had a few jaunts. She wrote to him, and when he was on leave again she'd wanted to get married. He went along with it as he doubted that he'd get through the war, so it didn't make any difference and he had to admit that it was a solace to feel that there was an anchor here in England. It was a big error. A relationship that suits isolated intervals during abnormal times isn't necessarily one that suits an ordinary everyday life, and they hadn't anything in common. That was how it was. They were stuck with each other. He had to fund her, which was why, ten to one, he wouldn't be able to do the mechanical engineering but would have to put his ambition into the garage. His wife liked company and going out and didn't want a husband who would be at night class and stuck in books.

Mary ran. She ran along the gravel paths up to the pagoda. Her chest burst with sobs and breathlessness. Frank caught her.

'I love you, Mary,' he said. 'I always have. It's you I love.'

She pushed him off as he kissed her, then kissed back and clung and sobbed as they withdrew into the dim pagoda.

And there he loved her. Though in her confusion and despair and sexual innocence, Mary wasn't sure what had happened. What mattered was that she was with Frank, that he loved her, but that he would be returning to Bowerby, to his wife.

Frank apologised. He ran his hands through his hair, said he shouldn't have done this. He should have been more respectful. Mary felt mildly surprised, and surprised that that was her main feeling about the act. What filled her awareness, banishing other concerns to an obscure periphery, was the fact that Frank was married to someone else and would soon be gone.

Thus, weeks later, Mary said to Tom one night, coming to his room in tears, 'I'm pregnant, Tom. I'm going to have a baby.'

She hadn't dared to go to the doctor. She had looked it up in the reference library.

CHAPTER XXVIII
Daniel

First day after the half-term break. Ade walking slowly up the school path, head down. Daniel jumped off the bus and ran up to him.

'Whooa Ade!'

Ade drew up but didn't greet him. Other kids jostled past.

'Hey, what's wrong?' Ade didn't look good.

'Somebody saw,' he said.

'Saw what? Who did?'

'Somebody saw the police raid. BB gun. The lot. They've told my mum.'

'Who saw it?'

'Dunno. She won't say. Some neighbour or other. My mum doesn't think it's funny. Neither does Oban now. She's chucked his BB gun and I'm grounded.'

'But it wasn't your fault.' Daniel bridled at the injustice of the punishment.

'It was. The police were at our house. She says she'd trusted me to behave responsibly.' He turned to Daniel. 'She works so hard, you know, Dan. Really long hours. And my dad. He does two different jobs. And it's so's me and Oban can have a better life than they did. They want us to get on. They've been so proud whenever I've done anything good, like at school. And now I've mucked it up.'

He looked as if he was going to cry. Daniel was alarmed.

'But it wasn't your fault,' he repeated. 'It was Neal who got that kicked off.'

'I was meant to be responsible for Oban. I should have stopped Neal.'

'Stopped him! Who could ever stop Neal?'

A fist in each of their necks jolted them.

'Hey children. Talking about your bossman?' Neal was on time for once.

Ade straightened up.

'That BB gun stuff. I'm in deep trouble at home.'

'Way-hey! That was classic, that was.'

'Not any more,' said Daniel. 'He's grounded.'

'Who by?'

'My mum.'

'Blurgh. Blank her. Go out the same. Do what you want. Why should you care?'

'Because I do.' Ade walked towards the school door.

'He's upset, Neal,' said Daniel in a low voice as they traipsed after. 'It's not because he's grounded. He's upset because his mum's upset. He thinks he's let her down.'

'Blah blah,' said Neal. 'Ade should man up. It's nothing. She'll get over it.'

Daniel didn't reply. The bell rang and they went in.

At the end of the school day, Daniel let Neal race for the early bus on his own and, while Ade systematically packed his bag in the classroom, waited for him so they could catch a later bus together.

When Lucy came home, Daniel was at the kitchen table with a large sheet of paper and an array of coloured pens.

'Danny, you're drawing!' she said in surprise.

'Mmm,' said Daniel, concentrating.

'You haven't drawn for ages.'

'I have at school.'

'At home. You used to draw a lot.'

She watched for a minute or two.

'That's Ade, isn't it?' she said. 'Ade skating. That's brilliant, Dan. It's just like him.'

'Thanks.' He changed pens.

'Why are you doing it?'

Daniel sat back.

'It's a present. A cheering-up present.'

'Does Ade need cheering up?'

'His mum won't let him go out skating or anywhere but school and church for four weeks.'

'Poor Ade. What's he done to get landed with that?'

'Zilch. But she's angry with him and he's unhappy, so since he can't go out skating, I'm making him a picture.'

'Then he can imagine himself skating even though he can't go?'

'Something like that.'

'It's thoughtful of you, Danny.' She spotted an envelope on the work surface. Posted from France. So soon. Lucy's reply to the previous one couldn't have been there long. 'I've got a letter from Becca. Will I distract you if I sit at the other side of the table?'

'No – I'd have done it in my room but the paper's too big for my desk so I had to come here.'

'I'm glad you did. I wouldn't have seen it otherwise.'

She picked up Rebecca's letter and sat down opposite Daniel. The pages were tear-stained. Serge had broken up with Rebecca. He'd been two-timing her, although she hadn't realised. She thought he'd been working extra-long hours, which he had, but not in the way she'd presumed. Becca was desolate. She had been used, humiliated. Her dreams had crashed. He was a swine. She was a fool. He'd been so beautiful.

'And Mme has been so kind again,' she wrote. 'I must have been a right pain for her this year what with the other and now this. The family has taken a villa outside Saint-Tropez for August. The final thing before I go back to England. They say I can ask a friend from home to join us. Will you come, Lucy? It sounds a lovely place and I would so like to have you there. I wish you were here already. We'll have to mind the children some of the time, but M and Mme will be on their holiday too and would like to be with the children on their own sometimes, and we'll be able to go out by ourselves.

'Let me know, Lucy, but say yes, won't you. Please come. I feel so alone. And stupid.'

'Oh no,' groaned Lucy.

'What's up?'

'Becca's been ditched by her French boyfriend. She really liked him. I'd better write to her.'

Lucy went off to her bedroom. Daniel drew on.

He felt calm, he felt safe. It was good to be doing this, the first time for ages that he'd drawn for himself, because he wanted to. He hadn't wanted to after Grandpa went. Drawing was part of being with Grandpa. Grandpa helped him and talked to him about art. Grandpa took him seriously. They drew together and Grandpa taught him how to do tricky things, like hands.

They're at Grandma's kitchen table, him and Grandpa, side by side with their paper pads and soft pencils. They've coloured in their drawings of Bucky O'Hare and his crew. Daniel has been concentrating on Willy DuWitt's peculiar feet, and Grandpa says that he's done a good job on them.

'You can tell how skilled a figure artist is by whether they can do hands and feet,' Grandpa was saying.

'What's a figure artist?'

'Someone who draws or paints people. Figure is a word for people-shape.'

'Hands are hard to draw.'

'Yes, they are. If they go wrong, the fingers are like a bunch of sausages.'

Grandpa stuck his hand out downwards, fingers straight and unnaturally splayed to resemble a bunch of sausages a bit, not a lot.

'It would be wacky to have sausages hanging off your arm,' said Daniel, drawing sausage-handed figures on his pad.

Grandpa chuckled. 'You could cook those for your dinner.'

Daniel drew a frying pan.

'How do you draw hands that aren't sausages?'

'You look hard at them and use your pencil to measure the different parts.'

He positioned his hand on the table in front of them and showed Daniel how. Together they drew their own hands and each other's, Grandpa's knobblier but strangely riveting, Daniel's appearing unused in comparison. Daniel had kept those drawings. He took them out sometimes.

Grandpa said that if you were doing a picture of a specific person your aim was to reveal what they were like, their nature. Daniel was aiming to do that with Ade. Ade was a wicked skater, but drawing the skating was the doddle part. He wanted to show the Ade he knew. It would be a completely different picture if I was doing Neal, he thought.

When Grandpa died, it was as if drawing died too. Without Grandpa, it became pointless. Now there was a point again, and it felt good.

He stood up to get the full effect of what he had drawn, gave a satisfied sigh and carried the picture off to lie flat on the sitting room floor until he could roll it up in a protective cardboard tube for Ade.

Beth came home with news too, which she held off announcing till the no-fuss quick risotto was on the table and being eaten.

'The big bulletin of the day,' she said cheerily, 'is that the agents emailed me this afternoon and we've got tenants.'

'We have?' said Lucy, her forkful of rice midway. 'Who are they?'

'They're an American couple. Two art historians from Boston. They're on a sabbatical.'

'What's a sabbatical?' asked Daniel.

'It means they've got time off work to do something else they'd like to do and they can pick up their old jobs again afterwards.'

'Lucky them.'

'Lucky all of us,' said Beth. 'They were already fixed up with renting elsewhere, but those arrangements fell through and they were apparently beginning to panic until the agents stepped in with our vacant house, and everybody's happy.'

'It still feels odd to imagine other people there,' said Lucy.

'In a way it's appropriate though. With them being art historians.'

'Grandpa's pictures are hanging up there,' said Daniel.

'Yes. I wonder what they'll make of them.'

'Maybe they'll want to buy them and you'll retire a wealthy woman,' said Lucy.

'He did sell some, you know.'

'There you are. Wealth for you, recognition for Grandpa.'

'If only.'

'They won't take Grandpa's pictures away, will they?' Daniel was perturbed.

'They're unlikely to want to,' said Beth. 'And they couldn't if we didn't want them to. They're only renting the house, Danny. Everything in it belongs to us.'

After dinner, as Beth was putting the packaging debris in the bin, Lucy whispered, 'Are you going to show Mum your portrait of Ade?'

Daniel was reluctant.

'She's got a lot of other things on her mind.'

'Go on. She'd like to see it.'

'I don't know.'

'What would I like to see?' asked Beth, overhearing.

Lucy tipped her head towards Daniel.

'It's just a picture,' he said.

'It's a terrific picture,' said Lucy.

'A picture, Dan? What of?'

'Ade.'

'Can I see?'

Daniel fetched the picture and held it up in front of his head.

'Oh Dan – it's so like him!' said Beth. 'It's marvellous. You've captured the essence of Ade. He's a good-hearted boy, and you can tell that from your picture. It's his portrait and it's fantastic.'

Daniel and his grandpa glowed, together.

CHAPTER XXIX
Beth

Beth sat at the end of the row, Desree at one side, the bar at the other. The function room above the pub was packed with clusters of college staff, shouting to each other over the music. Outside, the evening was warm: inside, the evening was sweltering. Beth tried to keep immobile, aware of the hair dampening around her forehead. She listened to Keisha, sitting opposite, excitedly describing the job she was going to, selling advertising space on one of the Sundays. A young team, dynamic. Expected to work like the clappers but great socially. Lunchtime out drinking, clubbing together, a lot of bants.

Beth congratulated her and felt old. Desree told Keisha that she had better hold off the lunchtime drinking. There were a lot of calories in alcohol and they were what had done for Desree's own weight control. That and too many patties. Keisha wiggled her boob tube and giggled.

The music faded and Colm climbed onto a table.

'Keisha!' he called. 'Where are you Keisha? Come up here. It's time to extol you.'

'The majority of those boys wouldn't say no to a bit of

extolling Keisha,' said Desree as Keisha slithered lithely through the crush and mounted the table to stand at Colm's side.

Colm praised Keisha adeptly, bringing in the customary references to amusing office incidents and good luck for the new job. He handed over the acre of card signed by everybody, and a gold gift bag containing the presents paid for by everybody, chosen by the young office friends who knew her best.

'Speech!' yelled someone.

'No. I can't talk,' said Keisha.

'Don't try that one on us. We know you. Come on. Speech!'

'I'd like to say thanks to everybody. I've enjoyed working with you and I'm going to miss you. Thank you. That's it.'

She got down. Colm clapped and everyone followed suit. The music started again. Beth sipped her lukewarm Chardonnay.

'Good speech,' said Desree, as Colm collected his glass from the bar.

'Thank you, ma'am.'

'Sit here and talk to your hard-pressed examination staff.'

'With great pleasure.' Colm sat on the chair vacated by Keisha.

'But don't talk about work. We've had it up to here with initiatives and appraisals and feedback systems and steering committees and whatnot. They are,' Desree took a delicate beakful of wine, 'downright boring.' She drank deeper.

'They certainly are.'

'So that's settled.'

Vincent, on the other side of Desree, detached himself from his football conversation.

'In a party mood, Desree?'

'You bet I am. It is a party, isn't it?'

'Come on. Let's strut your stuff.'

'Where?'

'Here. Let's get them dancing.'

'I'm trapped in. I can't get out.'

'Yes, you can.' Vincent swung the tables apart and clambered out. 'Come on. Show 'em girl.'

'I might just do that.' Desree rose with aplomb and held herself in to squeeze through the gap between the tables. She gave Beth a louche pout as Vincent guided her to a less crowded patch of floor, where they began to jig around.

'Desree's well away,' said Colm.

'That's because of Martin. He bought her a drink earlier. She asked for plain orange juice because she was thirsty, only he put a double vodka in without telling her and she'd downed it before she realised.'

'Sounds like Martin.'

They watched Desree's arms swaying in the air. Colm said, 'How are things with you, Beth? How's your mother doing?'

'So-so. They're caring at the Home, which is what matters. Most of the time she thinks she's somewhere else. Which is probably just as well.'

'Does she know who you are?'

'Occasionally, but no, she doesn't usually. She often behaves as if we're other people she's known. She thought Adam was her father once, and she sometimes calls Daniel Tom. That was my father's name.'

'She's time-travelling.'

'Yes. It's disconcerting. Especially with the Daniel–Tom thing, because Daniel and my father were very close. My dad was the nearest Daniel had to a dad of his own.'

'Is your father still alive?'

'He died four years ago.'

'Daniel must have been distraught.'

'He was.'

He was. He was.

'Let me get you another,' said Colm, as Beth fiddled with her glass. 'What were you drinking?'

'Chardonnay,' said Beth. 'I won't have more of that, thanks.'

'Too rich for this heat?'

'That must be it.'

'I'll get you something else.'

'Thanks.'

Colm stood behind Martin in the queue at the bar. An understanding man, Colm. Quick to cotton on to people's reactions. Like Daniel's, although Colm had never met him. But if office hearsay were accurate, Colm would be well acquainted with grief himself, his wife having died when the couple were quite young, repeated treatments being unable to prevent the tumours spreading. And oh yes, how the ten-year-old Daniel had been distraught. At first, he made no response when told of his grandfather's death. Tom had had a heart attack while sitting in the garden on a cold November morning, painting the fog in the trees. Daniel listened to how Grandma had called an ambulance and had rung Beth at work. How Grandpa had died doing what he loved. Daniel listened without comment and returned to his comic. Later, Beth found him under the bed in the room he shared with Adam. He was lying curled up round the blanket that Mary had crocheted for him when he was a baby. Beth, fragile herself and needing to get to her mother's, tried to winkle him out. He refused. Adam put in an arm, which was bitten. They lifted the bed. Daniel fought them off, kicking and thrashing around until he collapsed in Beth's arms, sobbing, 'Where is he? He's gone. He never told me he was going.' At her mother's house, Daniel and Mary sat with their arms round each other, rocking.

Although Beth thought that Daniel would be too young to go to the funeral, he was resolute. Mary had insisted on cremation, in a strange speech in which she talked of safety and protection as if she saw the fire as a preserving agent, keeping her beloved Tom in a safe existence away from the dangers of this world. She also wanted his ashes to be scattered over the river in Putney where Stefan's had been placed and where in due time, she said, she wanted her own to be.

On another grey, foggy day the family assembled by the edge of the river at low tide while Mary performed the ceremony. Beth was relieved there was no wind. Adam and Lucy stood by, but Daniel held out his hand to take part in the scattering. He picked a grey fleck from under his nail. 'Is this Grandpa?' he asked Beth, and solemnly ate it. Thankfully, thought Beth, her mother had not witnessed that. She shuddered and sipped the tepid Chardonnay.

'Was it as bad as that?' said Colm, returning. 'Perhaps you'll like this better.'

He handed her a new glass of wine and sat down again.

Keisha and the new man from Finance had joined Desree and Vincent in dancing.

'I'll be here in perpetuity,' said Beth, watching them. 'When it's my leaving do, I'll be dancing with a Zimmer frame.'

'You never know,' said Colm. 'You might be, there again you might not. I might be, but possibly not.'

'I can't argue with that,' said Beth.

'No, really. I might be the next to go. Don't say anything, it's not general knowledge. I've been shortlisted for another job.'

'Another job? Where?'

'Ssh. I'd rather it wasn't common knowledge for the moment. I might not get it.'

'What's the job?'

'It's at Westminster. University of, not Palace of.'

'Goodness! Congratulations.'

'Thank you. It is merely the shortlist.'

'It's an achievement to get onto a shortlist. When's the interview?'

'Monday. When I'm not in the office, that's where I'll be.'

'I'll have my fingers crossed for you. I'll transmit some good-luck vibes over there.'

'Good, good, good, good vibrations.'

'Those ones.'

'Too hot,' said Desree, tottering over. 'I'm getting past it.'

'Never,' said Colm. 'Can I get you a drink, Desree?'

'Vincent's getting them, thanks, Colm. Fit Vincent. Very, very, fanciable Vincent. What a loss for the world of women, baby-snatching me in particular.'

'Still sitting here?' Vincent put down the drinks. 'Look, Desree, do we or do we not set a trend?'

Many people had begun to dance.

'Cutting edge, boy.'

'Go on, Colm,' said Vincent. 'In the middle. Show them who's boss. Boss of the office, boss of the dance.'

'King,' said Desree.

'Eh?'

'King. It's King of the Dance.'

'Lord, isn't it?' said Beth.

'King. Lord. God. Whatever.'

'I lay no claim to deity,' said Colm. 'Would you like to dance, Beth?'

'You shouldn't sit in one posture without moving,' said Vincent. 'It gives you deep vein thrombosis.'

'He clinched the argument,' said Colm. 'Come on, Beth.'

He helped her out from behind the table and they made their way to the dancers.

'That's what I like,' said Vincent.

'What?'

'Ordering the boss around. Unless it's a party, you can't get away with it. You have to take advantage when you can, don't you?'

'If you say so, Vincent. If you say so.'

CHAPTER XXX
Lucy, Mary, Beth

Lucy laid the three birth certificates out on the floor of her bedroom. Three maternal grandparents; one mother: this was the family history. A history that was nowhere near as disturbing as had appeared when she'd first found the portraits but was nevertheless not the implicit version of family relationships she had grown up with, and it seemed that only Grandma Mary and Lucy now knew this. Grandpa Tom was not Grandma's husband, not Lucy's real grandfather, not her mother's father. And yet he was. He had been all those things. He had loved, supported, comforted and helped all the family. Grandpa wasn't devalued by not being their 'real' father and grandfather. Far from it. As Daniel had once said: being a real father is what you do afterwards. Daniel sometimes hit the nail on the head.

She took the green leather box from her chest of drawers and examined the locket with its photograph of her great-grandmother. Grandma hadn't inherited those features and neither had Lucy, with her pale lashes and beige hair. Nor Adam, come to that. But her mother had, and Daniel – lucky for them. And Grandpa Tom.

Who did Lucy look like? She got up and went to the cabinet in the sitting room, coming back with the photograph album brought from her grandparents' house. Taking the portraits of Tom and Mary out of the leather box, she compared them with the photos of her brothers and herself as children. Dan had always looked like Grandpa, that had long been a standard matter of comment, but the young Adam had something of the six-year-old Grandma about him. Adam had said that on his last visit to the Home Grandma had called him 'Father'. Were those features inherited from the strict Mr Pearson, owner of Midlands stores, as described by Mrs Smollett? As for the young Lucy, not much like either side.

These were important mementos but told her no more. She replaced the portraits, tissue and locket in the little leather box and put the packing back on top. The paper had become somewhat messily crumpled now, so she spread it out on her desk to smooth and refold: part of a retirement photo, lace-up shoes and wide trouser legs; part of an advertisement claiming that three minutes a day keeps busy hands lovely. The other side: Sydney Frank Lawton.

Lucy froze. Frank! So horrified by the contents of the box, so assuming that the newspaper was no more than convenient filler to keep those contents in place, she had never considered it as an item in itself. As a death announcement. Announcing the death of Sydney Frank Lawton, who had died 'tragically' in August 1951. Lucy did a quick calculation. Her mother was born in the following May. Frank must have died without even knowing he had fathered a child.

What was the tragedy? Who had placed the announcement? What would have happened if Frank had not died? Grandma must have cared about him or she wouldn't have kept the newspaper cutting in the box with other important keepsakes. Would it have been Grandpa Frank and Great-Uncle Tom for Lucy and her brothers as they grew up? The questions crowded in and there was no one to ask except Grandma, who must have been wrecked by this loss. Could Lucy risk asking her next time she visited?

Mary sat with her head on one side, a wistful expression on her face. Across the room, Hilda crumbled biscuits, rocking rhythmically in her chair. 'Oh dear. I *am* disappointed in you. Oh dear. I am disappointed in you. Oh dear oh dear. Oh dear oh dear.'

'Shut up!' shouted Sadie, toes flexed in her fluffy pink slippers. 'I said, shut up.'

'Ssh, ssh,' soothed the care assistant, going over from where she had been watering the plants.

'Don't you shush me. I speak my mind. Speak as I find.'

'That's poetry, Sadie. You're a poet and didn't know it.'

'Poetry! Huh!' snorted Sadie in disgust. She heaved herself by stages to her feet, stood for a minute, fingertips fanned out on the high arms of the chair to stabilise herself, and lumbered to the doorway as the carer hovered. There she came to a standstill, held on to the jamb with her left hand, and slowly rotated, transferring to a right handhold. Having untwined and repositioned her feet, she lumbered back to plonk heavily down again in her chair.

'Shut up!' she barked to the now quiescent room. She smacked her lips and subsided.

'Grandma,' said Lucy again, bending nearer to Mary. 'Grandma, who was Frank Lawton?'

Mary's expression didn't change and Lucy fluctuated between disappointment and release. Her only hope of learning more about Frank was if she could prompt her grandmother to utter a few snippets with which to construct some partial account. It wasn't just curiosity about her own descent. Not to know, to be indifferent to knowing, seemed a form of disregard, a further diminishment of the person who was, in any case, so diminished. To know was both a form of respect and a way of counteracting a total erosion of that previous life.

But if her grandparents' silent cover-up had been successful for all this time, both Grandma and Grandpa – Grandpa Tom – must have wanted the truth to remain concealed.

Lucy shouldn't be asking. She could have caused distress.

But if she, Lucy, couldn't find out the hidden story of Frank, it would soon be too late and nobody would ever know.

Which was presumably what Grandma wanted.

Who would benefit from knowing now who Frank was? Only Lucy with her project to find out. It was selfish to jeopardise Mary's peace for that.

Doors opening onto doors opening onto doors. Always something concealed, something yet to find out, always somewhere further. Unless you paused and let it go, stayed where you were, at least temporarily, and allowed the doors to stand shut.

At this stage in her life, Grandma was surely entitled to feel secure in her secret.

Enough. It was time to stop a search so fraught with the hazard of resurrecting bygone sorrow. Time to leave the past to its owners, to respect their reasons for concealment. Her mother, her brothers, herself – they had their own lives ahead and would probably find themselves making decisions they might not relish others probing in a further future. And Becca too. Enough. Stop now. Lucy could have caused distress.

She hadn't though. She hadn't noticeably caused anything much. Mary produced a social smile as Lucy told her about the email Beth had received from Adam. She told her what subjects Dan was choosing for his future exams. She told her about work, about the girl returning a jumper with what were obviously cigarette burns on it.

'Burning doesn't always damage,' said Mary. 'It can protect too. At the right time.'

'Can it?' said Lucy, caught on the hop as usual by a sudden pertinent contribution from Mary. 'When does it do that, Grandma?'

Mary looked enigmatic, and Lucy tried a joking continuation of the theme.

'It didn't protect the jumper, I'm afraid. Or her refund. She was quite annoyed that she didn't get one.'

Mary nodded and said nothing.

Lucy told her how she was going to the cinema with Maya that afternoon. She explained that Maya was her ex-colleague and was someone who would have had very firm things to say about the refund had she been working in the shop.

Mary smiled graciously.

Lucy talked about the weather, the sudden changes; how you never knew what to wear; how you wore what you should have been wearing the day before.

'Those eyes,' said Mary. 'I love those eyes.'

'Mine?' said Lucy, startled again.

Mary lifted her free hand and caressed Lucy's temple.

'I love those eyes,' she repeated, and let her hand fall again.

'That's nice of you, Grandma. I think they're too pale. You can hardly see my lashes naturally. Maya says I should dye them.'

'Kind eyes. Such kind eyes.'

Beth arrived. She bent down to Mary's level, being cheerful.

'Hello, Mum. How are you today?'

'Very well, thank you.'

'How is she?' said Beth to Lucy.

'I'm very well, thank you,' said Mary. 'I thought I said so. Didn't I say so?'

'You did. Yes, you did,' said Lucy and Beth together hastily.

'Kind eyes. Such kind eyes,' said Mary. Her gaze wandered to an indefinite spot near the end of the room where Hilda, having brushed away the biscuit crumbs, was pushing down and pulling up her knee-high stocking.

'It's about time you pulled your socks up, my girl,' she was saying sternly. 'You won't fulfil your potential unless you put in more effort.'

'You go now,' said Beth to Lucy. 'Enjoy the film.'

'Thanks,' said Lucy, getting up. 'Bye, Grandma. I'll see you soon.'

Hilda pushed down her stocking.

'I want to see better reports of you in future. Do I make myself clear?'

Lucy went to find a care assistant to lock the front door after her. Beth took over the chair and took up the hand. She told Mary that Lucy was going to the cinema with Maya. She explained that Maya used to work with Lucy until recently. She commented that Lucy wouldn't be doing that job much longer either and would be off to university, and how Beth would miss her.

The stocking was pulled up, up.

Beth told Mary how Adam had emailed her; that he was making new friends and enjoying his job. She described going to the parents' meeting at Daniel's school, and his choice of examination subjects. She produced a sanitised report of the office leaving party.

'Tom knew him through the business,' said Mary.

'Knew who, Mum?'

'Through the shop.'

'Is this Uncle Stefan, Mum? Are you referring to Uncle Stefan?'

'He liked him. He said he was a manifestly decent chap. Everyone liked him.'

'I liked him too, Mum. He was a lovely man. He was patient with me if I went to the shop or when he came to our house. He used to draw things with me. Of course, Dad did too.'

'He was a kind person.'

'They both were. It's strange that I've never been any good at art, considering my background. Daniel is though. He's inherited it.'

'Tom said he could go further.'

'Who, Mum? Dan? He was too young to tell, wasn't he? Or do you mean Stefan?'

'It was his situation. The way things were in those days. His people.'

'Oh, Uncle Stefan. Yes. He'd lost everybody, hadn't he. All his family. In the war. Terrible.'

'The war. Wars separate people.'

'And he never had children himself either.'

There was a series of annoyed yelps from the end of the room. Hilda had twined her fingers in the stocking top and was pulling in frustration, struggling to extricate herself. Beth went over to sort her out.

'Hello,' said Emma, from a nearby chair. 'Is it you? I asked him to see to it but I'm not persuaded that he has.'

'I'll investigate for you,' said Beth.

'That would be greatly appreciated.'

Hilda stopped tugging her entangled fingers.

'Oh dear,' she said reprovingly.

'Oh dear,' sympathised Beth.

'Now,' said Hilda. 'This instant.'

Beth unwound the stocking from the fingers. Hilda watched keenly.

'That was a competent performance,' she said as Beth smoothed her clothes back into place. 'You're a credit to the school. Well done.'

By the time Beth had crossed the room again, Mary's eyes were shut. Beth sat down and waited to see if she would re-arouse. Mary's eyes darted behind her lids.

Tom was speaking quietly, without moving his mouth. It was a technique they had used since childhood to talk to each other without being noticed. Tom had come home from work strained and preoccupied.

'I've got something to tell you.'

Mary bent her head fractionally and set the food on the dining room table. Their father ate in his deliberate manner, evaluating the day's trade and requiring analysis from Tom. Tom shifted his mouthfuls rapidly between unusually prolonged paragraphs, directing their father's attention to further commercial specifics with atypical finickiness.

After eating, he accompanied Mary to the kitchen with the dishes and, picking up a tea towel, stood by her as she ran the hot water into the sink.

'Mary, I heard—' he began.

Their father's footsteps.

'What's this, Tom?' he roared. 'Namby-pamby eh? Women's work, Tom. That's women's work. Mary is responsible for housekeeping. Our responsibilities have greater consequence. Come.' He held open the kitchen door, his other arm waving around to channel Tom from demeaning female tasks.

It will be Holly Hideout, thought Mary, as she washed the dishes. Holly Hideout – at our age!

She made her way there after she had tidied the kitchen. A summer sky spread high above the mass of spiked leaves, and a wood pigeon cooed from a tree. Shortly, as she had predicted, Tom arrived, pushing aside the boughs and crouching low.

'It's faintly ridiculous continuing to crawl in here for all these years.'

'I was thinking that.'

'In another way, it's comforting.'

'I was thinking that too.'

The hollow at the centre had enlarged along with the bush. Once inside, both Tom and Mary could stand up fully, but Tom's body edged and shifted as if to adjust to a painful position.

'What is it?' said Mary.

Tom hesitated. 'I wanted to tell you as soon as possible,

rather than try at bedtime. In case you heard by other means. I thought it better if I told you, on your own. Now I'm not sure that I should. It's something I heard in the office today.'

'What shouldn't I know? Why?'

'It's not that you shouldn't know. It's that…' He trailed off, uncertain.

'Whatever can it be? Go on, Tom. Tell me.'

Tom took a deep breath. 'You remember Frank? Frank Lawton?'

'Yes, I remember Frank.'

'After that awful ballyhoo, you know, years ago before the war, and he had to leave the warehouse and he went away… he was here in Fordham recently, visiting his aunt.'

'I know,' said Mary. 'I've seen him.'

'You've seen him! To speak to?' Tom stared at her.

'Yes, several times. I was going to tell you when I had the chance. We still like each other. It's the same, Tom.'

'My godfathers, Mary. That makes worse what I was going to tell you.'

'What? That he's married? I know that already.'

'No, not that. I didn't know he was.'

'What then?'

'He's dead, Mary. He was killed. Yesterday.'

Yesterday. Mary knew yesterday. Yesterday he had been going back to Bowerby. Living. Loving her.

'He was on the New Road, driving I mean – he's a mechanic apparently.'

'I know. I know.'

'Yes, of course. A car came out of the Creston junction straight into him. That was bad enough, but it also shunted him into an oncoming lorry. One of our delivery vans was on the road at the time and pulled over. Our driver recognised Frank from when he was in the warehouse. That's how I heard about it.'

Mary, too, knew Frank from when he was in the warehouse. From the midday walks in the park pre-war, and again in the past few days.

'He wasn't conscious, Mary. He wouldn't have known what had happened.'

Happened? What had happened?

'They took him to hospital. It was no good. He died in hospital.'

'He died.' The words at first held no meaning for Mary. He died. A sound of pain broke from her.

'He died,' she moaned.

'I know, Mum. I know.' Beth leaned forwards and put an arm round her mother's shaking shoulders. A tear ran down Mary's cheek.

'He died.'

Beth felt in her pocket for a tissue and wiped the tear away, and the others that followed. She ran a finger across her own nose.

'Tom brought me the paper. Tom showed me. I loved him.'

'I know you did, Mum. I know.'

A notice of Frank's death was posted in the family announcements section of the local newspaper. Tom brought the paper home for Mary and stayed with her in Holly Hideout while she gazed blankly at the words. That night, sitting up in bed, she read them over and over again:

SYDNEY FRANK LAWTON
Tragically taken from us
9 August 1951
Funeral to be held
Tuesday 28 August at 10.30
Bowerby Crematorium
No flowers please

Why no flowers? Why were they prohibiting flowers for Frank?

She couldn't have sent flowers. The funeral was being held in his wife's town, his town, attended by friends and family. She had no place there. She did not exist. Her love for the living, married Frank had been hopeless. Her love for the dead Frank left her excluded, with nothing of him except memories and his name in the newspaper.

Sydney Frank. She hadn't known about Sydney.

The people at Bowerby knew. They knew he was called by his middle name. They knew things about him that she didn't know. She was outside.

But she knew that it was Frank who loved her. Sydney felt like a different person, owned by Bowerby. Her Frank was Frank. Just Frank.

Who had died, though, all the same.

She sobbed at night. Her grey days of respectable, domestic routine grew greyer and heavier. As she lamented, she ridiculed herself too. She'd never had a future with Frank. Any thought that she might was an unrealistic fantasy. The reality was a mess with nothing for her. She ought to feel some brutal relief that the appalling accident had made impossible a future that was already improbable. It had let her out of the mess, and she should be paradoxically thankful and feel sorry for Frank's wife, whose prerogative it was to mourn.

She was crushed between what she ought to think and what she did feel. Both waking and sleeping were permeated by images of Frank – the pre-war Frank, gazing at her with his kind pale eyes as he helped her to wash the gravel from her hand in the fountain, the heavenly meetings in the park. The jolt of his sudden post-war reappearance in the television shop crowd. The hesitant, then loving trysts again. The pagoda. The crash.

She suppressed her sobs and felt exhausted by the effort and lack of sleep. She woke in the mornings with a dirty metallic taste in her mouth. A musty veil hung in front of her and she could scarcely bring herself to prepare food for Tom and her father, still less eat it herself.

The intense, complex anguish abated. The sick, debilitating exhaustion continued. After some weeks, a fear edged with ignorance began to nibble at her. She didn't know and at first she tried hard to resist knowing, as if knowledge would make it actual and ignorance could save her from what she feared.

Then one afternoon, changing her books in the public library, she left the loans section and climbed the staircase to the reference room. It was empty except for a scattering of old men reading newspapers by the windows. There a disinterested medical manual confirmed her fears. She, Mary Pearson, spinster daughter of a prominent authoritarian local businessman, was pregnant, pregnant with the child of a disgraced former employee who after the war became a garage mechanic, married someone else, and was killed in a road accident shortly after loving her once in the park pagoda.

She replaced the book and fainted. One of the old men and a librarian got her into a chair and called a female clerk, who put Mary's head between her knees and fetched a cup of tea. The librarian took her home. She went on feeling weak and dazed until that night, alone in her bedroom, the full import blasted through her.

How could anyone or anything redeem her? She opened her door soundlessly and, hearing her father safely snoring, crept down the corridor.

Tom was in bed reading and as usual turned back the bedding for her. She felt it would be easier to get the words out if she kept standing, braced and just said them. They were mere words, after all. At first, she couldn't. Tom thought her visit was because of Frank's death, that she had come into his room because she couldn't get to sleep, as had happened several times before. He got out of bed and put his arms round her and eventually she told him.

'I'm pregnant, Tom. I'm going to have a baby.'

She'd worried that Tom might reject her. It was scarcely imaginable, but what if he found her immoral, distasteful, or at best an embarrassment with which he did not want to be connected.

No. He was astounded, but as in great surprise, not as in judgemental revulsion. And although he was clearly aware of the enormity of the problem, there was also more than acceptance and compassion about him. There was a hint of excitement, as if his thoughts had moved on from the prevailing predicament. His eyes gleamed. He had already begun to devise their escape.

He told her next day, having planned with heightening enthusiasm throughout the night. An escape for both of them.

Mary's pregnancy could force them into doing something about the tedium and suffocation of their lives. They could go where no one knew them and where you could be what you were, live the life that suited you. It was an enormous leap into the unknown, but what was the alternative if they didn't? Especially for Mary – she must see that.

'I think we've got to go to London.'

Tom organised the day, the time, and primed Mary on what she should do. She packed a few clothes and the locket with their mother's picture. She packed the portraits of herself and Tom, the sole paintings to be saved from burning, laid between layers of tissue in her mother's old trinket box. She folded the page of newspaper announcing Frank's death and gently tucked that into the box too.

They went.

They managed it.

'We managed it.'

'What did you manage, Mum?' Beth had been about to leave, her mother having disappeared into that mysterious region inside her head where many of the other residents of the Home mainly existed. Was this what the future held for Beth too? An unpredictable swing in and out of reality, a vacancy, a reliance on others to care for you and to humour your disjointed mumblings? Was this what would be left?

'It worked out. In its own way.'

'That's good.'

Mary's head drooped and she disappeared into herself again. Beth decided that she would steal away home. As she rose to leave, Mary opened her eyes and joy flooded over her.

'Hello, Tom,' she said. 'Are you here already?'

CHAPTER XXXI
Beth

An expression of such delight, thought Beth as she got into her car and drove away. Such delight at seeing Tom. On this occasion it was herself who had given rise to the response, on others it was Daniel, both of them carrying Tom's features and easily generating Mary's confusion, when for her past and present were marbled together in coexistence.

Whoever was being Tom at that moment, there was no mistaking Mary's pleasure at his presence. That implicit quality of fulfilment had imbued Beth's childhood. Her father Tom going out to work each day at Uncle Stefan's art shop. Her mother Mary in the meticulously clean and tidy house, at home when Beth returned from school, cake from one of the tins on top of the kitchen cupboard, high tea when Tom came in. How tranquil, how uneventful. Enough for them. Her father went out sometimes, usually with Uncle Stefan. Her mother had hardly any social life outside the home. She would read, listen to the radio, later on watch television, and knit, sew or mend. Life progressed temperately, made up of insignificant everyday events. There was never any crisis, never any argument between her parents that Beth could recall. Nothing of moment happened to either of them but there was enough to be happy with then and to last into Mary's old age, a shining core through her life, there even now when everything else was falling away.

Not like Beth's own marriage. A spiked rod of irritation running through her life. Her heart sank when Tony breezed in, and her teeth clenched to hold in the forceful words that would hurtle out if given an opening. Her own children wouldn't recollect a stable, untroubled childhood. Grief, acrimony, shouting, withdrawal – that's what they'd been surrounded by in their early years, with intervals of peace at their grandparents'. That was over, but Daniel and Lucy came home to an empty flat, made their own snack, and in the week lived off fast food and the chill counter. Beth and Tom had always been given a cooked breakfast, whereas she had long taken for granted that everyone could pour from a cereal packet and add the milk themselves. All Beth's clothes had been ironed; even sheets and tea towels were too. Tom's collars and cuffs had been starched. Beth ironed the minimum and found that excessive. No sewing, no mending beyond the occasional button. Life as a continual rush, a perpetual sense that it was barely being held together. What an irony that having put in the effort to become autonomous and employable, she was now envying her parents' unflurried life. Yet within the envy and admiration, she found too a nugget of blame. Because there had been a precept in that self-effacement: don't dominate; keep out of the limelight; be unnoticed.

At which she had been remarkably successful. Throughout school she had been modest and unassertive. She went to a girls' school, where her friends were of the amenable stamp. There were no rows at home over late nights, clothes and make-up, as occurred regularly for the more spirited girls. She could wear what was fashionable, do what was done, but nobody in her group of friends went to extremes. Her parents didn't make issues of things; neither was there much to make any issue about. It was stress-free, lenient and loving and didn't spur her on to do anything of note. Many of the extreme girls went to university. None of Beth's friends did. They performed adequately, leaving school to work with children or in hospitals or offices. Before long, they got married.

Marrying Tony was the most daring thing Beth had done. She should have done it the other way round – been daring and challenging with her brain in school and sensible about her marriage partner. Why hadn't her parents intervened? It must have been obvious it was going to be a mistake. They couldn't have liked him, his brash confidence contrasting with their moderate tones. It had called for more control, more moulding, as opposed to dribbling along to nowhere other than disaster.

And here she was, a middle-aged woman trying to push responsibility for her own ill-judged decisions onto two gentle, tolerant parents, one of whom was dead, the other of whom was frail with only an intermittent grip on reality. Even if they hadn't channelled her, they had never deliberately tried to stymie her either. They had been a steadfast support throughout the traumas of Tony. Even him, even Tony, meant that she had the children, Adam, Lucy, Daniel. Even in the worst of times she had unfailingly had someone to love and be loved by. When she was about eight or nine years old, Uncle Stefan had come for a meal as he regularly did. Beth was wearing her red stretchy belt with interlocking buckle, highly desirable at the time. Stefan having gallantly admired this new acquisition, Beth told him the sad tale of her school friend whose older brother had taken his sister's similar belt without asking and adapted it for an Apache headdress by piercing a double row of holes for the feathers, and thus ruining it. Beth was glad that she hadn't anyone to spoil her things.

'When you were growing up,' she asked Stefan, 'did you have any brothers or sisters?'

'Two brothers,' said Stefan.

'Did you like them?'

'Oh yes.'

'Where are they?'

Stefan hesitated.

Mary intervened. 'Uncle Stefan lost his family during the war, Beth,' she said softly.

Beth was intrigued. How could Stefan have lost his family? The family might have lost him momentarily, she could understand that. Once, out with her mother, she had been lost in a large shop. She was in the process of asking an assistant, 'Have you seen a lady in a blue coat and hat?' when Mary came and took her hand. The loss had been temporary, not long enough to trigger scare on either side because her mother noticed at once and came for her. How could Stefan not notice that a whole family had gone? Why didn't they take better care of each other? As she opened her mouth to question, Mary raised her palm almost imperceptibly, a refraining gesture, which left Beth with an impression of negligence on the part of Stefan's family and an image of his brothers banded together in Never-Never Land with Peter Pan. It wasn't until adulthood that she realised what the implications of 'lost' were for a man of his age with an East European accent. There was no one left. Tom, Mary and Beth were the nearest he had to family, and when he died he left the business to Tom, who kept the name Stefan Szczepanski on the shopfront until he himself retired and the business was sold and the shopfront repainted.

With hindsight, thought Beth, what a pity that it was sold. It must have been pleasant to run that shop. It couldn't have made a lot, but it kept the family adequately and her father was always happy to be there. She should have taken it over. Although she wasn't artistic, she knew the shop and could have learnt the routines of stock and ordering. An opportunity lost because of her life being different in those days. So rather than fiddling around with tubes of paint and sketch pads, she fiddled around with exam entries and other people's coursework. Aye me.

Stopping at red lights, she found herself in front of the college building. It was Sunday. Instead of driving to her flat from the care home, she had taken the route to work and not noticed what she was doing. How many traffic lights had she stopped at on that journey? How many times changed gear? Waited for pedestrians? Signalled left or right? She had done it, presumably adequately, with no conscious awareness. Just as when driving back from the airport, she had been there and not there. This time she had been having her mother's cake in her childhood kitchen. She had been arguing with Tony, talking to Uncle Stefan. She had been envious, resentful, guilty. Loving, regretful, philosophical. And now she was – the lights changed – at college. Where she had unknowingly driven because she had not been where she was.

She drove past the college. The large building stood empty and purposeless, as if it didn't exist at this moment when it was not carrying out its function. She glanced up at the windows of the registry, at her window, the one by her desk. Shadow and light flitted across the glass, as if the movement came from within. Beth thought, What if I am in there? What if the college is full of students and staff? There's Desree parcelling up exam scripts. There's Colm's tall figure leaving his section to discuss something with her. There I am, my concentration sliding from the lines of abbreviations on the screen to imagine myself in this car, driving past on a misroute after visiting my mother. How do we know where we are or who we are?

What if, she thought, when her mother called her Tom and she was Tom for her mother, she did become Tom? What if you are wherever you think you are, and you are the person that other people think you to be?

What was she off about! Beth swung forcefully round the corner and began the route homewards. If she carried on like this, she'd get indistinguishable from her mother's state, and Lucy would be lumbered with both of them.

When Mary was Beth's current age, she had many future years left of living with Tom. Then, Beth was working in an office, doing the sorts of clerical jobs that no longer exist, and Uncle Stefan was alive. Tom and Mary looked after Uncle Stefan through his illness; they looked after Beth and the children in her Tony-created misery. There were always the two of them, looking after each other.

And how, thought, Beth, how shall I spend my future years? The children will be interesting and they'll come to see me but, as Tony considerately pointed out, they'll be living their own lives. It's supposed to be fashionable to live on your own, to be a singleton. That's not what I want though, thought Beth. I want a Tom to be with me. I don't want to be alone. I don't want to be alone.

CHAPTER XXXII
Mary

After Tom died, I burned his birth certificate. I burned mine too while I was at it. That was something that would stay a secret. I felt disoriented doing it, because I was reminded of years ago, when I burned Beth's birth certificate, the one with Frank as her father. I stood at the sink in our kitchen, watching as Tom's and my certificates caught fire, and one moment I was in our house and the next I was upstairs at Mrs Jessop's, flickering from one to the other as the flames flickered up the paper. Last time there was no more Frank. This time there was no more Tom and I didn't swill the residue away as before. I put it in with Tom's ashes, the charred remnants from both his certificate and mine. If I'd still had Beth's with Frank on it, I'd have put the burnt-up remains of that in too.

I put Tom's ashes in the river, where Stefan's had gone. I doubt it was the exact spot: Tom had wanted to be alone with Stefan's, and I didn't intrude. They had been friends for so long. It was Tom who decided on the river, but Stefan had told us, when he was ill, that he wanted to be cremated.

'That's what happens to my family,' he said.

Oh, that was a harrowing time. Stefan was in and out of

hospital, fading before our eyes, more grey and haggard by the day. And at the same time, Beth was desperate because of Tony's behaviour. We had the children to look after, and we had Stefan to look after, and we couldn't let Beth and the children know how worried we were about Stefan, nor Stefan know what was happening with Beth. Stefan died. Beth divorced. The children grew. And we went on.

I never heard a full account of Stefan's ordeals. He came from Poland after the war, his family gone. I knew the terrible general history, but I didn't know the specific details, not for Stefan and his family.

I said to Tom once, 'Does Stefan ever talk about it? About what happened to his people?'

Tom said, 'No. Never.'

And I asked myself whether I would want to, if I were in Stefan's place. Would I want to talk about it? I don't know.

I don't know.

Sometimes it's better not to ask. To let things be.

It made me feel chastened about my wartime experiences, which were at worst lonely and drab, especially with Tom not at home. He wasn't called up, because of his lungs, and I was grateful to the pleurisy that had almost carried him off as an infant but which made him exempt from active service. Tom reproached himself, though. The men of fighting age were disappearing from daily life. There were none left in the business, and Father made disparaging remarks about weaklings and milksops, and smug remarks about how he didn't shirk from doing his bit in the Great War. It wasn't Father's jibes that smarted – we were accustomed to those. It was Tom's conviction that he wasn't pulling his weight when others were risking their lives. We weren't at much risk. We had been issued with gas masks before war was declared, when Mother was alive. We never used them. The cellar was strengthened to use as a shelter in case of air raids. There were none. We weren't of strategic or industrial importance. We weren't historic or beautiful enough to get the Baedeker bombing. Planes flew over sometimes and people said they could tell from the sound of the engines whether they were ours or theirs. I couldn't. One or two bombs did fall, one relatively near, on a house a few roads away. That was unnerving, but it wasn't as bad as it could have been, because no one was in the house at the time. It would be dreadful to lose your home, but nothing in comparison to what was happening in the cities. That bomb was dropped, people said, because it was a left-over. If the Luftwaffe had been on a bombing raid and found they had a bomb or two left afterwards, they would tip it out randomly wherever they happened to be. The Luftwaffe obviously didn't have a Father in command. He'd have made them fly it back to base for future use. No wastage tolerated by Father.

In our household, we had spent our lives training for wartime restrictions. Five inches of water in the bath? Yes, it was less than we had been allowed before, but not a lot less. He would listen to the taps running to calculate the amount we were using. Fuel targets? Hadn't we always? Make Do and Mend? When not?

Food was the real problem. Although Father was economical, he did like his meals and he liked them to be proper food. That was the snag. There was scant proper food available, and it was my job to produce it. Before the war, we usually had the order sent up to the house: during the war, fuel restrictions and not knowing what might be available meant it was better for me to go and find out. Queues and queues. Father told his employees that we were to be treated like everyone else. It took a long time to do the shopping, and after that you had to fathom what to do with what you found.

It made you ingenious. I saved up to make a cake whenever Tom came home – chopped prunes and grated carrot and dried egg. As time went on, I became more adventurous and got the urge to ice it. Not with real icing – that was out of the question. I boiled up some butter beans until they were soft, mashed them thoroughly and added a few drops of almond essence. Marzipan! You felt triumphant if you managed to produce a concoction like that.

There was grated carrot in everything. They were never rationed, and apart from that we had Trimble digging up the garden, the top garden furthest from the house, where Mother used to paint. We had onions long after they had gone from the shops. Later, you couldn't get the sets either, and from then on we too didn't have onions. When we were running out, I would keep one over a glass of water until it sprouted, and cut snips off the shoot to use as flavouring.

The worst parts were that first winter of the war, without Mother, and with the furore over Frank not yet faded from Father's behaviour. At least the war deflected some of his outrage from that. It snowed for two months. The blackout was up, fuel was in short supply. I ached for Mother. I missed Frank. It was cold and it was dismal. And before long, Tom left too.

He was detailed to work in an aircraft factory outside Hull for the duration. It was wretched without Tom at home, worse than it was when he was a boy away at school during the week, because then I had Mother. I was worried about Tom too. If it was an aircraft factory, wasn't it a target for bombing? And Hull itself suffered terribly. Tom was sombre about the lost lives and destruction but gave no indication of being scared. Because he was living in digs and working long hours, he came home infrequently, and I must say that on his visits, he seemed to be thriving. He said that although he got dreadfully tired from the work and the air raids, he managed to find a few Jollies.

Jollies!

I felt quite jealous, partly because I scarcely knew what a jolly was, partly also because I did know that there were girls working in the factory, and I assumed they were part of the jolliness.

I said to Tom, 'Shall I be meeting your girlfriend one of these days?'

He said, 'No. No girlfriend.' He gave me a hug. 'No girl-friend, Mary. No girlfriend.'

Being away from Father would be jolly enough. When Tom went to the aviation factory, Father called me up to work in the office. I wasn't old enough for the women's forces, but Father said I could contribute to the war effort by releasing a man, i.e. Tom, to leave his peacetime occupation for war work. That way we felt better about not being in the forces. I went into the office, where both my father and Mr Hopkins were present. I filed and dealt with invoices and kept track of points and coupons. I taught myself to type from a library book. On Fridays, the employees would come to the office to receive their pay packets, lining up, shop by shop, in order of seniority or, in cases of equal seniority, alphabetically. Mr Hopkins gave out the wages through a hatch in the office wall, as Tom used to do.

I typed a little, and queued a lot, and grated carrots, and made corned beef into something else, and stuck up blackout, and patched sheets, and put out salvage, and gave in aluminium pans, and collected milk bottle tops, and squeezed slivers of soap together to make a new piece. Although that was something else Father had always made us do. And I worried about Tom, and I worried about Frank, missing them both so much.

In some ways life was worse, in some ways not overly different, and in some it was better than either before the war or afterwards. There was the wireless, for example. Father relinquished some of his control over it. That began because there was an early morning programme called *The Kitchen Front*. It came on at 8.15 to give recipes and domestic hints. Father instructed me to listen – part of my duty for the war effort – and it made me realise that I *could* use the radio, that it wasn't exclusively for him. He hadn't intended this, but that's what resulted. He listened to the nine o' clock news, and I listened with him because we were in the same room to save fuel. Usually it was precisely nine when he tuned in to the wireless, but on one occasion he was early and we heard the end of the previous programme. Oh, how I tried not to laugh over my darning! Father wasn't amused, being already annoyed because of getting the timing wrong. Tom told me the programme was called *It's That Man Again*, and when Father's Local Defence Volunteer service took him out on *ITMA* night, it was Tommy Handley and *ITMA* for me.

Later, I became a member of the Women's Voluntary Service. I liked that. We collected clothes to send to the bombed-out in the cities, and at Christmas we ran a toy exchange. Since there was a dearth of toys in the shops, we collected as many second-hand toys as we could and spruced them up. We allocated points to them, like the points on tinned food. Children could bring in an old toy to swap for points and we gave them a few extra points as an indulgence. They got a voucher for the points they'd earned, which they could then exchange for toys of the same value. It was a great success. The younger ones had never before in their lives seen as many toys together, and they were overwhelmed to begin with, becoming immensely excited as they realised how the system worked, finally absorbed and careful in making their choice.

Careful. Yes, you have to be careful.

At last the war was over and Tom came back. And Frank came back, although I didn't know it at first. My Frank. He was in the Royal Army Service Corps and he came through unharmed.

Frank.

Ah, Frank.

CHAPTER XXXIII
Beth, Daniel, Lucy

Beth logged on to her college computer and opened her emails. Examination boards, teaching staff, admin staff, and Colm. 'I got the job, Beth. I wanted you to know first, before it's officially announced. Now that I'm definitely going, will you let me take you out for dinner? You say when. If.'

Beth read Colm's email again, rubbing her chin with her finger. She sent her reply.

'Have you heard about Colm?' said Desree, putting down two plastic cups of coffee.

'Thanks,' said Beth, taking one. 'What about Colm?'

'He's leaving. Keith told me in the post room. I didn't know he was applying for jobs, did you?'

'He seemed happy enough here,' Beth sidestepped.

'Not happy enough. He's going.'

'Who's going?' asked Aysha, passing by.

'Colm. Keith told me. He's got a new job.'

'Has he? Where?'

'Westminster.'

'Oo-er. Is that better?'

'It's a bigger job. According to Keith.'

'What will we get in his place?'

'Good point,' said Desree. 'I hadn't got on to that thought. Colm's been universally all-round acceptable.'

'I know. We don't want some dictator. I had that in my previous job. It was why I left. We want another version of Colm.'

Aysha pulled a wry face and moved away.

Desree logged on.

'You know, you could do it, Beth.'

'What?'

'Colm's job.'

'Me?'

'Why not? Look how effectively you do this job. You know how the office as a whole functions. Everybody likes you. You'd be good at it.'

'It's too big a job.'

'Think about it. See how you feel when the specs are out. I reckon you'd be the People's Choice.'

'Probably not the interviewing panel's.'

'It's worth a go.'

'If I wanted it.'

'Don't you?'

'I don't know.'

Beth unlocked the examination cupboard and vetted the boxes of materials for the morning exams. It was the tail end of the session and it had gone reasonably smoothly this year. No nit-picking inspectors, no vomiting in the exam room, not many latecomers. Coming up to respite time.

'Heard about Colm?' said Martin, sidling round the cupboard door.

'Yes. Desree's been telling me.'

'Will you go for it, Beth?'

'What are you going for?' asked Palak, arriving to collect his box for the exam he was to invigilate.

'I haven't said that I'm going for anything.'

'You should.'

'What should she?'

'We've heard that Colm's leaving,' said Beth patiently.

'Colm? Is he? Where's he going?'

'Westminster.'

'Posher job?'

'Apparently.'

'More of the same, but more of it,' said Martin. 'We're trying to get Beth to go for his old job.'

'Agreed. You'd be ideal, Beth.'

'Thank you. Now, it's here in the box, Palak. They're mainly physics, with two others doing Italian. There were three candidates entered, but one was a no-show for the first paper so she's not going to be coming to the second. There'd be no point.'

'OK.' He took the box. 'And you categorically should go for Colm's job.'

'There you are,' said Martin. 'Another one on our side.'

'Colm's leaving hasn't been officially announced yet.'

'It has. It's on the bulletin board.'

'We don't know what the job description is.'

'Yes, we do. It's what Colm does.'

Beth laughed. 'So it is. Thanks for the vote of confidence.'

'Better the devil you know.'

'And thank you again.'

'See how popular you are,' said Desree as Beth returned to her desk.

'I'm the known devil, as Martin pointed out.'

'You're also known to be totally efficient.'

'So are you. Why don't you apply? You've been here longer than I have.'

'Not me.' Desree pushed the suggestion aside. 'I'm snug as I am.'

'I might be too.'

'And here's the main man!' called Vincent from the neighbouring section. 'Congratulations, Colm!'

Colm walked up the office, smiling as the staff spoke to him.

'You're a dark horse,' said Desree. 'We were taken by surprise. Weren't we, Beth?'

'Uh-huh,' said Beth.

'Anyway.' Desree had noticed. 'Congratulations. But we'd sooner you weren't leaving us.'

'You're very kind.'

'Will you give us some guidance, though?'

'I will if I can. What's it about?'

'We're persuading Beth to apply for your job. You'd give her a bit of coaching, wouldn't you? Let her know the secrets and tell her what they want to hear at the interview?'

'I'll try – if that's what you want, Beth.'

'I don't know.'

'You're welcome to ask me for anything.' He went on to his part of the office. Beth felt pink and also foolish at both the pinkness and at its implications.

'Any – thing,' said Desree knowingly, and began to hum the tune to 'Secret Smile'.

Beth pretended not to hear.

That evening when the table was being cleared after supper, she said conversationally, 'What are you two doing on Saturday night?'

'Can Ade come round?' asked Daniel immediately. 'He got *Star Wars Racer* for his birthday.'

'Is he allowed out?' asked Lucy as she put leftovers in the fridge.

'Yes, he is now. All done.'

'And did he like his picture? I meant to ask you about it before. Did he?'

'He did. He liked it a lot. He says Oban's clamouring for one too.'

'Not surprising,' said Lucy, ruffling his hair. 'You know what little brothers are.'

'Luce!' Daniel dodged her. 'Stop it. Can he, Mum? Can Ade come over?'

'I'd say yes but I was thinking I might have a night out and I don't want to leave you and Ade all evening on your own. Could you go to Ade's if I asked his mother?'

'I'll be here, Mum,' said Lucy. 'I can keep an eye on them.'

'That would help, Lucy.'

'You're a star, Luce.' Daniel put the salt and pepper away in the cupboard.

'It's no problem. I was going to come home straight after work on Saturday in any case. Are you and Desree out on the razzle?'

'No. Not Desree this time.' She paused. 'With Colm.'

'Colm? Who's she?' asked Daniel.

'Isn't he the office manager?' said Lucy quickly.

'Yes, he is. He's about to leave, so we're going out.'

'I thought your lot had parties when people left,' said Daniel.

'We'll be having a party for him too.'

'So this isn't a party?'

'No.'

'You're going out alone? Him and you?'

'That's it.'

'It sounds relaxing, Mum.' Lucy intervened again. 'Have a lovely time. Where's his new job?'

'Westminster.'

'I'm going to do my homework.' Daniel left the kitchen.

'Also,' said Beth, 'I've been asked to apply for Colm's job – the one he's leaving, I mean.'

'Clever Mum! Are you going to?'

'I haven't decided.'

'Would it mean a lot more work?'

'I don't entirely know.'

'You could ask Colm about it, couldn't you?'

'Yes. I expect I shall.'

Lucy was in the hall on her way to the bathroom when Daniel's bedroom door opened.

'Oy – Lucy.'

'Yes?'

He beckoned with his head. Lucy went over and was pulled into his room. It was transformed. The walls were covered with drawings and paintings as if in a gallery, the duvet was fully up and Adam's old bed was no longer a dumping ground. Daniel's homework books were open on an orderly desk and his skates together in the corner. Before she could comment, though, the worry emerged.

'What's Mum up to, Luce?'

'She's not up to anything.'

'Yes, she is. She's up to something with this Colm whazzit.'

'She's only going out with him, Daniel. He's a colleague. She's been working with him for ages and now he's leaving.'

'Why's she going out with him?' Daniel's thumbs were twisting together.

'Why does anybody go out? To have a good time. They probably like being with each other.'

'He likes her. They go out. Next thing we know there's someone else round here telling us what to do and it starts all over again. He might be horrible to her. She works so hard and Grandma and everything.'

He leaned a shoulder against the door, his lower lip quivering. Lucy realised how much older she was than him. She sat on the bed beneath Burlington Bertie.

'She deserves a bit of fun, Danny. And Colm sounds far from horrible. Mum would never have agreed to go out with him if he was. OK, it might develop into something. We don't know. I don't suppose she knows either, or him for that matter.'

'It's not the same for you, Luce. You'll be at university. You won't be here.'

'I will sometimes, but I get what you mean. But honestly, Dan, it won't be long before you're at this stage too.'

'It'll be ages.'

'It won't. It goes fast, trust me. Then what for Mum? We'll be off in our own lives. What about her life? On her own. Wouldn't it be better for her to have someone to talk to and go to things with? Better than being by herself at home lonely?'

Daniel toed the skirting board.

'I wouldn't want her to be lonely.'

'So why not let be? It won't stop her caring about us, you know.'

'I suppose.'

'You can talk to her about it later, *much* later, if – *if* things start to happen. Later on, not now. Let her have a bit of fun without having to be concerned about us, Danny.'

'OK, I will.'

'Promise?'

'Promise.'

'And don't worry. I think Colm might be all right, you know.'

CHAPTER XXXIV
The Family

Beth stood in the front garden of Mary and Tom's house, her childhood home. The house was clean and tidy inside and out, furnished and fully equipped, ready to receive its American tenants. She thought she might call on them when they came. Take them something English and welcoming. Invite them for supper. That would be the equivalent of a trip to America for her. America. Oh America. She wanted Lucy to have a treat, but so wished the treat wasn't going to be provided by Tony.

How placid had been the lives lived on the other side of that door, how blessedly uneventful. Those lives hung in the air of the house, pervaded its stillness with self-contained contentment. Whereas on this, her side of the door, outside in Beth's demanding world, came new uncertainties. That night she was going out with Colm, and she viewed the outing with a mixture of feelings. She liked Colm, his integrity and absence of flash. She was flattered and validated by his attention, yet there was a flutter of nervousness about living up to it and adapting to the change from Colm as part of a work group to Colm the personal individual. She felt vaguely silly too.

She was too old for emotion over a man. She wished she could skip the initial stages and slide directly into the type of relationship that was a known quantity, the worst already fathomed and the best too, the greater part lying in between with an unchallenging rhythm to it, trotting along an ordinary road as her parents had done, with a partner in companionship and affection. My, she was being middle-aged! Life drawn in from its edges. No sense of adventure. What a boring wimp.

Tired. Just tired.

After updating the Marriotts she drove home, toying with the possibility of ringing up Colm with an excuse. She arrived at the flats simultaneously with Lucy, returning from her week at work with the Maya-substitute. Beth and Lucy trudged into the hallway and up the communal stairs to their landing together.

'She'll do,' said Lucy. 'Niomi thinks she's dozy but that's because she's not as self-confident as Maya was. She'll get the hang of it. It's hardly genome sequencing, is it.'

'You're ready for something else.'

'Oh yes.'

'Have you heard from Maya?'

'She's frantically finishing her final assignment. She's left it a bit late. Niomi and I are going to take her out but she needs to get the assignment cleared off first.'

'And did you ever get what you wanted from Somerset House or wherever it is now? You know – your grandparents' birth certificates?'

'I didn't have enough background information.' Lucy evaded the specific question with a general truth.

'What a shame. You were so keen on it. That must have been disappointing.'

'No.' Lucy smiled at her mother. 'No, it's fine.'

They reached the flat door, which opened as if by itself. Daniel was standing in the hall.

'Hello,' he said. 'Please enter and take a seat.'

Nonplussed, Beth and Lucy walked in. Daniel held Beth's hand and led her into the kitchen, beckoning Lucy along as well.

Two mugs and a plate of biscuits were set on the table in front of invitingly positioned chairs.

'Coffee or tea?'

'Coffee please,' said Lucy.

'Me too,' said Beth, sinking onto a chair. 'This is lovely, Dan.'

'I thought you might be tired,' said Daniel. 'You've been working, I haven't.'

He made their coffee and poured orange juice into a glass for himself, then watched contentedly as Beth and Lucy each took a biscuit.

'Anything interesting happen today?' he enquired.

'Er... the house is ready for the Americans.'

'That's good. Anything else?'

'I got out of work a bit early,' volunteered Lucy.

'That's good too.'

There was a mystified hiatus. Lucy took another biscuit.

'What about your day?' asked Beth, sensing that something was required. 'Anything interesting for you?'

It was the moment Daniel had been waiting for.

'Yes!' he exploded. 'Yes! Look at this!'

He pulled an envelope from his pocket and waved it towards Beth.

'What is it?' she asked.

'Look, look.'

There was a letter and a leaflet in the envelope.

'Dear Daniel Kinnon,' Beth read out. 'Congratulations! On the basis of work put forward by your teachers, our selection committee has noted you as one of twelve young people in the borough who display exceptional artistic talent. We therefore have great pleasure in offering you a place at our future series of masterclasses for gifted young artists. The enclosed leaflet gives details. If you would like to attend, please ask a parent or guardian to complete and return the form below.'

'Wow, Daniel! That's fantastic!' She stood up and gave him a hug. 'Twelve chosen out of the entire borough and you're one of them!'

'Brilliant, Dan.' Lucy hugged him too.

'I can go, can't I, Mum?' He was radiant with happiness.

'Of course you can. I'll read the leaflet and get everything completed this weekend. Grandpa would be proud of you, Daniel Kinnon.'

Daniel drummed the table.

'Mum,' he said diffidently. 'There's something else. I'd like to change my name. A kid in my class did, and he says it's simple.'

'O—kay.' This was unexpected. 'What do you want to change it to? Leonardo?'

'No, Mum.' He grinned. 'Not that bit. Daniel's no problem. It's the other name. I'd like to change Kinnon to Pearson. You call yourself Pearson, and Grandpa and Grandma were Pearsons, weren't they? I'd like to be a Pearson too.'

'Oh Danny,' said Lucy. 'What a good idea.'

'Well,' said Beth, 'that's all right by me. I'll find out how to go about it. But it could be that your father would have to give permission too, so be prepared – he might not agree.'

'Oh, I think he might,' said Dan.

'Well, we can but try. And in the meantime we should celebrate your achievement, you know.'

'Pizza Express?'

'Whatever you like.'

'Great! Thanks, Mum.' He collected the plates, put the uneaten biscuits in the tin and replaced the tin in the cupboard.

Lucy said, 'I thought you were out with Colm tonight, Mum.'

'Ye-es.'

'Shouldn't you be getting ready?'

Beth rubbed her ear. 'I don't really feel like going.'

'Oh Mum, why not?'

'I'm too old for this. It's a bit silly.'

'What's silly about it?' said Lucy. 'You like Colm. What's silly about having a night out with someone you like?'

'Nothing, I suppose.'

'You're tired after getting the house ready. You should have waited till tomorrow and I'd have helped you. Dan too, probably.'

'Of course,' said Daniel, picking up the empty mugs and glass. 'You should go, Mum. You deserve a night out.'

Lucy smiled approvingly.

'When's Ade coming?' she asked.

'Soon. He's got to stay with Oban till his dad gets in.' He began washing up.

'What you could do with, Mum,' Lucy went on, 'is some cosseting while you're getting ready. I've got some new bubble bath you can use. It's meant to be rejuvenating.'

'And you can borrow my nail varnish,' said Dan.

'What have you got nail varnish for?' said Beth, amused.

'He hasn't,' said Lucy. 'It's mine. Come on, Mum, let's get you beautified. I'll start the bath for you. You sort out what you're going to wear.'

She led Beth away and went to run the bath. The door buzzer sounded. Beth, in her dressing gown, came out of her bedroom to answer it, but Daniel got there first and listened grimly. He put a wet hand over the mouthpiece.

'It's the Git. He's insisting on coming up. What shall I do?'

'You'll have to let him in. It might be important.'

'Like what?'

'Well – Adam.'

'He emails you. You'd know anything about him.'

'We can't keep him shut out.'

'Can't we?'

'Let him in, Dan.'

Dan pressed the opening button and Lucy turned off the bath taps. 'You get ready, Mum. We can deal with Dad.'

'I'd better see what he wants.' Beth opened the door and Tony came straight in.

'Excellent timing, Beth. Greetings *tout le monde*. What are you doing out here? Gathered to pay your respects, eh? Very touching but I'll go where there are chairs if it's all the same to you.'

He started for the sitting room, changed tack and went into the kitchen, where, after lowering himself with a huff, he reclined in his chair, ankle on knee, arms hanging wide and loose.

'No vino I'm afraid this time. It's not a planned stop. I was passing and thought I'd drop in. I could murder a cup of tea if someone would oblige.'

Beth made a move. Lucy clicked on the kettle.

'Not fresh water? Tea should be made with freshly drawn water, you know. With a warmed pot taken to the kettle.'

Lucy put a tea bag in a mug.

Tony clucked. 'Dear dear. Modern young women. Don't know how to make a cup of tea properly. Two sugars, sweetheart. *Muchas gracias.*'

Lucy put the tea in front of him.

'Silent night in here, is it? Come on, what's the news? How's the world of fashion retail, Lucy?'

'As usual.'

'Not for much longer, eh? You'll soon be quitting that job.'

'Yes.'

'And California here we come.' He shimmied his hands in the air like a minstrel singer.

'I won't be going to California,' said Lucy.

Beth held her breath.

Tony's arms froze and retracted. 'What? What did you say?'

'Thank you for the invitation. I've arranged to go elsewhere.'

'What do you mean elsewhere?'

'France. I'm going to stay with a friend.'

'Rebecca?' breathed Beth.

'If you agree, Mum. I'm invited to go on holiday with her French family.'

Tony stood up. 'France?' He moved his shoulders in derision. 'Old Frogland? You'd reject a trip to LA for a hop across the Channel? You can go there any time. You could near enough swim there. Get your priorities straight, girl.'

'I'm sure I have.'

'You'll regret it. It's a real experience, America.'

'The professors might invite me to go out and experience it.'

'What professors? What are you talking about?'

'We'll cultivate them,' Beth promised.

'Barmy,' said Tony. 'Barmy women. Don't know when they're on to a good thing. Still, makes no odds.' He put an arm round Daniel. 'It won't affect you, my old mucker. Lucy's making a bad decision, but I'll see that you get your skates.'

'Skates?' said Daniel. 'What skates are those?'

'The skates you wanted me to bring you from America, sonny. The best whatever-they-are. You just have to tell me. You can't have forgotten an offer like that.'

'No, no.' Daniel shook his head sagaciously. 'Not for me. There aren't any skates I want from America. There's more to life than skating.'

Beth gawped.

Tony clutched his brow. 'Are you barmy? You too? What's happened to you both?'

Daniel stepped away, acting sudden enlightenment. 'Ah,' he said. 'I know what might have happened. Perhaps you got your Daniels mixed up.'

'What?'

'You got your Daniels mixed up. You mistook me for Daniel. Easy mistake to make. Of course, I'm just Daniel.'

Tony shot a glance at Beth and at Lucy. Beth was regarding Daniel with puzzled amusement. Lucy looked Tony square in the eye, raising her brows. Tony broke the gaze, glanced again at Beth.

'Better get ready, Mum,' said Lucy. 'You'll be in a rush if you're held up any longer.'

Tony pulled himself together. 'Where are you off to, Beth,' he said, 'in your little dressing gown?'

'The bathroom, Tony.'

'You daft mitt. I mean, where are you going out to?'

Beth turned. 'Why?'

'I'm just asking.'

'Ah.'

'Into the bath, Mum,' cried Lucy. 'Go on. I've left the bottle in there. If the foam's begun to disappear put some more in.' She bustled Beth out. 'Bye Dad. We're rather busy.'

'Yes, bye,' said Daniel.

'Daniel,' said Tony in a low voice. 'What did you…?'

'Bye, Dad.'

'Yes, we'll have to move you on,' said Lucy briskly, re-entering and standing meaningfully in the kitchen doorway.

'All right. All right. Message received.' Lucy stood aside for him to pass through to the hall. 'I'll have a little chat with you two when you can find the time.'

The door sneck clicked.

'Roger and out,' said Daniel.

CHAPTER XXXV
Mary and Lucy

I went to Stefan and Tom's shop one day. I can't remember why. I didn't go often and I wasn't there for long – I expect I wanted to be home for when Beth came in from school. I was waiting for the bus when two young women went into the shop. After a while they came out with bags that showed they'd been buying art materials, and they joined the bus queue. Well, to be more accurate, the three of us made up the queue. There was no one else in it at that point. They were students at the art school and they were discussing their classes and some dissatisfaction they had with a teacher who was being snooty to them, and one of them said, 'Not like those two sweetie-pie fags in Szczepanski's. They're mega mellow.'

'Yes, they're a pair of treasures,' agreed the other, and went on to appreciate the advice she had been given about brushes or somesuch by a person who sounded like Stefan. Although what she said was complimentary, I felt uneasy. There was something about that conversation.

After Beth had gone to bed, I asked Tom.

'Tom, what does the word fag mean?'

He said, from behind the newspaper, 'It depends,' he said.

'It could be a cigarette, or something that's a nuisance or that's tiring. Are you doing a crossword?'

I was knitting.

I said, 'Not those meanings. If it's a person.'

He said, 'Oh, you know, senior boys at school have junior boys as fags. They're virtually servants, cleaning the senior boys' shoes, making toast for them and so forth.'

'But if it's an adult?'

He rustled the pages. 'In that case, it's a slang word for a man. Similar to chap or fellow. It's not a word you'd use. Where did you come across it?'

I said, 'I heard it somewhere recently, probably on the wireless.'

He looked round the edge of the newspaper. 'It would be an unusual word for the BBC, Mary.'

I left it at that. But there remained something unsettling about the girls' conversation that led me to the dictionary. And so for the second time in my life, a suspicion was confirmed in a reference library. I sat at the long wooden table opposite a man writing notes on the Act of Succession, and stared at the page with its unequivocal definition. I thought how often I'd worried that I had prevented Tom from marrying and having his own family, and how Tom had been unconcerned about it; how when we first came to London, he was the one who decided that it would be better for us to keep up the pretence of being Mr and Mrs Pearson, and how, when I'd worried that although it gave respectability to me and the baby, he might regret it later, he'd said he was happy with things just as they were.

Fags. Nothing to do with boring tasks or cigarettes.

'No. They weren't talking about cigarettes.'

'Who weren't, Grandma?' asked Lucy, attempting to enter the scenario indicated by Mary's sudden adamant statement, the first words she had spoken that visit.

'The girls.'

'Which girls?'

'Cigarettes!'

'Are you wanting a ciggy, Mary?' asked a carer cheerily, overhearing. 'I didn't know you smoked.'

'She doesn't,' said Lucy.

'Confirmed bachelor. They used to use that description.'

'Did they?'

'You were either married or single in those days. There was no open acceptance of other arrangements.'

'And now anything goes,' said the carer sympathetically.

'Not a cigarette. Not a boring task.'

'That's good. You don't want any boring tasks, Mary. You're here to take your leisure.' She smiled at Lucy and moved on.

'A chap. A fellow.'

'Who, Grandma?'

'A confirmed bachelor.'

'Who?'

Happy with things as they are. Tom had said that when we first arrived in London. Sitting there in the reference library, I realised why. And I thought of all that had come to pass since then. I thought of Beth, of our house, of the art shop and of Stefan with his unrevealed suffering, his unbroken courtesy to me, and his companionship for Tom, and I thought, It's none of my business. I don't want to know any more than I do. I know everything necessary – that Tom and I escaped from a wretched life with Father, that I eluded misery and shame, that we live as we do in our home with our daughter. Our daughter.

'And Beth is healthy and happy.'

'Yes, she is, Grandma. She'll be coming in to see you. She enjoyed herself when she went out last night.'

'It's none of my business.'

'Anyway, she's coming to see you.'

I don't want to know any more than I do. It worked out. We managed it. Why should I rock the boat? The heavy dictionary lies in front of me, a volume so thick that the pages begin to fall down and cover up the explanation I found in the rows of alternative definitions. Row, row, row. A librarian comes over and asks me if I need any assistance. I don't. I have all the assistance I need. It's Tom.

A very present help in trouble.

'That's true.'

'What is, Grandma?'

'A very present help in trouble.'

'That's the television. They always put the Sunday morning service on, don't they?'

There was a service for Stefan, at the crematorium. A lot of young people attended. Tom said they were from the art school. Among them were some of their teachers and, Tom said, former students whom he hadn't seen for many years. I didn't know any of them. Beth and I waited together as Tom spoke with them after the service. Such restraint. It was as if the intensity had gone into the flowers, burning white and rich with scent. Tom had chosen them. I watched him moving round methodically, grey-faced but composed as he had been since Stefan's death. Excluding the once.

Tom was with Stefan when he died. He came home from the hospital to tell me. I was in the sitting room, putting roses from the garden into a vase.

'Stefan's dead.' He said it without emotion.

'Stefan is dead,' he repeated in the same flat voice. Then he flung back his head and howled. It was an unearthly sound, raw with pain. I had never heard anything like it. I led him to the sofa, where he crumpled sobbing, his body racked by spasms. I couldn't help, and wept both for Stefan and for my brother in his agony of loss.

He stopped, quite abruptly. He sat up, his face streaked and his breathing jagged. He stiffened his shoulders and said in a factual way, 'Yes, he's dead. I must organise his funeral.'

He got up and went into the kitchen and made us both a cup of tea and was never like that again. He was as he was at the funeral.

Tom's own funeral was small, and was long after he gave up the art shop. He'd never changed its name after Stefan's death, but when Tom retired it went to a couple called Mr and Mrs Hislop, and they put their own name up in place of Szczepanski. They promoted Tom's pictures, and they had a friend with a restaurant who put them on the walls there, for sale. They came to Tom's funeral and they visited me sporadically afterwards, but it petered out. Some things do. Not everything.

'Time like an ever-rolling stream
Bears all its sons away.'

'You know the words, Grandma! Do you like that hymn?'

It did bear them away. The river. Stefan. Tom. It will bear me too. 'Gently down the stream.'

'Merrily, merrily, merrily, merrily,' Lucy joined in softly. 'You're singing again today, Grandma.'

That is my wish. That's how I want it to be. Borne away on the river like Tom. Like Stefan.

'That is my wish.'

'What is, Grandma? What do you want? Tell me. I can do it for you.'

You can worry and worry. Worry and worry and worry. But it works out. We managed it.

'Grandma? What would you like?'

Borne away by the river. With Tom. With Stefan. Gently down the stream. Elizabeth Frances, Beth. All is well.

'It works out. It all works out.'

'I hope so,' thought Lucy, watching her grandmother's eyes flicker behind the closed lids. 'I do hope so.'

Life is but a dream.

Perhaps.

ABOUT THE AUTHOR

Helen Stancey was born and brought up in Yorkshire but moved to London as a student and subsequently taught Psychology at various London colleges. Her two novels, *Words* and *Common Ground*, were published by Robin Clark Ltd. After focusing on academic and educational writing, she returned to literature with a collection of short stories, *The Madonna of the Pool*, the first of her works to be published by Fairlight Books.

FAIRLIGHT BOOKS

HELEN STANCEY

The Madonna of the Pool

*'I do not cheat others. Have I cheated myself? I
do not know who I am.'*

The Madonna of the Pool is a collection of short stories which
explore the triumphs, compromises and challenges of everyday
life. Drawing on a wide array of characters, Helen Stancey
shows how small events, insignificant to some, can resonate
deeply in the lives of others.

Richly poetic, deeply moving and entirely engaging, these
short stories demonstrate an exquisite understanding of human
adaptation, endurance and, most of all, optimism.

*'Stancey has pieced together a collection that feels subtle
and truthful to the human experience.'*
— *The Book Bag*

'Truly an excellent collection.'
— *Dovegreyreader*